THE CALEDONIAN BANDIT

Also Available from Valancourt Books

GASTON DE BLONDEVILLE
Ann Radcliffe
Edited by Frances A. Chiu

CLERMONT
Regina Maria Roche
Edited by Natalie Schroeder

CASTLE OF WOLFENBACH
Eliza Parsons
Introduction by Diane Long Hoeveler

THE VEILED PICTURE
Ann Radcliffe
Edited by Jack G. Voller

THE ITALIAN
Ann Radcliffe
Edited by Allen W. Grove

GLENARVON
Lady Caroline Lamb
Edited by Deborah Lutz

THE MIDNIGHT BELL
Francis Lathom
Introduction by David Punter

THE DEMON OF SICILY
Edward Montague
Preface by Jo Beverley

Gothic Classics

THE

Caledonian Bandit;

OR,

THE HEIR OF DUNCAETHAL.

A ROMANCE

OF THE THIRTEENTH CENTURY.

TWO VOLUMES IN ONE.

BY

MRS. SMITH,

OF THE THEATRE-ROYAL HAYMARKET.

A Tale of the times of old.

OSSIAN.

EDITED WITH AN INTRODUCTION AND NOTES BY

CAROL MARGARET DAVISON

𝕶ansas 𝕮ity:
VALANCOURT BOOKS
2010

The Caledonian Bandit by Mrs. Smith
First published by A. K. Newman in 1811
First Valancourt Books edition 2010

Introduction and notes © 2010 by Carol Margaret Davison
This edition © 2010 by Valancourt Books

ISBN 978-1-934555-74-3

Published by Valancourt Books
Kansas City, Missouri

Composition by James D. Jenkins
Set in Dante MT

10 9 8 7 6 5 4 3 2 1

CONTENTS

The editor would like to thank her research assistant, Ms. Betsy Keating, for her assistance in compiling the notes for this edition.

INTRODUCTION*

THAT Europe, on America's heels, witnessed an unprecedented socio-political revolution in the late eighteenth century, is a commonplace fact of history. Born of modern, rationalist, and Enlightenment ideas, the French Revolution was the watershed phenomenon in what has been characterized as the trauma of modernity, producing, among other things, a hugely significant reconfiguration of temporality (Lowenthal 96-97). According to Hugh Honour in his study of Romanticism:

> The French Revolution sharpened the historical sense in a way that no other event had ever done. No other event had ever seemed so cataclysmic. Creating between the present and the immediate past a gulf which was seen to widen with every year that went by from 1789 to 1815, it quickened awareness of the passing of time. (193)

That the Jacobins proposed a new calendar devoid of customary weeks and months that replaced the Christian year 1792 with the republican Year I (Fritzsche 1596), underlines and illustrates the contemporary sense of historical disjunction between the pre- and post-Revolutionary eras. Modernity thus fostered a pronounced sense of *no going back*.

Less well known to history is the fact that a cultural revolution transpired in Europe—identified and discussed as such in the contemporary periodical press—in reaction to modernity and the traumatic events of the French Revolution that has been variously theorized and whose impact was fairly significant and broad-based. Although "birthed" in 1764 by way of a quirky and unprecedented little volume by Horace Walpole called *The Castle of Otranto*, which was provocatively subtitled *A Gothic*

* As this Introduction reveals some details of the novel's plot, readers may wish to read it after completing the novel.

Story, the Gothic novel may be said to have entered a second phase in the 1790s, reaching its efflorescence in the wake of the French Revolution and its bloody aftermath. The Gothic novel, or *Schauerroman* ("shudder novel") as it was known in Germany, or *roman noir* as it came to be known in France, was re-energized by revolutionary violence and terror, and its original elements fittingly reconfigured.[1] As two satirical letters published in 1797 in *Monthly Magazine* and *Spirit of the Public Journals for 1797*, and a review published in *Gentleman's Magazine* in 1798, clearly attest, the Gothic connection to the French Revolution was not foisted onto history retrospectively by overly zealous cultural critics, but was actually identified and discussed by contemporary critics whose rhetoric was both unmistakable and resonant: the advent of Gothic literature in the 1790s is labeled a "wonderful" and "singular *revolution*" whose producers made "terror the order of the day".[2] According to the Marquis de Sade, a great admirer of the works of Ann Radcliffe and especially Matthew Lewis, the tale of terror was a predictable and even necessary cultural development that both emanated from and responded to the violent events of the late eighteenth century, in particular the Reign of Terror. In his now famous essay "Reflections on the Novel" (1800), Sade deems Gothic literature "the inevitable outcome of the revolutionary upheavals experienced throughout the whole of Europe," a literature of extremes conceived to rival French Revolutionary horrors (109).

This new cultural terror enabled imaginative, controlled play with terror and defied modernity's dictate of "no going back" by playing out collisions between pre-Enlightenment and Enlightenment values and belief systems. As such, it proved both extremely popular and lucrative. According to Robert D. Mayo, "[d]uring the years from 1796 to 1806[,] at least one-third of all novels published in Great Britain were Gothic in character while on the London stage one Gothic melodrama succeeded another" (766).[3] The Gothic novel was, veritably, "the major fictional form in English" in the 1790s (Carson 257). In an era when over seventy per cent of the books borrowed from circulating libraries were novels and less than one per cent were religious in nature (Outram 18) and women were producing and reading more novels than men,[4] 'Gothomania' was a guilty pleasure for many and a social concern for some. An explosion of Gothic abridgments, plagiarisms, and imitations, in the form of tales, fragments, and novellas published in magazines and 'bluebooks' or 'shilling shockers,' followed in the wake of Ann Radcliffe's tremendous success.[5] Donald K. Adams rightly comments that "the history of popular fiction throughout the 1790s is largely a chronicle of novelists striving to shape their romances in Ann Radcliffe's successful mold" (49). While these imitators may have helped to extend Radcliffe's powerful influence into the nineteenth century, most, sadly, plunged her work into disrepute (Spector, *English* 13). As Frederick Frank has noted, "Chapbookers, bluebookers, and periodical Gothics preferred not to sign their work to avoid justifiable charges of plagiarism" (142). Thus, as in the case of other cultural phenomena before and since, what began as dramatically groundbreaking and innovative—as much recent critical scholarship has cogently illustrated—was, at least in one of its main offshoots, drained of its radical energies by amateur copycats and reduced to a boring, predictable formula. (Some critics might scoff at and resist the idea of a radical Radcliffe, but the progressive nature of her work is indisputable when properly considered within its relevant socio-historical and cultural contexts.[6])

The clear winners during this era were the circulating libraries and such publishers as the Minerva Press who first published the present work—Mrs. Smith's *The Caledonian Bandit; or, The Heir of Duncaethal. A Romance of the Thirteenth Century*. It is important to note that the Gothic boom of the 1790s coincided with the great age of the circulating libraries. Starting in the 1770s with a single library in Leadenhall Street, London, Minerva Press's publisher William Lane established libraries in the fashionable resorts in the provinces, Scotland, and Ireland, and became the leading distributor of handsomely-bound yet relatively inexpensive double- and triple-decker volume Gothics (Frank 140). By 1810, Lane had also established libraries as far afield as New York, Jamaica, and India. Rather significantly, between 1795 and 1810, in keeping with the national production of Gothic novels (Mayo 766), a third of Lane's annual publication output consisted of Gothic titles, and the output was considerable: the Minerva Press catalogue included 10,000 titles in 1790 and nearly 17,000 titles in 1802.

Generally speaking, as Peter Garside notes, Minerva Press "was reactive rather than an originator of trends, and as such its history is especially useful as a barometer of taste" ("Romantic" 316). Given its incredible output and the tremendous expansion of the Gothic into the bluebook and chapbook markets—"mainly plagiarized abridgements, reductions, and condensations of the leading Gothic authors" that inundated the book-stalls and cheap printing shops in the 1790s (Frank, "Gothic Chapbooks" 139)[7]— Minerva Press was hugely influential in shaping public taste and reading habits from the 1790s into the 1810s. Lane ostensibly aimed to uphold public mores, claiming in his Prospectus in the *Morning Advertiser* (8 February 1794) that Minerva Press was "open to such subjects as tend to public good—the pages shall never be stained with what will injure the mind or corrupt the heart—they shall neither be the instrument of private damnation or Public Inquiry" (qtd. in Howells 82). Despite Lane's assertions, Minerva Press was frequently singled out and openly criticized for corrupting the public taste. Many even became hostile towards circulating libraries, considering them a "compact of sensationalism, sentimentality, and salaciousness" (Varma, *Evergreen* 16) due to their wide dissemination of Minerva Press-style publications, which were condemned generally as containing "an element of voluptuous lovemaking" (Sadleir 192). This assumption certainly held true for such Lewis-influenced works as Mary-Anne Radcliffe's *Manfroné; or, The One-Handed Monk* (1809), a novel of lurid sexual violence and dreaded hallucinatory terrors involving an irrepressibly violent father figure. *Manfroné*, however, was not representative of the mainstay of Minerva Press publications in the 1790s. Minerva Press authors generally copied Radcliffe's more sentimental Gothic rather than Lewis's more sensationalistic style. In fact, most Minerva Press publications, like Regina Maria Roche's *Children of the Abbey* (1796), were tame, sentimental rehashes of Radcliffe's Female Gothic romances. They contained little of what Montague Summers has nicely called "Gothic sauce" (*Gothic* 13). This changed, however, after 1810 when, in order to retain their well-worn readers' interest, Minerva plots grew increasingly sensational.

The present work, Mrs. Smith's 1811 publication, *The Caledonian Bandit*, is a fine example of this generation of Minerva Press productions. Lady Margaret Monteith, its unstoppable power-hungry female villain, is a wild and compelling creation who could only have been conceptualized after the début of Charlotte Dacre's scandalous Victoria de Loredani in *Zofloya; or, The Moor: A Romance of the Fifteenth Century* (1806). Although Lady Margaret's husband, the usurper and "tyrant" Duncaethal, is unarguably the novel's greatest villain, he is entirely overshadowed, simply by virtue of his gender, by his extremely passionate, ambitious, and proud wife whose future doom is sealed when she falls in love with a younger man, Donald, and audaciously discards propriety in expressing her desire to him along with her willingness to kill her husband. For readers in the early 1800s, Duncaethal's repeated sexual improprieties, coupled with his treacherous act of drugging his wife and arranging her murder, paled in comparison with Lady Margaret's violent and unrestrained passion, which is granted expression in her sexual indiscretion, unnatural gender cross-dressing, theatrical machinations, and her crowning, unrepentant acts of viricide and suicide.

Apart from its extreme characters and unpredictable, fast-paced plot, *The Caledonian Bandit*'s Scottish setting renders it of particular interest to Gothic scholars attentive to issues of genre history and national identity. According to Franco Moretti in his *Atlas of the European Novel, 1800-1900*, "Gothic stories were initially set in Italy and France, moved north to Germany, around 1800; and then north again, to Scotland after 1820" (16). Moretti's claim would support the case that Scotland became a popular Gothic locale only *after* the advent of Sir Walter Scott's Waverley series. While this claim may be true in the main, a good number of Scottish-set Gothic narratives pre-date 1820, among them John Palmer's *The Haunted Cavern: A Caledonian Tale* (1796), F.H.P.'s *The Castle of Caithness: A Romance of the Thirteenth Century* (1802),

Horsley Curties's *The Scottish Legend; or The Isle of St. Clothair* (1802), C.F. Barrett's *Douglas Castle; or, The Cell of Mystery, a Scottish Tale* (1803), Elizabeth Helme's *St. Clair of the Isles; or, The Outlaws of Barra* (1803), Mrs. Isaacs' *Glenmore Abbey; or, The Lady of the Rock* (1805), and Francis Lathom's *The Romance of the Hebrides; or, Wonders Never Cease!* (1809). In this regard, it is crucial to mention that the incomparable Ann Radcliffe, "the Shakspeare of Romance Writers" (Drake I. 359), set *The Castles of Athlin and Dunbayne* (1789), her very first work of Gothic fiction, in Scotland. Radcliffe's bloody tale of disinheritance and inter-necine strife would seem to have inaugurated the tradition. Its influence is discernible in numerous subsequent representations of Gothic Scotland,[8] including the aforementioned *The Castle of Caithness*, which features one Macmillan, an inhuman, tyran-nical, and "barbarous brother" (22) in a narrative resonant of Greek tragedy. Other "offspring" include *Douglas Castle*, a tale of dastardly fratricide involving a "tyrannical lord" whose subjects yearn for his overthrow (28), and *The Romance of the Hebrides*, which relates a drawn-out battle between cousins. Indeed, the representation of Scotland as a nation plagued by civil war in the form of clan feuds, and divided topographically, socially, and politically, was extremely popular in numerous Romantic cultural productions. This pejorative portrait notably possesses deeper historical roots. It found memorable dramatic expression, for example, in mid-eighteenth century Scotophobic propaganda disseminated in such venues as John Wilkes's *North Briton*. This representation of a chaotic and divided Scotland seems to have taken special hold, rather fittingly, in the Gothic with its special fixation on doubles and the theme of divided consciousness.

Various pressing questions arise in relation to this intriguing development in the Gothic novel, the first and obvious being, why Scotland? What, exactly, did that country offer the Gothic novelist during this era that a setting like Venice did not? Further to this, what were the implications—both aesthetically and ideologically—of these Gothic representations of Scotland in the late eighteenth and early nineteenth centuries? Finally, how did it come to be that, as Murray J. Pittock has noted, "[a]t the height of the Scottish Enlightenment, Scotland was presented as an anti-Enlightenment culture, to the delight of all Europe" (*Invention* 73)? Why is it that a romanticized portrait of Scotland furnishes its most "prevalent image" (31) despite that nation's noteworthy Enlightenment contributions and the fact that, as Katherine Haldane Grenier states, Scotland was to become "the leading industrial nation of the nineteenth century" (1)? Indeed, given that "it has been Scotland's fate to have become a Romantic object or commodity" rather than a site of Romantic production (Duncan, "Study" 2), Romanticism serves, as one critic has provocatively stated, as a spectre haunting Scotland (Hook 307).

In terms, solely, of practical issues, the Napoleonic Wars rendered Scotland virtually one of the only accessible, semi-foreign places that English tourists could visit safely in the late eighteenth and early nineteenth century (Haldane Grenier 35). As numerous, very famous contemporary accounts evidence, however, touring Scotland had become a popular enterprise on the heels of the Second Jacobite Rebellion, otherwise known as the Forty-Five (1745). Scottish tour narratives, which proliferated between the 1760s and the 1780s, touted the benefits of the Union and justified the Improvement project by showing that Scotland was safe for tourism. These "hymns to the values of improvement" (39) actually served two complementary agendas: the British national mission at home and the British imperial mission overseas.[9] Officially, "Improvement was a gospel of peace: 'Commerce and Concord', in a typical phrase, were to enter the Highlands hand in hand along the new roads" (Womack 118); however, this program effectively neutralized Scotland militarily and politically by draining the Highlands (in particular) of its young men in order to advance Britain's imperial contest with France (29). Thus did Scotland find itself in two seemingly oppositional positions during this era: the victim of British imperial conquest on one hand and its proponents and beneficiaries on the other.[10] Ironically and notably, while the Improvement program was designed to efface Scotland's historical distinctiveness (Womack 4), Tour accounts, "Gothic Scotland" narratives, and the later, hugely popular works of Sir Walter Scott, especially his Waverley

series, promoted a Romanticization/nostalgization of Scottish
history that served also to accent Scottish distinctiveness. The
sensational, international popularity of James Macpherson's
Ossian poems, published in the 1760s and advertised as the production of a Celtic Homer who chronicled that nation's glorious and Romantic past, rendered Scotland the Romantic nation
par excellence. This development, at the height of the Scottish
Enlightenment, resulted in a somewhat confused portrait of the
Scottish nation, one that makes better sense when one considers
that enlightened modernity and the pronounced sense it engen-
dered of "no going back" often went hand-in-glove with a nostal-
gic romanticization of the past.

A brief overview of post-Culloden Scottish Tour narratives
helps to set out the broad contours of a semiotics that was
later parlayed into portraits of a Gothic Scotland. These works
were greatly influenced by Daniel Defoe's mid-1720s post-Union
evaluation of Scotland, *A Tour Through the Whole Island of Great
Britain*. This former spy and propagandist for the Union informs
his readers in his Introduction that he will provide, in stark contrast to his Scottish precursors, a realistic account of Scotland
that, he suggests, could only be provided by an Englishman (560).
Armed with his Gospel of Improvement, which Peter Womack
has cogently illustrated works in covert complementarity with
the increasing romanticization of Scotland fostered throughout the eighteenth century (3), Defoe anticipates the Scottish
Enlightenment concept of stadial history as he deems Scotland
to be representative of England at a much more primitive stage
(560)—a truly Gothic relationship if ever there was one: Scotland
assumes the role of England's benighted past that, forever strain-
ing against England's border, continues to haunt her progress.
As Defoe casts a commercial and imperial eye over Scotland and
compiles an inventory of her marketable resources, much like
his beloved Robinson Crusoe upon arrival on "his" island,[11] all
seems ripe for improvement with one formidable and irrepress-
ible exception—the Scottish Highlands. No more treacherous
locale does Defoe encounter than what he terms the "Northern
Highlands", wild, unruly, and uninhabitable lands, which he

describes as "frightful territory" (661) out of which he, turning
to the "pleasant and agreeable country" of the Lowlands (674),
at one point in his journey, is thankful to be extricating himself.
True to his vow neither to make a paradise or a wilderness of
Scotland (561), Defoe opts to make a paradise out of the improv-
able Lowlands and a wilderness—often romanticized—out of
the possibly unassimilable, unimprovable Highlands. In such a
manner is Scotland divided and the spectre of a Gothic Scotland
raised, a spectre that is magnified in Defoe's generally dry and
composed account by chilling memories of Anglo-Scottish
warfare evoked by place and landscape.[12] Although a generally repressed, bloody history of warfare and rivalry continues
to haunt the English-Scottish union, Defoe's Tour narrative
nonetheless affirms *British* identity and the newfound security
granted by the Union: one can now travel peacefully through the
Highlands (Haldane Grenier 7, 18), formerly a region of lawlessness and "pure violence" (Womack 11, 35).

Despite the passing of half a century and the definitive defeat
of Jacobitism, the Gothic Scotland spectre remains intact in the
tour of Scotland undertaken by Thomas Pennant, a renowned
naturalist and member of the Royal Academy, who pens what
has been described as "the fullest travel account of Britain to
that point" (Haldane Grenier 16). Although Pennant foregrounds
Scottish Civil War as opposed to Anglo-Scottish warfare and
insists that Scotland is now in a "very improving state" (50),
Scotland remains, in Pennant's account, a bloody nation in thrall
to mantology. As with numerous other Scottish Tour narratives
of this period, tales of bloodthirsty clan battles and revenge
punctuate the account (Haldane Grenier 138-139). Notably,
Pennant promotes the established "idea that the inhabitants of
Highland Scotland, and of the Hebrides in particular, regularly
saw, or believed that they saw, spirits, ghosts, and the phenomena of Second Sight.[,] . . . a fairly well established feature of
the metropolitan knowledge of the Highlands by the mid-eighteenth century" (Womack 87). Further to this, Pennant articulates a very specific agenda in his 1769 tour through Scotland—
namely, to preserve information about Highland customs and

superstitions in order to teach the "unshackled and enlightened mind the difference between the pure ceremonies of religion and the wild and anile flights of superstition" (Pennant 67).[13] Thus is Scotland, a nation then in the process of establishing and developing major ideas in Enlightenment philosophy, represented as a region of unenlightened superstition, a portrait, it must be noted, that was also advanced by some Scottish Enlightenment thinkers themselves.[14]

Dr. Samuel Johnson, another self-described rational Englishman, advances a demeaning portrait of a benighted, war-plagued Scotland in his infamous Tour narratives *A Journey to the Western Islands of Scotland* (1775) and *The Journal of a Tour to the Hebrides* (1785). He establishes a division between a post-Union "time of universal peace" (86) produced under English law and Scotland's pre-Union instability when feudal chieftains governed by the sword (109). In a move designed to support the idea of a primitive, unenlightened Scotland, Johnson strategically elides references to Edinburgh and the Scottish Enlightenment. He also undermines the authenticity of the Ossian poems that lent credibility to the idea of a literate, ancient Scottish culture. And the rational Doctor cannot resist painting the Highlands black. In a move calculated to undermine the connection between Scotland and any sense of loftiness, Johnson disputes the notion of Highland sublimity. This treacherous land replete with memorials, he says, is marred by a blood-soaked history of clan warfare and can literally, he maintains, kill people (61), an idea far removed, in his view, from any sense of transformative sublimity. Johnson even explicitly links Scotland and the Gothic when, travelling through Talisker one gloomy evening, he considers the possible terrors that could beset a solitary wanderer and remarks, "The fictions of the Gothick romances were not so remote from credibility as they are now thought" (88). In such manner does Johnson's Tour anticipate future literary encounters with "Gothic Scotland" and promote such titillating encounters, in this post-Jacobite era, as a desired objective. It is important to note, however, that it is the *frisson* of Gothic terror that is wanted and not the actual experience of bloody violence and horror.

Such *frissons* are certainly on offer in various "Gothic Scotland" novels published between the 1790s and the 1820s. Written predominantly by English women, such works suggest that Scotland—with its entrenched superstitious worldview, bloody history, and innumerable ruined castles—serves as the natural and obvious choice for a Gothic locale. The Highlands may be said to furnish the jewel in Scotland's Gothic crown given that they are home to Britain's most sublime scenery and its foreign, Gaelic-speaking, Roman Catholic, tyrannical, banditti-like Highlanders. The Gothic's transition from the Roman Catholic continent to British "home" territory could not have been smoother. Thus did some British writers trade in the image of a Romanticized and sublime yet divided Scotland at war with itself and, rather significantly, often under the yoke of morally and/ or physically "monstrous" women. When Victor Frankenstein agrees to create a monstrous female companion for his lonely, demanding Creature, Mary Shelley's selection of Scotland as the site for this purpose is not without noteworthy precedent. In fact, several key works—both literary and otherwise—made Scotland the natural choice for the location of female monsters. John Knox's venomous diatribe, *The First Blast of the Trumpet Against the Monstrous Regiment of Women* (1558), which was aimed primarily at undermining the authority of Mary Queen of Scots, did much to establish the association between female monsters and Scotland. In Knox's words, such powerful, authoritarian women were nothing short of an abomination—"repugnant to nature" and subversive "of good order" (9)—a philosophy that also served to justify the brutal persecution of so-called Scottish "witches" a century later.[15] Likewise, William Shakespeare's domineering and ambitious femme fatale, Lady Macbeth, was inextricably linked to that nation.

Perhaps most importantly for Mary Shelley's novel is the fact that several British Gothic works published in the decade prior to *Frankenstein*'s publication employed Scotland as the site of female monsters. In these narrative scenarios where rational benevolence is often opposed by vengeful malice, these authors present phallic, enterprising femme fatales who embrace the latter standpoint and seem to take such figures as the fictitious, stereotypical Scottish witch, Lady Macbeth, and Mary Queen of Scots as their models. Francis Lathom's *The Romance of the Hebrides* (1809), for example, is set against the backdrop of a superstitious Scotland where the greatest threat is sorcery. The novel's most terrifying and bizarre character is the "dreaded Abdeerah" (I, 179), "the famed witch of Iona" (I, 153) who is essentially half-woman, half-beast. At least one hundred years old, Abdeerah is a cave-dweller garbed in a wolf's hide and ragged tartan who possesses unearthly red eyes filled with rheum, pointed, beastlike fangs, and talon-like fingers (I, 179-180). She is also a prominent player in an argument about the capabilities of female rulers, which is notably one of the novel's principal debates. When Ulina, the daughter of the Laird of Cornic from Lewis, seeks Abdeerah's assistance in getting pregnant because her husband, Starno, threatens to annul the marriage otherwise, Abdeerah readily assists, enabling Ulina to give birth to a daughter. When Starno contests the claim that women can properly rule a country on the grounds that "the capacities of a female mind are ill-adapted to the weighty task of governing a state" and "a scepter swayed by the hand of a woman can never reflect honour on herself, or prove a blessing to her subjects" (I, 201), Ulina vigorously disagrees, citing numerous examples of countries flourishing under queens. She suggests that her daughter may be an intelligent woman of sound judgment. Starno's response that such a daughter would be nothing short of a prodigy echoes Knox's position (I, 202), a stance ultimately undermined by the nature and actions of Ulina's daughter, the Lady Alexandra, who, after consistently exhibiting sound judgment and faithful devotion while facing tremendous persecution, is gloriously installed as a ruler by novel's end and her greatness proclaimed (III, 252).

Not every "Gothic Scotland" work, however, embraces a Wollstonecraft-style agenda to challenge the female monster category, a category into which Wollstonecraft was herself placed by Horace Walpole, the grandfather of the Gothic novel, who dubbed her a "hyena in petticoats."[16] Most use the female monster, as in *The Caledonian Bandit*, in a more figurative fashion and for dramatic effect as opposed to feminist ends. Scheming, power-hungry women abound in these works. In Regina Maria Roche's *Children of the Abbey* (1796), Lady Greystock, a former Scottish servant with grandiose marital aspirations, is revealed to be the nasty schemer behind this torturously lengthy novel's action. She later confesses and repents. Likewise, a courtesan named Helena (6), an "infamous woman" (28) who is noteworthy by her absence in the narrative, controls the novel's despotic murderer in *Douglas Castle* (1803) and, in *St. Clair of the Isles* (1803), the manipulative and vengeful Countess Roskelyn confesses at novel's end that she conceived the novel's hero out of wedlock and cruelly denied knowledge of him to his father. It is said of this "wolfish" mother (17) that "if ever fiend dwelt in a woman's form, it is in that of the Countess" (74).

The choice of Scotland as a breeding-ground for such female monsters was perhaps a function of women's elevated social and legal status in that country in the late eighteenth and early nineteenth centuries. The domestic power of Scottish women had been "remarked on by foreigners as early as the fifteenth century, [and] did in fact have some implications at law: for example, 'when a wife was eventually granted a divorce, she was put in possession of her jointure lands and was free to marry again'" (Pittock, *Inventing* 131). Women were able to divorce on the grounds of adultery or desertion throughout the eighteenth century "(347 cases came before the Edinburgh Commissary Court between 1708 and 1780, initiated roughly equally by men and women and across a range of social classes)" (86) and, remarkably, "When the Anderson's University (now Strathclyde University) was founded in Glasgow in 1796 to educate those in work, women were permitted to attend its lectures" (131).

The popular image of Scotland as a nation inhabited by female monsters and a site of gender subversion in much early nineteenth-century British Gothic fiction was further bolstered by established propaganda that ambivalently represented Scottish men. While John Wilkes's virulently anti-Scots newspaper, *The North Briton*, frequently pumped up the volume on Scottish sexual potency in the mid-eighteenth century, it also traded fast and loose with the image of the effeminately skirted, filthy, famine-plagued Scot. Although set in the thirteenth century, *The Caledonian Bandit* registers a quintessentially eighteenth-century transition in relation to masculinity. As it does repeatedly in the works of Radcliffe, male conduct takes centre stage alongside female conduct. Donald, the novel's hero, is a religious, patriotic soldier, and anachronistically placed man of feeling. As such, he stands opposite the sinister Duncaethal, an inveterately corrupt gambler and womanizer. These issues of character are even mapped onto the landscape for, while Duncaethal's exact regional origins remain unclear, he woos Lady Margaret, rather fittingly, in the Orkneys, her homeland. In Smith's regional semiotics, this remote group of islands off Scotland's North coast seems, erroneously, to be figured as Scottish territory in the thirteenth century.[17] As such, the Orkneys function as a fittingly Gothic Highland locale of extremes, a wild site of lawlessness associated with the novel's notorious outlaw duo of Duncaethal and, especially, Lady Margaret of Monteith. Mary Shelley will likewise associate the Orkneys with female monstrosity in *Frankenstein*, as it is to the Orkneys that Victor retires in order to create a "wife" for his lonely Creature (136). The upright Donald's situation near (the entirely fictitious) Castle Bosmora in the Scottish Borders, adjacent to England, signals his greater Anglicization and superior capacity for civilization and improvement. That he ultimately succeeds in getting and saving "the peerless Matilda" and settling in a happily transformed Castle Bosmora illustrates the case.

Mrs. Smith's regional awareness of Scotland, albeit basic, is matched by an equally murky sense of that nation's history. This would have been fully in keeping with the popular cultural treatment of Scottish history in the eighteenth century, post-Ossian, which tended towards the romantically obscure. Scotland emerges as mistily history-less. In the astute words of Kathleen Haldane Grenier, "In an era of rapid, continual, and sometimes unsettling change, Scotland—the Highlands in particular—seemed fixed, rooted, and constant. Indeed, tourist literature sometimes suggested that Scotland was immune to the passage of time" (135). This immunity, Haldane Grenier argues further, "deprecate[d] Scotland's modern developments" (136) and served an agenda grounded "in specific cultural needs and anxieties which emerged in both England and Scotland in the beginning of the industrial era" (11). Scotland was repeatedly held up as a nostalgized, romanticized, pre-modern domain of seemingly untouched and sublime natural scenery that stood in contradistinction to the bleak and unnatural industrial landscapes of Northern England.

Notably, however, and as its subtitle *A Romance of the Thirteenth Century* intimates, *The Caledonian Bandit* seems somewhat historically attentive. Indeed, Smith would have been hard pressed to select a more explosive watershed era in Scottish history. The end of the thirteenth century witnessed the dramatic Scottish Wars of Independence involving Robert the Bruce and William Wallace when Scots of various ranks fought—sometimes against each other—to resist English domination. Curiously, however, no reference to such events is made in Smith's novel. This could be due to her ignorance of Scottish history, an ignorance that might have served her well with a post-Union Scottish readership uncomfortable with references to a historic English invasion and Scottish civil war. Or perhaps Smith's lack of more specific historic detail functions in a subtler manner to suggest greater post-Union peace in *North* Britain. While much is made of warfare in the novel's opening pages—the loyal peasant Donald pledges to fight the battles of his Sovereign and Matilda's brother is slain in battle (2)—the nature of these battles and the identities of their opponents remain unspecified (4-5). This is in keeping with the nebulously otherworldly atmospherics of the works of Ossian—popularly cited here as chapter epigraphs—which pay tribute to a vanished heroic age and the ephemeral nature of love and life. The fact that the King's soldiers arrest the criminal usurper Philip Duncaethal at novel's end intending to subject him to a trial judged by Scotland's top nobles, however, suggests a certain national unity in Scotland at the time of the novel's setting. In this final reestablishment of order, Scotland proves to be the home of morally upright men and not just the domain of "tyrants or servile lackeys" (Finlay 148). Notably, the battles that Donald does manage to undertake are actually personal, involving matters of the heart. He valiantly risks life and limb to save Matilda from the clutches of both the treacherous Duncaethal and Darthalgo, the persona of his vindictive, enterprising wife Margaret.

While the Gothic has engaged with the trajectories and lessons of history, both individual and collective, since its inception, Smith fails to capitalize on this. Radcliffe, who developed various key innovations in this regard—namely, fleshing out her female protagonist's individual history in relation to those of her ancestral foremothers—would never have passed up such opportunities. Indeed, they constitute the very meat and muscle of Radcliffe's œuvre. Mrs. Smith, however, was an actress who seems to have chosen Scotland primarily for its post-Ossianic romantic atmosphere and its fashion possibilities. Items of plaid clothing litter the landscape from the opening page and are worn by moral and immoral characters alike. Perhaps unknown to Smith, the plaid was erotic and political and, therefore, doubly illicit, just decades prior to her novel's publication. The plaid was "something of an erotic symbol because so many ballad heroines are 'row'd' in it . . . and it was, itself, a prohibited garment between 1746 and 1782" (Womack 13) having been outlawed after the Second Jacobite Rebellion. It would appear that by 1811 and the publication of *The Caledonian Bandit*, this signpost of Highland allegiance and defiance had been depoliticized and, thus, divested of such radical and risqué associations, all of which contributed to Scotland's role as an innocuous, history-less black hole in the early nineteenth century.

Despite the fact that they are sometimes misquoted and/or their sources misidentified, Smith's epigraphs evidence her better knowledge of literature—especially theatre—and Gothic convention as opposed to national history. Resonant and atmospheric citations from such Scottish romantic works as James Macpherson's Ossian poems and John Home's *Douglas* are interspersed with passages from dramatic works by Shakespeare, Cibber, and Otway. Despite this very self-conscious framing,

The Caledonian Bandit never approaches the tragic heights and depths of the aforementioned works. The narrative's pacing is also frequently rushed, resulting sometimes in confusion as to chronology and character identity. These deficiencies—which are especially prominent in the opening chapters after which Smith gains a better footing—seem to be due to Smith's background in the theatre and that medium's emphasis on episodic action. Notably, the novel's crowning sequences are framed as moments of theatrical spectacle featuring the impassioned Lady Margaret. In the first, Smith takes a page out of Lewis's *The Monk* as Lady Margaret assumes the role of a Bleeding Nun figure. She appears in the guise of a lamp-bearing, blood-soaked spectre with wounded breast who, when the imprisoned Matilda rejects an amorous Duncaethal's marriage offer, reminds him of his dastardly crime of uxoricide. (In this instance, it is interesting to note that, according to Devendra Varma, Smith had played the role of Ursula in *Raymond and Agnes; or The Bleeding Nun of Lindenberg*, a drama adapted from *The Monk*.) In her unlikely disguise as the dreaded and aggressive bandit Darthalgo, Lady Margaret later kidnaps and threatens the upright Matilda and, in the novel's closing scene, reveals her true identity by tearing off "her false hair and counterfeit beard", kills her husband, and then commits suicide (87). In the light of these adeptly conceived and spectacular sequences, one wonders why Smith opted to recount her tale in novelistic, as opposed to dramatic, format.

Smith's knowledge of the Gothic is on exhibit throughout *The Caledonian Bandit*, lending some support to Montague Summers's claim that this work is "Gothic in the highest degree" (*Gothic* 368). Characters whose names derive from signature works in the Gothic tradition such as Matilda (Walpole) and Agnes (Lewis) inhabit animated, contested castles that house groaning portraits and various dark secrets in the form, principally, of brutalized and imprisoned women. The Gothic Castle, which is virtually a character in much Gothic fiction, is a site of radical transformation in Smith's novel that nicely mirrors the nature of its varied owners and circumstances. According to Simon Schama, castles are ambivalent locations that may serve as "citadels of authority in peacetime, *engines of terror* if need be in times of civil war" (107, emphasis added). Both the Castle of Bosmora and that of Duncaethal live up to this billing in the course of Smith's novel as they are converted from sites of peace and mirth to sites of imprisonment and battle, and vice versa. Extending Clara Reeve's innovation of the castle's secret, fatal chamber, Smith creates a space of generationally sedimented oppression. The kidnapped Matilda is held in the chamber "of the late lady Margaret" (33) where the latter was drugged in preparation for her murder. The room contains a portrait of Matilda's mother Mabel who died, tragically, after her daughter's birth, and serves as a shrine to the ill-fated Agnes Maclean who is later discovered by her long-lost son Donald to be a life-long prisoner in Duncaethal's castle. Smith provides a noteworthy variation on this Castle-as-Bastille theme when she places Donald in the traditional Female Gothic heroine's perilous position as potential seduction victim. Donald claims that Lady Margaret's passionate declarations to him in this fatal chamber and her vows of revenge subsequent to his rejection of her advances, haunt him until story's end. Only then, on the heels of Lady Margaret's shocking suicide, can he finally relate—and, thus, unburden himself about—the traumatic episode.

In keeping with Radcliffean tradition, *The Caledonian Bandit* also serves as a disguised conduct guide whose overarching suggestion seems to be that parents are not entirely blameworthy for the creation of monstrous children. Most Gothic fiction—including all of Radcliffe's works and Lewis's *The Monk*—serves as a warning to misguided and overly indulgent parents. *The Caledonian Bandit* promotes this idea to some degree in Lady Margaret's case as the reader is informed that the Earl of Monteith, "a man of most excellent qualities", possessed a single failing—namely, that of over-indulging his daughter, "whom he had loved even to a fault" (183). As a result, the "fiendlike" (22) and "masculine" (12) Margaret serves as "a dreadful example of the bitter effects of an ungoverned temper and unrestrained passion" (167). This is, tragically, coupled with a marriage undertaken to gratify her ambition, a decision that further perverts her passionate sensibility. Margaret's abuse at the hands of her heartless husband is rendered in an unsympathetic manner as an appropriate comeuppance. Much like Charlotte Dacre's *Zofloya*, however, *The Caledonian Bandit* advances contradictory standpoints regarding the recipe for monstrous children as Duncaethal is described as an inveterately evil youth whose desperate parents' concerted efforts at reform have the opposite effect: Duncaethal's trip to Venice for improvement results in his apprenticeship in libertinism and gambling. It would appear that some individuals are inherently evil and all attempts at their reformation prove futile, an unsettling message for Smith's middle-class readership and their faith in the transformative power of proper moral education.

In the final analysis, "Gothic Scotland" narratives like Mrs. Smith's *The Caledonian Bandit* testify to the tremendous popularity of Radcliffe-style Gothic into the early nineteenth century and beyond. With the advantage of hindsight, literary scholars can now see that Minerva Press Gothomania, with its predictable, recycled narrative recipes, proliferated in the form of twentieth-century Harlequin-style costume Gothic works. As I have argued at length elsewhere, contrary to the established critical view that the 1810s and 1820s witnessed the death of the Gothic, that form was actually in the process of being spectacularly revived in innovative, psychologically-focused ways in novels like Mary Shelley's *Frankenstein* (1818) and Charles Robert Maturin's *Melmoth the Wanderer* (1820).[18] Perhaps most intriguingly and pertinently given the Gothic Scotland image advanced in such works as Smith's *The Caledonian Bandit* is the fact that Scottish experimenters with the Gothic in the nineteenth century, ranging from Sir Walter Scott, James Hogg, and numerous contributors to *Blackwood's Edinburgh Magazine*, to Robert Louis Stevenson and Margaret Oliphant, rejected the Gothic Scotland image in favour of their own compelling formulations of a Scottish Gothic literature, works that counter Tom Nairn's contentious claim that there is next to no literature worthy of attention produced in Scotland between 1820 and 1885 (112). Drawing on key precepts of the Scottish Enlightenment and its attendant idea of "enlightened" progress, these authors engage with Scotland's own historic bogeys including such issues as the Calvinist/Covenanting spectre and a certain national "schizophrenia" induced by the Union. But that, as they say, is another story and the subject of my next critical study tentatively titled *Gothic Scotland/Scottish Gothic: The Poetics and Politics of a Cultural Tradition.*

CAROL MARGARET DAVISON
University of Windsor

January 5, 2010

CAROL MARGARET DAVISON is Associate Professor of English Literature at the University of Windsor. She is the author of *The History of the Gothic, 1764-1824* (University of Wales Press, 2009), *Anti-Semitism and British Gothic Literature* (Palgrave/Macmillan, 2004), and the editor of Bram Stoker's *Dracula: Sucking Through the Century, 1897-1997* (Dundurn Press, 1997). She is currently at work on *British Gothic Casebook: A Compendium of Critical Reviews of British Gothic Literature, 1764-1824,* and *Gothic Scotland/Scottish Gothic: The Poetics and Politics of a Cultural Tradition.*

NOTES

1   There are different schools of thought as to the exact chronology and nature of the Gothic's inter-continental cross-fertilizations. In the 1950s, Devendra P. Varma, for example, disputed Montague Summers's claim that continental writers directly influenced the British Gothic novel's development. In *The Gothic Flame*, Varma contentiously positioned the British Gothic—in both its novelistic and theatrical forms—as the progenitor of both the *Schauerroman* and the *roman noir*. Certain it is that, despite the tremendous popularity of the British Gothic novel in France, the *roman noir* came later. See Maurice Lévy's essay, "English Gothic and the French Imagination: A Calendar of Translations, 1767-1828," which provides a detailed bibliography of the English Gothic novel in French translation. For the best available concise overview of the development of the novelistic subgenre known as the *roman noir*, a marginalized tradition within the French Romantic movement, see Terry Hale's essay on the "*Frénétique* School" in *The Handbook to Gothic Literature*. As numerous British Gothic novels from the 1790s evidence in contradiction to Varma's claim, the German terror-novel or *Schauerroman*, which blended 'political and magical ingredients' and focused on 'the activities of powerful secret societies' (Tompkins 281), served as a significant influence (Hall 169). As Robert Kiely has rightly commented, these narratives "generally brought more explicit eroticism and violence to the realm of the English Gothic" (100). For more detailed analyses of the impact of the German *Schauerroman* on British Gothic fiction, see Robert Ignatius Le Tellier's *Kindred Spirits*, Terry Hale's chapter devoted to continental influences in *The Cambridge Companion to Gothic Fiction*, and Daniel Hall's *French and German Gothic Fiction in the Late Eighteenth Century*.

2   The first author laments the extent of his nation's obsession with "the horrid massacres which disgraced France during the tyranny of Robespierre":

> But, alas! so prone are we to imitation, that we have exactly and faithfully copied the SYSTEM OF TERROR, if not in our streets, and in our fields, at least in our circulating libraries, and in our closets. Need I say that I am adverting to *the wonderful revolution* that has taken place in the *art* of novel-writing, in which the only exercise for the fancy is now upon the most frightful subjects, and in which we reverse

the petition in the litany, and riot upon "battle, murder, and sudden death." (A Jacobin Novelist 299-300; emphasis added)

The author of the second piece likewise wields the motif of terror when he or she alludes to "the great quantity of novels with which our circulating libraries are filled, and our parlour tables covered, in which it has been the fashion to make *terror* the *order of the day*, by confining the heroes and heroines in old gloomy castles, full of spectres, apparitions, ghosts, and dead men's bones" (qtd. in Mudge 98; emphasis added).

3 This statistic actually squares with that provided by Franz Potter in relation to William Lane's Minerva Press in roughly the same period. According to Potter, "between 1795 and 1810 more than a third of the books published by Lane had Gothic titles" (15). Peter Garside's research about this "undeniably buoyant" genre ("English" 55) concurs with these figures (56). Garside's statistics do not take account of Gothic chapbooks and stage melodramas (57). As regards Gothic serials ("penny dreadfuls") and mini-novels ("bloods"), Bradford K. Mudge intriguingly points out that the "pulp Gothic dominated the working-class market during the 1820s and continued to grow throughout the 1830s and 1840s" (100).

4 Drawing on the research in Peter Garside's *The English Novel 1770-1829: Bibliographical Survey of Prose Fiction Published in the British Isles* (2000), Robert Miles notes that "[b]etween the years 1785 and 1820, women produced more novels than men, gradually at first but accelerating to 1814, when women-authored novels reached 66% of new novels published, where the gender of the writer has been established" (181 n.1). As Pam Morris rightly states in the light of the revolutionary shift of the household from a site of production to one of consumption, "Women, as both readers and writers, played a significant role in the expansion of print culture" (xi).

5 According to Montague Summers, "The Gothic novel, a lengthy affair, in its four volumes or three volumes, as the case might be, was abridged, compressed and imitated upon a small scale, and the cheaper presses began to pour out in undiminished spate legions upon legions of "bluebooks" which were the lineal descendants of the earlier chapbooks, and which were bought in infinity by exactly the same class of purchaser" (*Gothic* 82). Bluebooks were, effectively, "the poor man's Gothic novels, often a crude six-penny leaflet, bound in blue covers" (Robert K. Black, qtd. in Varma, *Evergreen* 80). According to Angela Koch, based on her examination of the

Corvey collection—an extensive collection of early British fiction held in the Princely Library of Corvey Castle near Höxter in North Rhine Westphalia—Gothic bluebooks were not a consecutive but a contemporaneous phenomenon of the Gothic craze. The best study of this branch of Gothic production remains William Watt's 1932 publication, *Shilling Shockers of the Gothic School*. As Summers notes elsewhere, the "influence of Mrs. Radcliffe on her contemporaries can hardly be over-estimated" (*Essays* 23). As regards the calibre of those derivative works, however, Robert Spector claims that while Radcliffe may have granted great respectability to the genre, "her multitude of followers quickly plunged it into greater disrepute" (*English* 14). Michael Sadleir likewise refers to the "throng of imitators and exaggerators of the Radcliffian romance, for whose lack of restraint and very miscellaneous talent Jane Austen could have felt neither respect nor tenderness" (172). Some authors who failed to embrace the vogue drew greater attention to their works by signalling their lack of Gothic credentials. See, for example, Rachel Hunter's *Letitia; or, The Castle without a Spectre* (1801) and Mary Goldsmith's humorous title page for her domestic novel, *Casualties, A Novel* (1804) which reads, "No Subterranean Caverns—Haunted Castles—Enchanted Forests—Fearful Visions—Mysterious Voices—Supernatural Agents—Bloody Daggers—Dead Men's Skulls—Mangled Bodies—Nor Marvellous Lights, from any Part of the present Work; but will be found, on Perusal, to arise out of Natural Incidents."

6   See my discussion of Radcliffe in chapter 3 of *History of the Gothic: Gothic Literature, 1764-1824*.

7   For more on the fascinating phenomenon of Gothic bluebooks and chapbooks, an intriguing and valuable study in its own right, see the works of Potter, Koch, William Watt's *Shilling Shockers of the Gothic School* and Frederick S. Frank's chapter devoted to "Gothic Chapbooks, Bluebooks, and Short Stories in the Magazines (1790-1820)." Frank estimates that tens of thousands of bluebooks and chapbooks were published in this period (143).

8   Radcliffe's first novel, *The Castles of Athlin and Dunbayne* (1789), is notably like *The Castle of Otranto* in its peasant hero's discovery of his true, aristocratic identity. Set during the Middle Ages, *The Castles of Athlin and Dunbayne* involves the tale of two warring Scottish clans. Like Walpole's Theodore, Alleyn, a peasant captured during a clan attack on Dunbayne castle, discovers that he is a nobleman. He also discovers two women imprisoned in the castle's

subterranean passages, who turn out to be his mother and sister. The evil Malcolm Dunbayne had killed his own brother (Alleyn's father), stolen his lands, and imprisoned his wife and daughter. After his defeat, a double wedding concludes the narrative whereby each hero marries the other's sister.

9 Katherine Haldane Grenier persuasively discusses tourism's "imperial tendencies" in Scotland and notes how claims of expertise about Scotland were "a form of imperial takeover" (4).

10 In *Scotland, Britain, Empire: Writing the Highlands, 1760-1860*, Kenneth McNeil underscores the nature of Scotland's ambivalent position within the British Union. Problematic in terms of its ascription of a type of national consensus to the Act of Union, McNeil's claim is that "Scots accepted the loss of political autonomy in return for something that would prove more beneficial to the nation in the long run: access to new overseas markets and the wealth of empire" (10). In its representation of a conscious trade-off, McNeil's claim remains contentious. Certain it is that Scots—especially Highlanders—provided a great deal of British imperial military muscle while many reaped the benefits of the Empire by establishing trading posts in the colonies (11-12).

11 It is ironic that Defoe fails to recognize that touring, the very activity in which he is engaged, will prove to be of huge commercial value in years to come for this seemingly worthless territory.

12 The Battle of Bannockburn, for example, is evoked by the frightening hills Defoe passes en route to Stirling where the Bruce defeated the English army (611).

13 It bears commenting that the word "anile" is a gendered term that, effectively, links women to irrational superstition, a longstanding pairing in the Western cultural tradition. According to the OED, "anile" means "Of or like an old woman, old-womanish; imbecile."

14 Murray J. Pittock notes, for example, William Robertson's suggestion that "Popery" and "superstitious terror and credulity" were especially appealing in Scotland ("History" 90). Richard J. Finlay considers the propensities and agendas of various Scottish Enlightenment thinkers from a wider perspective, noting that, in their eagerness to create a North British identity, "There was a head long rush to divest the nation of its previous 'barbarisms'" (147). In this regard, the Highlands were especially embarrassing. Their modernization would evidence Scotland's post-Union progress (147).

15 While the Witchcraft Act dates from 1563, the most intense period

of witch-hunting in Scotland took place a century later between 1658 and 1662.

16 Walpole also deemed Mary Shelley's father, William Godwin, "one of the greatest monsters exhibited by history" (qtd. in Sterrenburg 146). Ironically, Thomas de Quincey declared, looking back at the 1790s, that "most people felt of Mr. Godwin with the same alienation and horror as of a ghoul, or a bloodless vampyre, or the monster created by Frankenstein" (qtd. in Sterrenburg 147).

17 Orkney was only pledged to the Scottish crown in 1468 and the title resigned by Earl William Sinclair to James III in 1470 (Crawford 467).

18 See chapter 7 in my *History of the Gothic: Gothic Literature, 1764-1824.*

WORKS CITED

A Jacobin Novelist. "The Terrorist System of Novel-Writing (1797)." *Gothic Readings: The First Wave, 1764-1840.* Edited by Rictor Norton. London and New York: Leicester University Press, 2000. 299-303.

Adams, Donald K. "The Second Mrs. Radcliffe." *The Mystery & Detection Annual.* Edited by Donald K. Adams. Beverly Hills, Calif., 1972. 48-64.

Barrett, C.F. *Douglas Castle; or, The Cell of Mystery, a Scottish Tale.* London: A. Neil, 1803.

Barrow, G.W.S. *Kingship and Unity: Scotland 1000-1306.* Edinburgh: Edinburgh University Press, 1981.

Carson, James P. "Enlightenment, Popular Culture, and Gothic Fiction." *The Cambridge Companion to the Eighteenth-Century Novel.* Edited by John Richetti. Cambridge: Cambridge University Press, 1996. 255-276.

Crawford, Barbara. "Orkney and Caithness, earldom of." *The Oxford Companion to Scottish History.* Edited by Michael Lynch. Oxford: Oxford University Press, 2001. 467-470.

Curties, T. J. Horsley. *The Scottish Legend; or The Isle of Saint Clothair.* London: Minerva Press, 1802.

Dacre, Charlotte. *Zofloya; or, The Moor: A Romance of the Fifteenth Century.* 1806. Peterborough, Ont.: Broadview Press, 1997.

Davison, Carol Margaret. *History of the Gothic: Gothic Literature, 1764-1824.* Cardiff: University of Wales Press, 2009.

Defoe, Daniel. *A Tour Through the Whole Island of Great Britain.* 1724-26. Harmondsworth: Penguin, 1986.

Drake, Nathan. *Literary Hours: or, Sketches, Critical, Narrative, and Poetical.* 1800. New York: Garland Publishing, 1970. 2 vols.

F.H.P. *The Castle of Caithness: A Romance of the Thirteenth Century.* London: Minerva Press, 1802.

Finlay, Richard J. "Caledonia or North Britain? Scottish Identity in the Eighteenth Century." *Image and Identity: The Making and Re-making of Scotland Through the Ages.* Edited by Dauvit Broun, R.J. Finlay, and Michael Lynch. Edinburgh: John Donald Publishers, 1998. 143-156.

Fox, J. Review of *Santa Maria; or The Mysterious Pregnancy: a Romance. In Three Volumes. Gentleman's Magazine* 68 (September 1798): 786.

Frank, Frederick. "Gothic Chapbooks, Bluebooks, and Short Stories in the Magazines (1790-1820)." *Gothic Writers: A Critical and Bibliographical Guide.* Edited by Douglass H. Thomson, Jack G. Voller, and Frederick S. Frank. Westport, Conn. and London: Greenwood Press, 2002. 133-146.

Fritzsche, Peter. "Specters of History: On Nostalgia, Exile, and Modernity." *The American Historical Review* 106 (2001).

Garside, Peter. "The English Novel in the Romantic Era: Consolidation and Dispersal." *The English Novel 1770-1829: Bibliographical Survey of Prose Fiction Published in the British Isles.* Vol. 2. Oxford: Oxford University Press, 2000. 15-103. 2 vols.

—. "Romantic Gothic." *Literature of the Romantic Period: A Bibliographical Guide.* Edited by Michael O'Neill. Oxford: Clarendon Press, 1998. 315-340.

Haldane Grenier, Katherine. *Tourism and Identity in Scotland, 1770-1914.* Aldershot: Ashgate, 2005.

Hale, Terry. "French and German Gothic: The Beginnings." *The Cambridge Companion to Gothic Fiction.* Edited by Jerrold E. Hogle. Cambridge: Cambridge University Press, 2002. 63-84.

—. "Frénétique School." *The Handbook to Gothic Literature.* Edited by Marie Mulvey-Roberts. Houndmills, Basingstoke: Macmillan, 1998. 58-63.

Hall, Daniel. *French and German Gothic Fiction in the Late Eighteenth Century.* Bern: Peter Lang, 2005.

Helme, Elizabeth. *St. Clair of the Isles; or, The Outlaws of Barra.* 1803. London: Frederick Warne and Company, n.d.

Honour, Hugh. *Romanticism.* 1979. Harmondsworth: Penguin, 1991.

Hook, Andrew. "Scotland and Romanticism: The International Scene." *The History of Scottish Literature.* Vol. 2. 1660-1800. Edited by Andrew Hook. Aberdeen: Aberdeen University Press, 1987. 307-322.

Howells, Coral Ann. *Love, Mystery, and Misery: Feeling in Gothic Fiction.* London: Athlone Press, 1978.

Isaacs, Mrs. *Glenmore Abbey; or, The Lady of the Rock.* London: Minerva Press, 1805.

Jenkins, James D. "Introduction" to *Barozzi; or, The Venetian Sorceress* by Catherine Smith. Chicago: Valancourt Books, 2005. vii-xiv.

Johnson, Samuel and James Boswell. *A Journey to the Western Islands of Scotland and The Journal of a Tour to the Hebrides.* 1775 and 1786. Harmondsworth: Penguin, 1984.

Kiely, Robert. *The Romantic Novel in England.* Cambridge, Mass.: Harvard University Press, 1972.

Knox, John. *The First Blast of the Trumpet Against the Monstrous Regiment of Women.* 1558. New York: Da Capo Press Inc., 1972.

Koch, Angela. "Gothic Bluebooks in the Princely Library of Corvey and Beyond." *Cardiff Corvey: Reading the Romantic Text.* Edited by Anthony Mandal. 9 (Dec. 2002). CEIR, Cardiff University 21 Oct. 2005 <http://www.cf.ac.uk/encap/corvey/articles/cc09_n01.html.>

Lathom, Francis. *The Romance of the Hebrides; or, Wonders Never Cease!* London: Minerva Press, 1809.

Le Tellier, Robert Ignatius. *Kindred Spirits: Interrelations and Affinities Between the Romantic Novels of England and Germany (1790-1820).* Salzburg: Institut für Anglistik und Amerikanistik, 1982.

Lévy, Maurice. "English Gothic and the French Imagination: A Calendar of Translations, 1767-1828." *The Gothic Imagination: Essays in Dark Romanticism.* Edited by G.R. Thompson. [Pullman, Wash.]: Washington State University Press, 1974. 150-176.

Lowenthal, David. *The Past is a Foreign Country.* Cambridge: Cambridge University Press, 1985.

Macpherson, James. *The Poems of Ossian and Related Works.* Edited by Howard Gaskill. 1996. Edinburgh: Edinburgh University Press, 2003.

Mayo, Robert D. "Gothic Romance in the Magazines." *PMLA* 65 (1950): 762-789.

McNeil, Kenneth. *Scotland, Britain, Empire: Writing the Highlands, 1760-1860.* Columbus: Ohio State University Press, 2007.

Miles, Robert. "What is a Romantic Novel?" *Novel* 34 (2001): 180–201.

Moretti, Franco. *Atlas of the European Novel, 1800-1900.* London: Verso, 1998.

Morris, Pam, ed. General Introduction. *Conduct Literature for Women.* Vol. 1. London: Pickering & Chatto, 2005. ix-xxxii.

Mudge, Bradford K. "The Man with Two Brains: Gothic Novels, Popular Culture, Literary History." *PMLA* 107 (1992): 92-104.

Nairn, Tom. *The Break-Up of Britain: Crisis and Neo-nationalism*. London: NLB, 1981.

Outram, Dorinda. *The Enlightenment*. 1995. 2nd edition. Cambridge: Cambridge University Press, 2005.

Palmer, John, Jr. *The Haunted Cavern: A Caledonian Tale*. London: B. Crosby, 1796.

Pennant, Thomas. *A Tour in Scotland, 1769*. 1769. Edinburgh: Birlinn, 2000.

—. *A Tour in Scotland and Voyage to the Hebrides, 1772*. 1772. Edinburgh: Birlinn, 1999.

Pittock, Murray J. "History and the Teleology of Civility in the Scottish Enlightenment." *Enlightenment and Emancipation*. Edited by Susan Manning and Peter France. Lewisburg: Bucknell University Press, 2006. 81-96.

—. *The Invention of Scotland: The Stuart Myth and the Scottish Identity, 1638 to the Present*. London: Routledge, 1991.

Potter, Franz. *The History of Gothic Publishing, 1800-1835: Exhuming the Trade*. Houndmills, Basingstoke: Palgrave, 2005.

Probatum Est. 'Terrorist Novel Writing.' *Spirit of the Journals for 1792*. London: James Ridgway, 1802. 227-229.

Radcliffe, Ann. *The Castles of Athlin and Dunbayne*. 1789. Oxford: Oxford University Press, 1995.

Radcliffe, Mary-Anne. *Manfroné; or, The One-Handed Monk*. 1809. Kansas City: Valancourt Books, 2007.

Roche, Regina Maria. *The Children of the Abbey*. 1796. London: Minerva Press, 1798.

Sade, Marquis de. "Reflections on the Novel." 1800. *One Hundred and Twenty Days of Sodom*. Translated by Austryn Wainhouse and Richard Seaver. London: Arrow Books, 1989. 91-116.

Sadleir, Michael. *Things Past*. London: Constable, 1944.

Shelley, Mary. *Frankenstein; or, The Modern Prometheus*. 1818. Oxford: Oxford University Press, 1993.

Smith, Mrs. *The Caledonian Bandit; or, The Heir of Duncaethal. A Romance of the Thirteenth Century*. London: Minerva Press, 1811. 2 vols.

Spector, Robert Donald. *The English Gothic: A Bibliographic Guide to Writers from Horace Walpole to Mary Shelley*. Westport, Conn.: Greenwood Press, 1984.

Sterrenburg, Lee. "Mary Shelley's Monster: Politics and Psyche in *Frankenstein*." *The Endurance of Frankenstein*. Edited by George

Levine and U.C. Knoepflmacher. Berkeley: University of California Press, 1974. 143-71.

Summers, Montague. *Essays in Petto*. 1928. Freeport, N.Y.: Books for Libraries Press, 1967.

—. *The Gothic Quest: A History of the Gothic Novel*. 1938. London: The Fortune Press, 1964.

Tompkins, J.M.S. *The Popular Novel in England 1770-1800*. London: Methuen, 1932.

Varma, Devendra P. *The Evergreen Tree of Diabolical Knowledge*. Washington: Consortium Press, 1972.

—. *The Gothic Flame*. London: Arthur Barker, 1957.

—. Introduction. *Barozzi; or, The Venetian Sorceress*. Vol. 1. New York: Arno Press, 1977. v-xiii. 2 vols.

Walpole, Horace. *The Castle of Otranto*. 1764. Oxford: Oxford University Press, 1982.

Watt, William W. *Shilling Shockers of the Gothic School: A Study of Chapbook Gothic Romances*. New York: Russell & Russell, 1932.

Womack, Peter. *Improvement and Romance: Constructing the Myth of the Highlands*. London: Macmillan, 1989.

NOTE ON THE TEXT

The Caledonian Bandit; or, The Heir of Duncaethal was first published in two volumes by A. K. Newman of London in 1811 under the Minerva Press imprint. Only two copies of the first edition are known to exist: one at the Corvey Collection in Germany, and the other in the University of Virginia's Sadleir-Black Collection of Gothic Fiction. The present edition, the first since the novel's initial publication, reproduces the text of the original edition from a microfiche of the Corvey copy. The text used in this edition reproduces verbatim the original text, with the exception of a small number of obvious typographical errors, such as omitted closing quotation marks, which have been silently corrected. No attempt has been made to modernize or standardize spelling or grammar.

The Publisher gratefully acknowledges the assistance of his sister, Laurie Grove, who undertook the arduous task of transcribing the text of the novel from the microfiche.

THE

Caledonian Bandit;

OR,

THE HEIR OF DUNCAETHAL.

A ROMANCE

OF THE THIRTEENTH CENTURY.

TWO VOLUMES IN ONE.

BY

MRS. SMITH,

OF THE THEATRE-ROYAL HAYMARKET.

A Tale of the times of old.

OSSIAN.

VOL. I.

LONDON :

PRINTED AT THE

Minerva-Press,

FOR A. K. NEWMAN AND CO.

(Successors to Lane, Newman, and Co.)

LEADENHALL-STREET.

1811.

ADDRESS.

THERE are so many motives for writing, that it is usual to satisfy the reader's curiosity, by a statement of the cause in so doing. Reasons the most laudable first induced the author to attempt the following humble pages.

For the liberal encouragement which she received from the publisher, on her submitting the MS. to his consideration, she is truly grateful.

What most she ought to dread, are the reviewers' disapprobation; but they are her countrymen; and though, by habit and education, strict judges of style and composition, they will, in pity, *spare*, if they cannot praise.

Critics, I deprecate your anger; and though this first offspring of my brain* possesses neither brilliancy of character, nor beauty of language, I trust, if you cannot let it flourish in the warmth of your smiles, you will in mercy forbear to crush it with your frowns.

THE

CALEDONIAN BANDIT.

CHAP. I.

What needs there
A stronger breast-plate than a heart untainted?
Thrice is he arm'd that hath his quarrel just;
And he but naked, though lock'd up in steel,
Whose conscience with injustice is corrupted.

SHAKESPEARE.*

A HEART-RENDING sigh burst from the fair bosom of the beautiful Matilda, as she cast a rich embroidered scarf of tartan plaid across the form of the graceful Donald;—"Receive this, beloved youth," said she; "and when you meet the eye of the fierce and terror-striking Duncaethal, let it inspire thee with tenfold strength to crush thy foe, and return to thy Matilda, crowned with the laurel-wreaths of victory." A drop like the dew of morn glistened in her soft blue eye, as her taper fingers twined the knot which fastened her gift. "Farewell," said she, "and sometimes, in the battle's rage, remember Matilda."

The youth arose from his knee, exclaiming, while the feeling of his heart shone in his expressive countenance, "Farewell, sweet maid! and when I face my enemy, this arm shall prove that he who feels like me is doubly armed—who fights alike the cause of gratitude and love. The unknown Donald, fierce Duncaethal's scoff, shall prove his heart as brave, and as great a stranger to ignoble fear, as though he stood acknowledged sprung from princes. And since I am blest with thy dear love, I envy not the greatest sovereigns of the world!" Thus saying, he again sunk on his knee, and pressing her hand to his lips, sealed on it a burning kiss; then tore himself away, followed by his faithful squire.

Matilda hastily ascended the west turret of the castle, following him with her eyes as he rode through the forest's maze, until its gloom enveloped him from her sight; quick tears then chased each other down her fair cheeks, as she again sought her chamber, when sinking on her knees, she offered up prayers for the protection of the heroic Donald.

CHAP. II.

Instantly I plung'd into the sea,
And buffeting the billows to her rescue,
Redeem'd her life with half the loss of mine;
Like a rich conquest, in one hand I bore her,
And with the other dash'd the saucy waves,
That throng'd and press'd to rob me of my prize.

OTWAY.*

A low-born man, of parentage obscure,
Who nought can boast but his desire to be a soldier,
And to gain a name in arms.

HOME.*

EAST of the Cheviot Hills, on an eminence, stood the ancient but grand Castle of Bosmora; it seemed to bid defiance to the destroying hand of Time, as it frowned, in sullen majesty, on the surrounding scenery. It had, for centuries, been inhabited by ancestors of the present possessor, who were no less famous for their deeds in arms, than for their benevolence and hospitality. Their vassals were numerous, and, at the call of their laird, were ready to protect his rights with their lives, not for the fear they bore to him, but their love; for while, with the dignity of a baron, he made them remember he was their lord, he never, by severity, taught them to forget their respect for him as a man. About twenty years previous to the commencement of this period, he obtained the hand of Mabel Duncaethal, who was beautiful, accomplished, and sprung from a race as noble as her consort's. The laird, her father, had one foible, that somewhat obscured his many excellent qualities, an immoderate share of ancestorial pride; he doated on his son, the twin-brother of Mabel, as he hoped he would transmit his name to posterity: but Heaven ordained it otherwise—for when he went forth to repel a chieftain with whom his father had commenced hostilities, he fell in battle, and crushed at once the hopes and life of his unhappy father; nor did he alone sink by the weight of grief—the lovely Agnes Maclean, an orphan who had been reared under the protection of his sire, loved him; and when the fatal news arrived that he was slain, she sunk into a profound melancholy—the rose of her cheek gave place to the lily, as she

"Sat, like Patience on a monument, smiling at grief."*

Long had she loved the youth Alexander, and he returned her passion with all the glowing ardour of a first affection; but when his father heard of his ignoble passion, as he termed it, he treated it with ridicule; and when he found that had no effect, he bade him forget her, or he would cast him out, an alien to his blood; for though he loved him so passionately, he could not give him such a proof as to admit a union with an orphan obscure and poor.

The amiable and lovely Agnes had been placed under the care of the baron by her father, a descendant of the house of Maclean, when on his deathbed: she was the only fruit of an inauspicious marriage; her birth sent her mother to an early grave, and her father survived her but five years. The baron brought home his little charge, and had her placed under his immediate eye, with his own daughter, who was three years more advanced in age. As they grew up, they loved each other with the affection of sisters; Mabel often said she felt not less affection for Agnes than her brother; and Alexander looked upon both equally as his sisters; till age taught him the difference of the sensations he felt for the ward of his father, and those he felt for Mabel: long did he struggle with his growing passion, until he found it in vain, when gaining courage from desperation, he ventured to declare it to his father, when the confession was received in the manner already related. Though the baron was not blind to the good qualities of Agnes, but as Alexander was the heir of his name and titles, he had other views, and hoped to unite him to the heiress of Cathloda, who was equal, not to say superior, in the pride and wealth of ancestry.

While he was thus endeavouring to realize his hopes, Alexander was indulging in all the melancholy of despairing love. About this period the castle was visited by Bosmora, who, being struck with the beauty of Mabel, offered her his hand, which was accepted with joy on the part of her father, and becoming modesty on hers. All was now hilarity and mirth in the castle, save in the breasts of Agnes and Alexander; the ancient halls resounded with songs of the minstrels, as, with flying fingers, they kissed the golden strings of the lyre, and chaunted an epithalamium in honour of the nuptials of Bosmora and the peerless Mabel; who, at the end of a short time, left Duncaethal for the castle of her lord.

A few weeks after, her brother was slain in battle, as before premised. At the commencement of her father's illness, Mabel was sent for to the castle; and, upon his demise, she would fain have conducted Agnes to Bosmora, as Duncaethal now fell to a far-distant branch of the family, and the succeeding heir had arrived to take possession of his rights; but on his signifying he should absent himself for a few weeks, she requested permission to remain for a short time, as she wished to indulge the poignancy of her grief in solitude. Mabel acquiesced, after a promise of her following in a few days.

In the meantime, the former was recovering gradually her usual spirits; for though she tenderly loved her father and brother, she was not of a disposition to mourn beyond measure for what was without remedy. She found in Bosmora a truly tender husband, which contributed to the mitigation of her sorrows, and compensation of her losses; and she looked anxiously forward to that blissful period when she was to produce a living pledge of their mutual affection; though her anticipated joy was severely checked by learning the loss of Agnes, who, in a short excursion into the fields, was precipitantly thrown from her palfrey, who had taken fright from the rushing of a flight of birds, into a roaring flood which flowed near the castle, and met with a premature death. Many tears were shed for the hapless fate of her friend, till Heaven sent her consolation in the being of a lovely son, which weaned her from her sorrows, to taste the most transcendant joys of maternal love.

The castle now echoed with shouts and joyous acclamations, with which the numerous vassals greeted the birth of their future laird; but scarcely had six months elapsed, ere all mirth was converted into grief, by the sudden death of their anxious hope, the new-born heir: the unhappy mother was almost frantic, while the father, though less violent, felt equal sorrow; and summoning all his philosophy, endeavoured to bear his loss with a pious resignation.

At the expiration of a few months, Mabel again proved pregnant; the baron's hopes were once more revived, and he looked forward to the rapturous period with joy undisguised: but, alas! how often human hopes of happiness terminate in sorrow; and we oft anticipate, as the greatest blessing, what, in the end, may prove a curse; thus it was with the baron. While he was fondly indulging the hope of having an heir to his name, he forgot the attendant dangers—what, then, was his distraction, at seeing the death of the lovely and most truly affectionate of wives, in bringing into the world a daughter!—he was frantic and despairing by turns; nor could he be brought to look upon the innocent cause of grief, then so poignantly felt; but shut himself in his apartment, and would see no one except his servant Andrew.

He engaged attendants for the care of his infant daughter, and appropriated the east wing of the castle for her particular use.

Several years passed on in the same gloomy and monotonous manner, when one day, as the baron was crossing the corridor leading to his apartment, he suddenly met his daughter led by her nurse; glancing instantly his eyes upon her infantile countenance, a thousand new and tender emotions were raised in his heart, by her strong likeness to her mother; he caught her in his arms, and, for the first time, imprinted upon her cheek a father's kiss; then took her into his chamber, where her innocent prattle amused, and yet, at times, distressed him, as she would oft make observations which reminded him of her mother's loss. He, however, from this day, grew as fond of her society as he had before avoided it, nor would scarce suffer her to be a moment from his presence; she repaid his affection by a thousand puerile endearments.

As she advanced in age, her necessary tuition would sometimes deprive him of her company, but he felt the loss repaid by her rapid progress in all the studies and accomplishments which adorn her sex.

At the time when she arrived at the age of fifteen years, walking one day in the adjacent forest, and approaching too near a river, which with rapidity sought its course, by quickly turning round to speak to her maid, she lost her equilibrium, and was plunged into the foaming deep; a loud shriek burst from the lips of her terrified attendant, as she looked round in vain for assistance, and seeing no one, left her hapless mistress to her fate. Hastening towards the castle, the first person she saw was Andrew, to whom, as fast as terror would permit, she recounted the dreadful accident; but ere she had finished, her loud sobs attracted the attention of the baron, who, on learning his daughter's dreadful fate, was rushing towards the spot, when he perceived a youth of about seventeen, bearing in his arms the object of his solicitude. He received the insensible form of Matilda, and conveyed her into the castle, where, by proper applications, she was soon restored to her senses, to the great joy of her father.

After a shower of tears, in which she recalled the danger that had passed, she inquired for the youth who had delivered her from her perilous situation; this reminded the baron, that he had failed to reward, or even to thank him for his intrepidity; he now summoned Andrew, and inquired the name of the noble-minded boy, who had saved his daughter's life at the extreme hazard of his own.

"'Tis Donald, so please you, my lord," says Andrew.

"Donald," replied the baron; "and who is he?"

"He is the son of Allen and Jannet, your vassals, who dwell in the white cottage hard by the glen."

"Call him to me," said the baron.

"I will, your honourable lordship," answered Andrew, and immediately left the apartment for that purpose. The baron then ordered the attendants of his daughter to convey her instantly to bed, and seating himself on a couch, waited, with some degree of interest, for the youth's appearance. In the course of a few minutes, Andrew tapped gently at the door, when being desired to enter, he came in, leading by the hand the young peasant.

"Well, young stranger," said the baron, "you have done a brave and gallant action—accept of this as a small token of my gratitude;" at the same time presenting him a purse of gold; which the youth declined, with a graceful bow, apologizing, at the same time, for his refusal, by saying—"My lord, I have done but my duty; I should have acted the same, had it been one of my fellow-vassals, where I was sure of no reward, save the heartfelt satisfaction of having saved a fellow-creature's life; then how much more must my joy be augmented, in preserving the daughter of our noble laird!"

While he delivered thus his sentiments, the baron gazed on him in the greatest surprise; that a poor peasant boy should, when offered, refuse a purse of gold, was, to him, the source of the highest admiration, and that, added to the language which he uttered when declining it, made him conclude he had received somewhat more than a common education.—"Are you the son of Allen and Jannet?" interrogated the baron.

"I am, my laird," replied the boy.

"Wonderful! there are few young men possess your generous ideas; pray who has instilled into your mind such exalted sentiments?"

"If my sentiments are indeed exalted," says he, while a modest blush suffused his cheek, "I am indebted for them to Father Peter, of the convent of St. Andrew; he has, gratuitously, been my instructor, as my parents were too poor to procure for me that knowledge for which I am beholden to his great good-nature; therefore, my laird, if my actions indeed merit the high encomiums you are pleased to bestow, they are due to him who taught me to *know* myself, and love my fellow-creatures."

The baron grew more and more astonished as he contemplated the animated countenance of the speaker; for when he mentioned the name of Father Peter, a tear trembled in the corner of his eye, as, with enthusiasm in his voice and manner, he endeavoured to express the gratitude which he owed him.— "How old are you?" asked the baron.

"Seventeen, my laird," replied Donald.

"It is a pity you should pass your life in the seclusion of a cottage—is it your choice? are you content?" reiterated the baron.

"I wish to bear arms in the service of my country, and would fain leave home to fight the battles of our sovereign; but my fond parents will not consent to it."

"If you can gain their permission, you shall reside in the castle, and be the knight of Matilda, and guard that life which you have so gallantly saved."

Donald dropped on his knee; surprise and joy deprived him of speech, as he respectfully raised the hand of the baron to his lips.

"Spare your thanks—I see what you would utter; receive this ring, and remember, from this time, your name shall be enrolled with the warriors. Andrew shall instruct you in feats of chivalry; and when your studies are complete, you shall depart from Bosmora to the wars, in a manner worthy thy brave and noble spirit."

After endeavouring to express his thanks, Donald arose and left the room; then, swift as the winged arrow from an archer's bow, he sought the cottage of his parents, to whom he recounted the morning's wondrous adventure. Allen and Jannet listened with surprise and wonder, the latter frequently thanking the Virgin for the good fortune of her darling son; and after receiving their benedictions, he left their humble roof for one more suitable to his noble aspiring mind.

CHAP. III

Arise, black Vengeance, from th'unhallow'd cell!
Yield up, oh Love! thy crown and hearted throne
To tyrannous hate! Swell, bosom, with thy fraught,
For 'tis of aspic's tongues!

....

Oh, blood! blood! blood!   SHAKESPEARE.*

THE bell at the convent of St. Andrew had chimed the hour
of vespers, when Father Peter received a message, desiring
his attendance at the castle on the following morning; he was
the confessor of the baron, and the latter wished to make some
inquiries respecting the youth he had taken under his protection.
Upon his arrival, he related many circumstances, which tended
to exalt the boy still higher in the favour of Bosmora. When he
was departing for the convent, as he crossed the court-yard of
the castle, he was accosted by Donald, who had now thrown off
his peasant's guise, and appeared in a dress worthy of his exaltation; the father was surprised; he scarcely, at the first glance,
recognised his pupil, such an advantage did he derive from his
present habiliments, which consisted of a kilt of rich plaid, and
a tartan plaid which hung pendant from his shoulder, and, with
various folds, encircled his graceful form; on his head he wore
a bonnet of Saxon green, on which nodded a plume of black
feathers, that gave a shade to his open brow; a girdle of glossy jet
leather buckled round his waist, from which a sword of curious
workmanship was suspended, gave a martial appearance to the
garb of the beautiful youth. The father contemplated him with
tears of joy, as he entertained for him a real affection, almost
equal to a parent's; many admonitions did he offer in regard
to his future conduct, all of which were received with humble
respect and attention by Donald.

A series of time now passed on, without any change in his
fortune, save that he grew more in favour with his lord; nor did
the fair Matilda view him with an impartial eye; at first she felt

for him only gratitude as the preserver of her life; but it soon ripened into a more tender affection, an affection which she dared not confess even to herself.

At the period when she attained her eighteenth year, the baron gave a *fête* in honour of the event. Numerous lords and ladies assembled at Bosmora on the occasion; among others came Duncaethal, who, since the death of the baroness, had travelled to distant countries, and had but lately arrived at his inheritance, the castle, bringing with him his beautiful lady, the heiress of Monteith. They were welcomed with the usual hospitality of the baron, though he recalled many unpleasant recollections into his breast by his presence, as the last time he had beheld him was on the death of his lamented lady's noble father, by which he became possessed of the name and fortunes of Duncaethal.

The manner of this chief checked all familiar intercourse; his face wore a gloomy and ferocious appearance; his form, though noble and commanding, was to be remarked more for an air of unbending pride, than any natural dignity. His lady, Margaret, was his counterpart in mind, as she also resembled him somewhat in person; her features were strictly beautiful, though masculine, and ill suited the air of languor which she endeavoured to assume; her piercing black eyes seemed more calculated to command homage, than win admiration; and her person, though at once dignified and elegant, was rather above the common stature;—such she was at the time she paid her first visit to the heiress of Bosmora.

The morning of Matilda's natal day was proclaimed by the songs of minstrels, while the beautiful object of these rejoicings was discovered on an exalted seat, by the right hand of her father; on his left was lady Margaret. There could not be a greater contrast than that exhibited in the appearance of those noble females; a rich bandeau of rubies, set in gold, confined the hair of the latter; while a crimson velvet robe, embroidered with gold, and fastened with rich jewels, gave more than usual dignity to her appearance: Matilda wore a pale blue vest, confined round her sylph-like form by a cestus of pearls; a tiara of the same encircled her arched brow; while her auburn tresses waved on her shoulders in graceful ringlets; her arms were bare, except bracelets of the richest pearl, which were only to be rivalled in whiteness by the snowy skin of the wearer, which they were meant to adorn.

The harpers, at an appointed signal, struck their instruments, and, with inspiring voices, chaunted the following words:—

> Hail, flow'r of great Bosmora's race!
>   Hail, Matilda, young and fair!
> In our peerless lady's praise
>   We chaunt the loud inspiring air.
>
> May she all her days possess
>   Her mother's beauty—spotless fame;
> And her great sire shall ever bless
>   The fair descendant of his name.
>
> Chaunt still louder, louder praise!
>   In beauty's cause the song we raise:
> Ceaseless honour—endless fame,
>   Crown Bosmora's mighty name!

At noon the company withdrew to an elegant saloon erected for the occasion, in the eastern wing of the castle; there, seated in a balcony, they were to behold the dexterity of the youths who were about to try their skill in feats of archery. The ladies Matilda and Margaret had the office of presenting the prizes to the victors. The first who approached to claim his reward, was Malcolm, heir of Ross. Matilda, who was to present the first prize, involuntarily heaved a sigh, as she had secretly hoped the victor would have proved Donald.

After the congratulating shouts the spectators raised in honour of the young champion had subsided, the second in skill advanced, and she had the mortification of beholding, at the feet of lady Margaret, Donald himself, who gracefully knelt to receive from her hands the prize due to his skill—it was a beautiful rosary, from which was suspended a rich cross of St. Andrew; an indefinable sensation disturbed her breast, as she saw him gallantly press the gift to his lips; and it was the more augmented, when she beheld the looks of admiration with which he was regarded by lady Margaret; her heart sickened, and she anxiously longed for the commencement of the masque, which was to conclude the festivities of the day.

At the end of the banquet, the visitors retired to assume the characters they intended to represent; when the pavilion being thrown open, glistened with a thousand lights, and admitted the motley group. Donald was arrayed as a knight of St. Andrew, and wore the cross he had received from lady Margaret; he could nowhere distinguish, amongst the crowd of beauties which thronged through the place, the beloved object of his soul, the fair Matilda, and withdrawing to an unoccupied corner of the pavilion, watched anxiously for her appearance. He had not remained long in this situation, when he heard his name pronounced in a low voice, and looking round, perceived, at the left of him, a tall figure, enveloped in a long cloak of plaid. "Follow me, youth!" said the stranger; and instantly issuing from the entrance, and turning into a dark walk overshadowed with trees, suddenly disappeared.

Donald, for a moment, was irresolute, when curiosity gaining the preponderance of caution, he followed his mysterious guide, who proceeded, by a circuitous route, to the left entrance of the castle, and beckoning him to advance, entered an apartment appropriated to the use of some of the visitors, but to whom was to him unknown.

His conductor now being seated on a couch, seemed, for a moment, at a loss to disclose the purport of this nocturnal meeting. In the mean time, Donald remained standing by the entrance of the door, which the stranger had secured: at length the latter seemed to be making a powerful effort to overcome sensations which were evidently painful, and turning to Donald, desired him to be seated, at the same time motioning him to take part of the couch. The stranger then continued—"You are, no doubt, in surprise, at my bringing you here; and perhaps, when I discover who has thus far forgot the dignity of birth, to gain an interview with one unknown, it may be converted into contempt; and yet it lies in your, and only *your* power, to ease the torments of a heart become a burthen to the bosom it inhabits."

The voice of the unknown became agitated with contending emotions, while the sympathizing Donald replied—"Oh, stranger, if it is in the power of so poor a youth as I to allay the sorrows you struggle with, I should feel happy; freely would I sacrifice my life to save a fellow-creature's, nor ever did their miseries by me meet with contempt!"

"'Tis well," said the unknown, "and disguise is no longer necessary;" at the same time throwing up the slouch bonnet which had concealed her face, and casting aside the cloak which had covered her dress, arrayed in an elegant habit, stood before the astonished eyes of Donald the lady Margaret Duncaethal; his amazement was increased tenfold, when he heard her unblushingly declare for him a passion, forgetful of her own and her husband's honour.

With all the uprightness becoming a man, he withstood the temptation—exhorted her to banish from her breast so guilty a passion, and reminded her of the duty due to her noble lord. She regarded him not, but bent on him ardent looks of love; and finding him still remain cold and inflexible, vengeance flashed from her dark eyes—then endeavouring to stifle the revenge which agitated her bosom in convulsive throbs, burst into a flood of tears. He now endeavoured to sooth and calm her perturbation, when recovering in some degree, she earnestly requested him never to divulge the purpose of the meeting.

"If that will give you any satisfaction, you may firmly rely that I never shall."

"Nay, but swear to me," she urged.

"By what oath would you have me bind myself?" asked Donald.

"Swear to me, by the honour of the knighthood you now bear, upon any occasion whatever, to mortal ears never to mention this meeting!"

"I solemnly swear that I never will!" said he; and raising the cross he then wore to his lips, imprinted upon it a kiss to ratify the vow.

"I am now secure," she exultingly replied; "you dare not break your oath—full well I know you dare not violate it!"

Horrid passions combated in her breast, while her dark features were distorted with marks of vengeance, as, with a tight grasp, she held him by the arm: in dreadful sounds she exclaimed— "Learn, thou proud upstart, that, in rejecting my proffered love, thou hast aroused my bitter hate; and from this moment I will prove thy direst foe, for I will revenge myself for the slight thou hast offered me, in a way that shall rend thy heart-strings, and make thee curse the hour in which you first beheld me! Full well know I the cause of this insult—love for another! Matilda! she is the object of thy *chaste* adoration! Heavily will I wreak on her all my vengeance, and when in vain you seek to save her from destruction, in bitterness of soul you shall utter—'This is the revenge of a disappointed woman, who will not bear an insult with impunity!'"

Her ravings now became so loud, that he was fearful lest she should be overheard by Duncaethal, whose apartment was contiguous, and possibly he might then be within, as he had sent an apology for being unable to attend the masque, by reason of a sudden indisposition. Donald ventured to expostulate, and expressed his fears of her exposing herself to the rage of her lord.

"Thou shallow boy," said she, "dost thou foolishly think that Margaret ever acts by halves? think thou I should venture to procure this interview, if I had not been certain of being free from interruption, and still worse, the interruption of a hated husband?—follow me, and be a witness of my security."

She now led him into the adjoining chamber, where, in a deep sleep, lay Duncaethal, unconscious of his dishonour. Donald was going to recede, but holding him by the arm, with a frowning look of contempt, she exclaimed—"*Coward!* what, art thou afraid to approach, when thou seest no terror mark my cheek? he shall not wake till I command!" then lowering her voice—"and if I will it so, he shall sleep for ever!—Now begone! and learn from this, that I have both the will and power to execute my threats!" Thus saying, she led him to the entrance, and closing the outer door, in a voice that struck to his heart, bade him *remember his oath!*

Donald could scarcely believe but that all he had been a witness of was only the effervescence of an imagination proceeding from an oppressed mind; but as the sound of the last words of Margaret, sounding in his ears, recalled to him the remembrance of the dreadful threats she had vowed against the innocent Matilda, and though he would fain persuade himself that she would not dare to put them in practice, yet it cast upon his mind a gloom, which he in vain endeavoured to dispel.

In the mean time, the idol of his soul was endeavouring to account for the reason of his absence from the entertainment, which was on the point of concluding, when he again entered the pavilion, where he beheld the lovely Matilda habited as a nun, (a character she had assumed by reason of its requiring so little spirit to support, being a stranger to that gaiety with which she was surrounded).

Donald now approached, and, in a voice of tender solicitude, inquired if he should conduct her to her apartment, as she appeared unwell? when giving him an assenting smile, and presenting her hand, he proceeded with her to the door of her antichamber, and then gracefully bowing, retired.

Matilda had not been there many minutes, ere she was attended by her woman, Venella, who, perceiving her mistress look pale, inquired if she was ill?

"Rather indisposed," replied the former. "Go to the baron, and inform him that I have retired for the night."

"I will, my lady," said the latter, and withdrew for that purpose.

On the departure of her maid, Matilda relapsed into a train of thoughts but little calculated to tranquillize her troubled spirits. Her reverie was interrupted by Venella, who returned with the baron's and complimentary wishes of the guests for her recovery; which, when she had delivered, with a look of vast importance, and in a tone of half whisper, said—"You know, my lady, you asked me, when you was dressing for the masque, if I had seen sir Donald. I had not seen him then, Madam, but I have since—and where do you think it was, my lady?"

"Nay," said Matilda, as she listened, with the greatest emotion to the chattering Venella, "I know not."

"Why, my lady, he was in the apartment of lady Margaret."

"Impossible!" said Matilda; "what should he do there?"

"Ah, my lady," said Venella, "that's what I should like to know myself. I would not have the sins of some folks to answer for— no, not for that beautiful blue robe I put on your ladyship to-day."

Matilda could scarcely help smiling at the conclusion of this speech of her attendant, though she endeavoured to check her free observations on the lady Duncaethal, by saying she must have mistaken some one else for Donald.

"What! does your ladyship think," said Venella, "that I have lived all these years in the same place, and not know him when I see him?—why, my lady, I should have known him in the dark— and besides, he had on that fine beautiful cross he won to-day by shooting at the mark—the one which lady Margaret herself hung round his neck. Ah! she looked then just for all the world as if she was in love with him;—I thought so, and it seems I thought right.—'Ah,' said I to myself——"

"Silence, I desire you!" exclaimed Matilda.

"Why, holy Virgin! my lady, do you think sir Donald would have gone if he had not been sent for?—No, I am sure he would not; and I saw lady Margaret her own self lead him to the door; she had a taper in her hand, and laying her arm upon his, she said something to him—what it was, I don't know, but I thought to myself, at the time, it was no good, and so——"

"And pray where did you behold all this without being seen yourself?" inquired Matilda, wishing to find the tale untrue, and yet she felt inwardly convinced there was no mistake on the part of Venella.

"Where did I see it, my lady! why I was going through the garden, to take a peep at the fine doings that were going forward in the pavilion, when I heard someone open the door of lady Margaret's chamber; so I stepped behind a pillar of the corridor; I should not have done this, only that I saw sir Donald, and I thought I should hear what he said; but for once I was out in my reckoning, for he never said one single word—no, not one, but walked through the garden; why I was close behind him, my lady, and saw him come up and speak to you, and then lead you to the castle; why, my lady, I wondered to myself how he dared come to a lady so chaste, and so beautiful, and so handsome as yourself, when he knew he had just visited that good-for-nothing, shameless, and——"

"Peace!" said Matilda; "you forget you are talking of my relation."

"Why then, my lady, don't she behave like you? would you have had a man in your chamber at midnight?—no, my lady, that you would not: besides, she has a husband; and though my lord Duncaethal does look so fierce, he is a handsome man: besides, what matters if he is a little older than his lady?—you know he is a baron, which argufies a great deal, my lady; for though we are all ordered by your ladyship's honourable father to call the son of old Allen and Jannet *sir* Donald, yet he is *but* the son of Allen and Jannet; therefore I think the lady Margaret the more to blame, my lady: now if it had been a lord, or an earl, indeed, why it would not be half so shameful; but to act as she has done with a poor peasant, 'tis very shameful indeed—don't you think so, my lady?"

"What then," said Matilda, "you would not think her conduct blamable if Donald had been a lord?—oh, fie, Venella!"

"Oh no!" stammered she; "but I meant if she had not been already married, my lady."

Matilda smiled at the confusion which she perceived in the countenance of her loquacious attendant, who remained silent till she was asked if she had mentioned this affair to any one else?

"No, my lady, not to no living soul: why I have seen no one but the baron your father, and your ladyship is sure I should not mention it to him."

"Then," said Matilda, "you would oblige me very much, by never hinting the subject to any one."

"That I am sure I will not, my lady, if you desire it, for perhaps my lord Duncaethal might call sir Donald to account, for being alone with his lady at that time o'night; now it is a chance if he could account for it, much to his own credit, or to lady Margaret's either—therefore, my lady, it will be best to say no more about it, though I am sure I need not be silent for the sake of sir Donald, for he never said a civil thing to me in his life—no never! so I am sure I have no occasion to like him."

"Why I thought I often heard you say you had a great affection for me," said Matilda.

"Oh, the Virgin! and so I have, St. Andrew be my witness!—but I did not know because I loved you, my dear lady, I was obliged to love sir Donald too."

"You seem to forget," said Matilda, piqued at the remark of her attendant, "that sir Donald saved my life, when, walking with you, I unfortunately fell into the stream, and must inevitably have perished, but for the intrepidity of him you speak of so slightingly."

"I speak slightingly! Oh, St. Andrew forbid! no, indeed, not I. To be sure, I forgot—yes, my lady, he did indeed save your ladyship's life, when I was terrified out of my wits, and left you, to run to the castle for assistance; but you would have been lost, my lady, ere I could return, but for sir Donald, who was returning from the convent of St. Andrew, and was just passing the old oak, when he heard my screams, and I believe he called to me, but I was so frightened, that I dared not look back. Then, to be sure, it was very brave of him to jump into the water, for all the world just like Juno the great dog; but then he knew he could swim: then, my lady, old Andrew scolded me for leaving you, to run so far as the castle—but what could I do? I saw no one near; and if I had jumped in after you, my lady, and caught you by the robe, which I at first thought of doing, I remembered me I could not swim, therefore we should have both gone to the bottom together;—so, in spite of what Andrew said, I think I showed better judgment in flying to the castle; don't you think so, my lady?"

"A very safe one, at least," replied Matilda, smiling.

"Oh, as to that, my lady, if I had been sure of saving your ladyship's life, I would have done my best; but as I knew that was impossible, why I thought it would do no good to drown myself too."

"Very true," said Matilda, who, in spite of the depression under which she laboured, could not refrain indulging in a fit of laughter, at the wise rhetoric of her attendant, whom she now desired to assist in undressing her, and then dismissed her for the night.

Matilda, now left to herself, recalled to herself the wonderful communication made by her attendant, whose veracity she could no longer doubt; now did she fatigue her mind with fruitless conjectures of the purpose for which the visit of Donald could be made to the chamber of Margaret in that mysterious manner, and at that secret hour of night, when the castle was supposed to be entirely evacuated, all the company being assembled in the pavilion; in vain did she endeavour to find some plausible pretext for this conduct; she would have given worlds to have cleared her breast of the painful suspicions with which it laboured; but after a long time spent in ruminating to no purpose, she was obliged to conclude her reflections, very little in favour of the honour of lady Margaret.

Morpheus now cast over her his somniferous veil, and she awoke not till a late hour the next day.

CHAP. IV.

Ha! soft!—'twas but a dream;
But then so terrible, it shakes my very soul;
Cold drops of sweat hang on my trembling flesh;
My blood grows chilly, and I freeze with horror!

SHAKESPEARE.*

DONALD retired to bed as soon as he had left Matilda, but not to rest; no sooner had he closed his eyes, than horrid images flitted across his imagination—the fiend-like looks of lady Margaret, with her dreadful vows of revenge; sometimes he beheld Matilda in the grasp of her unrelenting enemy, calling for his aid in vain; for when he would have flown to her rescue, an unknown power rivetted him to the spot; he then beheld the keen poniard pierce her snowy bosom, and her soft blue eyes closed in eternal sleep.

A deathlike shiver pervaded his whole frame, as he endeavoured to shake off the poppy influence which reigned over his senses; then starting from his couch, repaired to the window of the apartment, and opening the casement, the picturesque view which met his eye in some measure caused the perturbation of his spirits to subside: to his left arose the lofty hills of Cheviot, meeting the first kiss of the ruddy goddess, as she peeped forth from her rosy chamber—it was a fine clear morning, and her disk appeared a bright orb, darting forth rays of refulgent glory, the radiant brightness of whose splendour confounded the curious eye which would discover the *spots* philosophers maintain are on that heavenly luminary; flocks innumerable cropped the grassy carpet of nature, and, by their gambols, seemed to greet the opening day with that gratitude to the Omnipotent, too often neglected by the part of the creation he has stamped with his own godlike image, and endowed with the divine attribute of reason, and pour forth their thanks to the great Dispenser of all things.

Donald now closing the casement, prepared to attire himself, and walk forth to enjoy more fully the beauties of the morn; he strolled towards the cottage of his parents, as the duties which he owed them he never failed to pay. In his way he passed by the spot where he had rescued Matilda from a watery grave; the feelings of delight rushed into his breast, as he praised the dispensation of that Providence who had made him the instrument of preservation to that lovely maid. A horrid idea now rushed across his imagination, as the recollection of lady Margaret again obtruded itself.—"And have I," exclaimed he, "preserved the most lovely of her sex from a fate like this, to meet a still worse from the unjust rage of a fiendlike woman, the disgrace of herself and her lord—forgetful of the sacred ties of honour and religion! Shall she presume to rule the destiny of the angelic Matilda!—no; perish such a thought! I will instantly unfold the——" He started; for, as he raised his hand, in an energetic manner, it came in contact with the cross he wore suspended from his breast, and seemed to say, in a language more powerful than speech—"Remember your oath!" His blood ran cold, large drops bedewed his brow, and his trembling limbs could scarce support him, as, in a low voice, he said—"Yes, I must be silent;" and recalling his scattered spirits, he proceeded to the cottage, and was redeemed with all the parental tenderness the authors of his being never failed to express.

When Jannet, for the first time, beheld that beautiful cross—
"Oh, holy Virgin! where did you get that? Look," said she to
Allen, whose eyes were also rivetted on it, "if that is not the very
jewel which——"

A forbidding look from her husband stopped her prattle, to
the disappointment of Donald, who asked if she had ever seen
the jewel before?

"Not that I know of; for, now I look again, it is not the same I
thought: but how did you come by it, son?" again asked she.

He now explained the means by which he possessed it.

"Oh, holy Virgin! that ever I should live to see you excel all the
young knights in feats of archery! So pale and thin as you looked,
when I saw you with that cross hung on your neck, and——"

"Silence!" said her husband, angrily; "hast forgot what thou
art talking of?"

"I believe I have," said Jannet, in confusion.

Donald, all this time, stood in the greatest surprise, but as
he saw his father wished to drop the subject, he forbore further
question; though Jannet's unguarded words aroused his curiosity, and he was determined, at a fit opportunity, to find out the
meaning to which she alluded.

He soon after took his leave, and returning to the castle,
arrived just as the company were sitting down to their morning
repast. At table he beheld the lady Margaret; when he perceived
her gentle demeanour, and heard the languid tone of her well-
modulated voice, he could scarce persuade himself it was the
same being, who, by the violence of her passions, had caused
him so much uneasiness. While these thoughts passed, in quick
succession, across his mind, and he was gazing at the object
who had caused them, he turned and beheld the lovely eyes
of Matilda earnestly rivetted on him; as soon as she perceived
herself observed, she withdrew them in the greatest confusion;
a vermilion tint heightened the colour of her cheek, as, quickly
turning, she addressed some question to her father, at whose
side she was seated. Lady Margaret paid her more than common
attention, like the concealed snake, that waits a proper opportunity only to sting the deeper. Secretly did Donald rejoice, as he

heard Duncaethal name the following day for their departure; and when Bosmora, in the voice of friendship, requested their longer stay, earnestly did he pray the invitation might not be accepted; his wishes were propitious, for he heard Duncaethal say he had business which could no longer be delayed, and turning to his domestic, bade him make preparation for the journey.

Heavily did the hours lag on till that period arrived, when Donald, with a joyful heart and ready hand, assisted lady Margaret to mount the steed which was to convey her from Bosmora.

What a weight was lifted from his heart, when he once more saw the castle free from visitors! Now did he again enjoy the sweet society of Matilda, either by rambling in the adjacent forest, or, when seated by her father, she charmed his enraptured ear, by playing, with a skilful hand, harmonious strains upon the sweet-sounding lute. Often, in their walks, was she on the point of breaking into the subject of his visit to lady Margaret, but the words died upon her lips, as an innate shame prevented her utterance; and, at length, she almost forgot the occurrence, as she felt convinced Donald could not be guilty of any action base or dishonourable.

Several months passed on with the usual serenity, when one evening a messenger arrived at the castle, with information that the father of Donald lay apparently at the point of death. The youth flew, in the greatest agitation, towards his parent's cottage, and, sinking on his knees by the side of the bed, on which sat the weeping Jannet, he seized the hand of his father, and pressed it fervently to his lips, as the quick tears that chased each other down his cheeks deprived him of the power of utterance.

"My son," said Allen, "I feel the approach of death; and I cannot depart in peace, till I have disclosed a secret on which your future welfare must, in a great measure, depend; for I never so easily should have given my consent to your residing at the castle, had I not thought you had some claim to the exaltation which, by our noble baron's munificence, you now possess; for know that I have no natural claim to your duty—you are not my son!"

"Not your son!" said Donald. "Oh, my father! then will you,

on your deathbed, disown me?—you surely are my sire; for since my earliest days, you have tenderly loved me!"

"Indeed, dear youth, I am not," said Allen; "nor can I tell who are your parents; but whatever I know upon the subject shall not be concealed from you."

Donald now sat, with an attentive ear, while Allen proceeded in the following words.

"About twenty years since, I resided in a vale some miles distant from this place. One evening, as the rain poured down in torrents, the rushing waters from the hills overflowing all beneath, and tremendous peals of thunder shook the firmament, a loud knocking was heard at the door of our hut. 'The Holy Virgin protect the wretched being who is obliged to wander such a dreadful night as this!' said Jannet, and proceeding to the door, admitted a man, bearing in his arms a babe about a month old—I need not add you was that child. The stranger seemed almost sinking with fatigue, and delivering you into the arms of Jannet, who stood ready to receive you, requested lodging for the night.

'Marry! I have but sorry accommodation,' said I; 'but you shall have the best that I can afford.'

'Well, 'tis no consequence; for when I have quenched my thirst, and refreshed my limbs a little,' said he, 'I will pursue my journey.'

'But you will not think of taking this poor babe out such a night as this?' said Jannet.

"The stranger considered a moment, then said—'Good woman, you appear affectionate—will you take this child to nurse? you shall be paid for it annually, receiving the first year in advance.'

"My wife looked at me with a beseeching eye; we had never been blessed with children, and that, together with the pity I felt for your helpless state, made me resolve to accept the proposal; when producing a well-stocked purse of gold, he put it in my hand, with a promise, that, at the end of the year, we should receive another, if you lived, which was rather doubtful, as you appeared sickly and declining: the stranger then kissing you, was about to depart, when a rich cross, which was fastened round your neck by a string of small beads, attracted his attention; he seemed to ruminate earnestly for a few moments, then quickly seizing the necklace, he separated the jewel from it, and bore it away with him; whether this was for fear it should, by any means, lead to a discovery of who you were, or that he was afraid to entrust such a valuable ornament in the hands of poor people like us, I know not, but *thought* the latter.

"In the mean time, you improved in health and beauty. The stranger expressed great satisfaction at your altered appearance, when he again came, which he did at the expiration of the promised time: he asked how we had accounted for your sudden appearance to our neighbours? We told him we had said you was the child of a distant relation of Jannet's. This did not seem to satisfy him, so fearful was he of a discovery; and he begged we would remove to a distant part, to rear you as our own, at the same time exacting from us an oath of inviolable secrecy, with a promise of a satisfactory and ample reward. We then left our dwelling and came to this cottage, which we let him know by my meeting him at a spot appointed for that purpose.

"Year after year rolled away, and we never saw or heard of the stranger more. We loved you as if you were indeed our son; and I often regretted that it was not in my power to give you learning equal to what I felt inwardly convinced your birth demanded:— how joyful was I then, when you gained a friend in father Peter, that good man who is now no more! I was many times on the point of disclosing the mystery concerning you unto him; but the remembrance of my oath, and the hope of once more seeing the stranger who had consigned you to my care, restrained me. Nineteen years have now elapsed; during that I have never again beheld him; then judge, my dear child, how great must have been my astonishment, when you visited us the morning after our young lady's birthday, to behold on your neck the very cross which the stranger took from your infant bosom, when you was first entrusted to our care! I doubt not but you recollect the astonishment Jannet betrayed when it first met her wondering eye; and how it should come into the hands of lady Margaret, is a source of surprise, that only serves to convince me that I am right in my conjectures in supposing you are the offspring of some noble family, who, for unknown reasons, disclaim you, and withhold from you your rightful inheritance."

Allen now ceased, being quite overcome by the disclosure he had made to Donald, who sat quite absorbed with surprise and wonder; yet he could not help thinking they had made some mistake in regard to the ornament he had worn when they first beheld him, and the one presented him by lady Margaret; but he was determined to make inquiries, on his arrival at the castle, of the baron, who, he believed, had given the prize for her to present; but the illness of Allen would not allow him to leave the cottage that night, for he loved the old man with all the filial duty of a son, and therefore was determined to watch by his bedside during the night, as the aged Jannet was ill calculated to bear the fatigue.

Towards morning Allen fell into a slumber, and awoke, about noon, in a state of convalescence, to the great joy of Jannet and the affectionate Donald, who, soon as the glow of health appeared on his cheek, took his leave, to return to the castle, where, on his arrival, he requested a private audience of the baron, to whom he unfolded the wonderful relation which had been disclosed to him, at the same time producing the row of small beads, (as Allen had called them, and which, in reality, were fine pearls,) to corroborate the truth of what he had spoken. The baron listened with silent attention, and, at the conclusion, expressed his great surprise; but agreed with Donald in saying that Allen was mistaken in respect to the cross, which, he affirmed, had belonged to his late lady, the baroness, and, at the important period mentioned, was in the castle;—"Though," added he, "I have no doubt but that you are the descendant of some noble family, who, for selfish and unknown reasons, have thus shamefully deserted you: but be not dejected, sir Donald," added he, "for Heaven will, no doubt, one day or other, discover the mystery which envelopes you; and remember you have a friend and father in Bosmora."

"Oh, my lord," said the grateful youth, "you have indeed ever been a parent to me, when those on whom I had a natural claim cast me out, an alien wretched and forsaken!" A tear forced itself into the corner of his eye, as he continued—"Oh, may it one day be in my power to prove how gratefully the remembrance lives in my heart!"

At that instant a slight rap at the door announced the approach of some one, and, on its being opened, there entered the lovely Matilda. She blushed on beholding Donald, as she was unacquainted with his being in the castle; and when she perceived that he had been in earnest conversation with her father, was about to retire; but the baron requested her stay, and, on her being seated, he recounted to her the tale of Allen. During the recital, numberless sensations arose in her breast, the foremost of which was joy to think that her preserver was not the offspring of a peasant; and she flattered herself that if the veil which now obscured his origin was once removed, her father would gratify the hope she had long cherished in her bosom; for she was convinced that Donald long had loved her, and had only been restrained from declaring his passion, through the hopelessness of ever obtaining her hand, knowing that the baron, how much soever he might esteem him for his virtues, would never consent to bestow on a peasant's son the heiress of Bosmora.

CHAP. V.

I am too sore enpierced with his shaft
To soar with his light feathers, and so bound
I cannot bound a pitch above dull woe;—
Under love's heavy burden do I sink.

SHAKESPEARE.*

....

But let each bind on his mail, and each assume
his shield—let every sword be unsheath'd, for the foe
returneth in his strength.   OSSIAN.*

MONTH after month passed on, but still nothing occurred by which Donald could gain any clue by which he might come at the knowledge of his birth. Allen had perfectly recovered, and was each day visited by his son, as he still continued to call him, who, trusting in Providence to aid his cause, and bring to light the authors of his being, felt resigned to his fate, and once more recovered his usual serenity.

One night, as the castle-clock loudly announced the silent hour of midnight, a tremendous knocking at the gate alarmed its peaceful inhabitants. Old Andrew, repairing the portal, demanded who was there, and their business at that unreasonable hour?

"'Tis Dargo," answered a rough voice; "I have brought a packet for the baron, which must be immediately delivered."

Andrew, knowing the speaker to be one of Duncaethal's servants, unbarred the gate and instantly admitted him.

"I had been here by noon," says he, entering, "had it not been for the freaks of my horse; confound the jade! she took fright, and ran out of the way some miles with me, nor would have stopped till now, I suppose, if her career had not been arrested by a shepherd catching the reins. I was to have delivered this packet to the baron by noon, as I expect my lord Duncaethal will be here tomorrow."

"Lack-a-day!" said Andrew, "we shall be sadly harrassed for want of proper notice, as I suppose he will bring a score attendants with him."

"Not he, indeed; he does not want so many now, since he has lost his lady."

"Lost the lady Margaret!—why where is she gone?"

"Gone! why to the tomb of her ancestors."

"Oh, gramercy!" said the astonished Andrew; "what, is she dead?"

"Why dost think a lady of her spirit would go there while she was living? or, mayhap, you did not know her so well as I."

"Ah, Dargo, thou wert always a joking knave; but come in, and I will deliver your packet to my lord."

Dargo now followed to the hall, where some remaining embers, which Andrew blew into a flame, and a flask of wine, which he placed on the table, made the former completely happy. The old man then repaired to the chamber of his lord, whom he found anxiously expecting him—"Now, Andrew, who is it?" said he.

"Marry, my lord, 'tis only Dargo; he has brought this packet for your honourable lordship; and the reason he came at this unseasonable hour, is because his horse ran away."

"Well," said the baron, "go and make him welcome, while I peruse this packet; and when he has refreshed himself, conduct him to a chamber."

"I will, your honourable lordship," said Andrew; and leaving the room repaired to the hall, where seating himself and filling Dargo a bumper, he said—"Do tell us where lady Margaret *died*, how long it is *since*, and of what *complaint?*"

"That I will, Andrew," said his companion, drinking off his bumper; "for I know you love to have your curiosity satisfied:— as to the *when*, why 'tis since you last saw her; as to the *where*, why in bed; and as to the *how*, why it was e'en by the stoppage of her breath."

"Pish!" said the disappointed Andrew; "why, thou madcap, canst not be serious for a moment?"

"Well then," said Dargo, "about four months since, she died of a disorder *sudden* as it was *violent*—a raging fever, which carried her off in a few hours; and of so malignant a nature, that my lady's confessor, a priest of the monastery near Duncaethal, would scarce suffer her to be approached by any but himself; and, soon as her eyes were closed, she was put into a coffin, and conveyed to Monteith by my lord, who saw her deposited in the tomb of her ancestors; when, after spending the last three months in mourning for his departed lady, he called me into the chamber yesterday, and put in my hands the packet which I brought tonight; but though he did not condescend to acquaint me with the contents, why I think I can partly guess: but come, let us have another cup of wine, for sorrow and talking together makes me thirsty."

"Ah, so it does me," said Andrew, filling up a goblet, and lifting it up, said—"Here's to the health of lady Matilda, my lord's daughter!" When Dargo exclaimed—"I will pledge you—here's to the health of Matilda, *my lady* that is to *be*."

"What!" said Andrew, dropping the uplifted goblet, "is our baron's daughter to be your lady? Marry how?"

"Why by becoming the wife of my lord, to be sure," answered Dargo.

"Matilda the wife of your lord! that she will never be. Why dost think she'd marry a man old enough to be her father?—no, no!"

"That will be as her sire commands," said Dargo.

"And dost thou imagine my lord will ever command her to marry a man she does not love?—ah, you don't know him!"

"Not much of him," said the other; "and yet I think he will not refuse a powerful nobleman like my master."

"Powerful! who made him powerful? why the death of Matilda's uncle; for had it not been for the unfortunate end of Alexander, he never would have been lord of Duncaethal; previous to the possession of which he was poor enough, I believe, for he was of a very distant branch of the family; and if, after his son's death, the old baron had lived to have another heir, why it would never have been his."

"Ah well," said Dargo, "we shall soon see who's right; in the meantime, I wish you would let me lie down a little, as that jade of a horse has made me feel the effects of her mad ramble through the forest."

Andrew, now taking a taper, preceded Dargo to a chamber, and seeing him in bed, betook himself to his own, to finish his night's sleep.

Not so his lord; for the packet he had received from Duncaethal at once astonished and perplexed him—it contained an offer of himself and fortune to the fair Matilda; concluding with an intimation that he himself should follow in the morning to receive his answer personally: it was couched in language almost amounting to haughtiness. This irritated the baron, who was used to receive the most servile adulation from him, when formerly he wished to ingratiate himself into his favour. As yet, no one had ever presumed to offer themselves as candidates for the hand of the heiress of Bosmora, even in the most respectful manner; yet did this upstart lord, who was indebted to the family for the honours which he bore, disdaining solicitations, dare to proceed in terms which seemed to say—"I will not be refused!" The baron formed an instant resolution not to consent to this preposterous union, which was but at the best a sacrifice, in consigning his young and lovely daughter to a man in age equal with himself. He had, moreover, often thought of presenting her hand to Donald, as he long observed a mutual passion between them, should the latter ever attain that elevated rank which he was inwardly convinced was his due by birth.

In the morning he sent for his daughter, and informed her of the death of lady Margaret, with the subsequent offer of Duncaethal; when a sudden flood of tears which gushed from her lovely eyes, and streamed down her now pallid cheek, convinced the baron of the repugnance *she* felt at the proposed union.

"My beloved Matilda," said he, taking her affectionately in his arms, "dry your tears: my dearest child, I did not say I had any intention to give Duncaethal hopes, or that I should to (I will not say) his solicitations, for he has almost dared to demand of me your hand; add to which, I think that you have not the least liking for him, but, if I mistake not, entertain a secret passion for another."

During this speech, he fixed on her a penetrating eye, while her lovely face underwent alternate changes from the rose to the lily; then hiding her blushing countenance, she convinced him that he was right in his conjectures; when pressing her with a parent's fond embrace, he thus continued—"'Tis Donald, my child, whom you love."

"Oh! my dear, honoured father!" dropped, in sounds almost inarticulate, from her trembling lips.

"Compose yourself, dear Matilda," added he; "I am not displeased with you; but tell me, has he ever made to you any professions of love?" As he spoke, a slight frown passed across his features, lest Donald had so far presumed upon his bounty and benevolence.

"Alas! no, my lord, it is utterly unknown to me whether he has ever thought of me at all, but with respect, as the daughter of his benefactor."

"'Tis well," said Bosmora; "I have, for a moment, wronged the noble-hearted youth; and yet, my child, I am convinced he tenderly loves you; I have long observed it, but cannot say the discovery just made of your returning his passion at all offends me; for should he, by the goodness of Providence, ever be discovered and acknowledged by his race, I will not withhold my consent to your union; but while the least mystery involves him, and conceals *his* birth, I cannot, in respect that is due to *mine*, bestow on an unknown youth the heiress of Bosmora. The first opportunity that occurs, after the departure of Duncaethal, I shall make him acquainted with my sentiments in his favour; and, in the interim, I shall expect that your conduct will bear the usual marks of polite reserve towards him."

Matilda spoke not; a thousand tumultuous but grateful thoughts prevented her utterance, and respectfully taking the hand of her father, she pressed it to her lips; then flying to her apartment, threw herself on a couch, and, for a considerable length of time, indulged the most delightful sensations she had ever experienced.

Donald had risen at an early hour, and directly seeking out Andrew, with whom he was a great favourite, inquired the reason of the knocking at the castle-gate on the preceeding night, which had disturbed all its inhabitants?

"Oh," said Andrew, "what reason indeed! why a very pretty one, if you did but know all;—why would you believe, the lord Duncaethal is coming here to-day, to offer his hand to the lady Matilda—yes, indeed, to my dear young lady; and sent his servant forward with a packet to my lord, containing his intentions.—Oh that ever——"

"Impossible!" said Donald, interrupting him; "why he is already married!"

"He was, you mean, sir Donald," answered the other, "but the lady Margaret is dead."

"What did you say?" asked the latter.

"Why I say that she is dead—defunct," replied Andrew, with a look of the greatest communication.

"Indeed!" said Donald; "how long since?"

"Why," returned he, "Dargo says 'tis about four months since; and, marry, I think he must be main fond of matrimony, when he is in so great a hurry to marry again; but I think he had better seek elsewhere, for I am sure our sweet young lady will never be happy with such a man of his age—No, no! I know better than all that: I have not lived as long, but that I can tell what's what!"

"No," said Donald, as a heavy sigh escaped him, "the lovely Matilda was never formed to be the wife of a man like Duncaethal!"

"Ah, well," said Andrew, "perhaps my lord never may consent to give her hand to a man that she does not love—and I am sure she does not love *him*."

"Ah!" said the former, "how do you know, pray?"

"Why, marry, because I know who she does love, sir Knight;" at the same time fixing his eyes upon the face of his interrogator, and seeing the colour rush into his cheeks, he added—"Ah! and so do you, sir Donald!"

"Indeed I do not," said the still more confounded youth.

"Don't you? why then you can give a pretty shrewd guess," said the other. "Well, well! you saved her life; and though she is richer than you, yet her riches would have been of no use without life to enjoy them, and——"

"Andrew, you are mistaken," said Donald, earnestly, "if you suppose that——"

"Ah! ah! you are afraid that I should tell!—ah! ah! ah! marry, that will I not; but you must not think to deceive old Andrew; for though I am not in love myself, I can tell who is, and in those affairs I can see as far as most folks."

"I have the greatest respect in the world for your penetration, Andrew; in this, however, I repeat that you are mistaken," said he, emphatically.

"Ah! ah! go to, go to! I did not suppose you were such a novice as to kiss and tell. Ah! ah! when I was your age, I was a wag myself;" and went off, exulting in his skill of penetration, sing-ing—"I once was young and gay, but now am old, &c." leaving Donald in the deepest vexation, fearful lest his garrulity should bring upon him the anger of the baron.

When he had in some degree recovered from the surprise which the strange intelligence just communicated had thrown him into, recollection brought to him the death of lady Margaret, and he felt a sensation of pleasure, which he thought it impossible ever to experience in learning the loss of a fellow-creature; for though a long time had elapsed since the night she met him at the masque, he had not once forgot her horrid looks and fiend-like vows; nor did he ever pass near the fatal chamber, but that a cold shiver would run through his veins at the bare recollection.

He now sought his chamber, and in solitude ruminated on the morning's unwelcome intelligence; a heavy weight oppressed his spirits, as he found the hopes which he had so long cherished within his breast for ever crushed by the object of his soul's adoration becoming the wife of another.

A loud noise in the court-yard aroused him from the reverie into which he was plunged, and stepping towards the window, he perceived Duncaethal had already arrived, who, surrounded by a train of attendants, was making his way into the castle. "Oh!" faintly ejaculated Donald, "when he departs, he will bear away with him as his bride the angelic—the peerless Matilda! Oh, happy, enviable man! to enjoy a bliss which gods might envy, and the greatest monarchs contend for! while I, the unfortunate Donald have been prevented declaring my adoration, by the inexplicable veil my adverse fate has thrown on my birth! Oh! I had still remained happy, had I never beheld her lovely form; but to feel the dreadful pangs of secret love is more than I can bear. Oh Heaven! give me fortitude to endure those painful ills with a becoming resignation!"

Thus did he soliloquize, till the bell rang which summoned him to attend the banquet, in the saloon where sat Duncaethal on the right of Bosmora. When he entered, he expected the baron would arise from his seat, and present to him the future husband of Matilda; but no such movement being made, he fondly began to hope that he declined the offer of marriage *made* by Duncaethal; a thousand palpitations agitated his breast, which, by turns, felt the most lively hopes and the dreadful torture of despair. His fears were again aroused, when the latter broke the silence which prevailed, by saying—"My lord Bosmora, time wears apace, and I wish to receive your sentiments on the subject already proposed; will you grant me a *private* audience, or is sir

Donald so great a favourite, that you have no desire to conceal from him the purport of your intentions?"

The latter part of his speech was spoken in a tone so malevolent, that Donald, instantly rising from his seat, and bowing respectfully to the baron, requested permission to retire.

"You need not," said the latter, mildly, "as I will attend lord Duncaethal to a private apartment."

The two chiefs arose, and repairing to the study, Duncaethal impatiently demanded of the baron, if he consented to his proposal of the alliance between himself and Matilda? To which, in a voice of restrained anger, the latter replied—"My lord, the abrupt, not to say haughty, manner in which you first made the proposal, would almost determine me to refuse, even if it had met the acceptance of my daughter; but as she feels an utter objection, you will excuse me, if I say I must decline the honour you intend me."

"You refuse me then? 'tis well!" exclaimed the offended chieftain; "you then refuse me your daughter, to bestow her on an unknown?—I perceive your views—you would unite her to Donald—an outcast, as dishonourably born as the tale of his consignment to Allen false, which he has deceived you with, in hopes of your bestowing on him your daughter, and so enrich himself, with the old dotard who forged the lie, at the expence of your credulity; but, my lord Bosmora, do not suffer yourself to be imposed upon, which, if you will, beware how you refuse me! Now I again make the offer—beware!"

"How!" replied the baron; "beware!—beware of whom? and darest thou add threats to thy presumption? Know, thou proud lord, Bosmora can be as quick in resenting an injury as thou art in giving one; and, further, know I alike despise thy friendship or thy hate!" Then ringing the bell, he ordered Andrew, who attended, to summon Donald and his daughter to his presence, and turning to the enraged Duncaethal, continued—"Sooner would I give her to that *unknown wretch*, as you are pleased to term him, even if I was assured he was no other than the offspring of a peasant, rather than link her to a man, who, from his pride or his passions, seems so little calculated to render her happy."

The door now opened, and he was interrupted by the appearance of his daughter, who entered the room with trembling apprehensions, fearing that Duncaethal had won her father over to his wish; she was closely followed by Donald, who imagined he was about to see the beloved object of his heart consigned for ever to the arms of another. "Ah!" mentally exclaimed he, "the baron little knows the feelings of this breast; for he is too noble to think of adding to my miseries, by making me a witness of a scene like this." What then could equal his joy and surprise, when Bosmora addressed him in the following words—"Approach, young man; behold this maid, my daughter—the heiress of a noble house—receive her from my hand as your destined wife; take her, for she is yours: nor do I give her to you more to recompense your many virtues, than to convince this haughty lord that I defy his utmost malice."

Duncaethal hastily arose, rage sparkling in his eyes; and uttering the most dreadful threats of revenge, hastily left the castle.

Matilda and Donald cast themselves at the feet of the baron, to pour forth their gratitude, and receive from him his blessing, which he failed not to bestow, and then addressed them in the following manner—"My dear children, the conduct of the haughty lord Duncaethal has compelled me, in some measure, to adopt the method I have now taken; but I feel perfectly assured the high mind of Donald is too noble to wish to unite himself to my daughter, until he has obtained some clue to the mystery of his birth: in the meanwhile, until that period arrives, which I hope, through the help of Heaven, will not be far off, you have my permission to look upon Matilda as your destined bride; and I doubt not but that your future, as well as your past conduct, will merit that title. In the mean time, it will be necessary to adopt proper measures for repelling any attack which may be made on the castle; for I have no doubt that Duncaethal, from the threats he uttered, will commence a feud, to revenge the affront he supposes he has this day received; therefore it will be wisest, at all events, to put the castle in a state of defence."

He was interrupted by a billet from Duncaethal, in which he informed him that if he did not send his written consent by the following day, to prepare to meet him as his foe.

Orders were now issued to make speedy preparations for resistance; a centinel mounted the watch-tower, which commanded a view of the adjacent country; the vassals now, with an alacrity that evinced the love they bore their laird, made preparations; the armourers began to repair the long-neglected shields and helmets; the archers their arrows; all within the castle was a busy stir, attended with the clank of arms; the drawbridge was raised; the ramparts filled; and Bosmora, that had so long wore the smiling face of peace, now assumed the terrific look of war.

CHAP. VI.

Take thou thy armour, and rush to the first of thy battles!—be thy course in the field like the eagle's wing! Why shouldst thou fear death, my son? The valiant fall with fame— their shields turn the dark stream of danger away—renown dwells on their aged hairs.   OSSIAN.*

THE utmost vigilance was continued within the walls of the castle; but nothing in particular occurred to disturb the peace of its inhabitants, until the evening of the fourth day after the departure of Duncaethal, when the centinel stationed on the watch-tower that commanded the forest gave notice of the approach of a band of armed men seemingly towards Bosmora.

Donald, to whom this intelligence was communicated, immediately mounted the parapet, where, at a distance, he beheld the clan of Duncaethal, with martial step, winding through the intricacies of the forest; for some time they were hid from view, within its labyrinths; then suddenly again appearing, the red bright rays of the departing sun, gleaming upon their bright helmets and polished shields, made their appearance at once glorious and terrific.

Donald now retired to the armoury, and equipping himself with a helmet and breastplate of steel, drew forth his two-edged trusty sword, and waited, in anxious expectation, their nearer approach. He was joined by the baron, who had been informed by Andrew of the enemy's appearance.

When they arrived nearly within bowshot of the castle, a herald stepped forth from the opposing army, and, with gigantic strides, advanced to the foot of the drawbridge; with heavy strokes he thrice struck the ponderous shield of war, whose sonorous sounds made the castle ring, and surrounding glens re-echo back its martial clash; he then, in the name of his lord, loudly demanded a parley; which being granted, he thus addressed Bosmora:—"In the name of the most noble and illustrious baron Duncaethal, I, his honoured servant, now stand forth, and, speaking with his mouth, propose saving the effusion of blood, which must this night be shed, should he proceed in his intention of attacking this fortress; and as our brave and humane lord would fain spare the lives of the unoffending vassals, he challenges Donald, son of Allen and Jannet, to single combat; and though he is so much inferior to our great lord in birth, yet he will descend, for once, to wave his dignity, and meet him in the field on equal terms. Should this proposal be accepted by Donald, let him so signify, and to-morrow, at sunrise, our lord shall meet him, to prove, by force of arms, his claim to honour, attended only by his armour-bearer, and Malcolm, earl of Ross, who shall play the umpire between the challenger and challenged. If this arrangement satisfy not Donald, and he does not confide in the impartial arbitration of lord Malcolm, he is at liberty to bring whom he chooses, provided he is a man of unstained honour, and bears the dignity of knighthood. The spot proposed for the combat is the vale of Aldo. Long live our noble lord Duncaethal!"

The herald now ceasing, the baron stepped forth, and thus answered for Donald—"In the name of the saint of whose order he has the honour of bearing the dignity of knighthood, sir Donald, the future son of Bosmora, shall accept the terms; and I, the baron, will accompany him to the fight: bear back from me this message to thy haughty lord."

The herald departed, and returning to the clan of Duncaethal, delivered the acquiescence of Donald; and, after a pause of a few minutes, the clan then wheeling round and clashing their shields, with warlike sounds and martial steps returned through the forest.

In the mean time, Donald, with his utmost eloquence, endeavoured to dissuade the baron from accompanying him to the combat, adding—"My lord, I can fully confide in the honour of earl Malcolm; and as the faithful Robert will accompany me, there will be no fear but I shall meet with justice:—if I conquer, I shall at once revenge the insults offered to my benefactor and myself—if I fall, it will be in the cause of gratitude and love; for since I have received the sanction of my honoured lord to love Matilda, I will maintain the glorious claim, while life remains, or perish in the cause."

Bosmora being, at length, convinced of the inutility of himself attending, consented to his departing only with Robert.

The intervening time was spent by Donald visiting Allen and Jannet, and preparations for the important moment, when, for the first time, he was to prove his prowess in deeds of arms. When the hour drew near, he went to bid Matilda and the baron adieu, when the former, being agitated by the ceremony, gave utterance to the words as recorded in the first chapter; and, soon after, he bade farewell to the inhabitants of the castle, whose good wishes for success went with him.

Frequently did Matilda, on her knees, offer up her earnest prayers for his safety; and often did she send Venella to the turret, to see if she could descry his appearance—but in vain; hour after hour passed away in the most torturing suspense, and yet no signs of his return: Sometimes thinking Venella did not look carefully, she would ascend the castle walls, and partake with her a station on the turret, till the gloomy approach of night, and the fast-falling dews, which descended in thick clouds of mist, prevented her anxious eyes from distinguishing objects at the distance of a bow-shot from the castle; she then sought her chamber, and seating herself at the window, which looked over the court-yard, with palpitating heart, agitated with hope and fear, then listened, with eager ear, for the notice of his arrival. As every tedious hour was proclaimed by the castle-clock, she would exclaim—"Ah! he has too surely perished!" At length the bell sent forth the lengthening sound that announced the hour of midnight, when being no longer able to contain her fears, she rushed down to the apartment of her father, and throwing herself upon his bosom, exclaimed—"Oh! my dear lord, he has too surely fallen a victim to the treachery of Duncaethal! for had he perished in the fight, Robert, ere this, would have returned. Ah! little did his noble spirit consider the wily nature of his foe! Wretched Matilda! well, well did my heart forebode that I had beheld him for the last time! It is for me—for me he has perished! for had it not been for this wretched form, he never would have encountered the vengeance of the fierce Duncaethal!"

Thus did she indulge in the most frantic grief, unrestrained by the presence of her father, who in vain endeavoured to console her. He said he had sent some vassals in search of him at the approach of night, fearing lest some false play had been offered.

He was interrupted by a loud knocking at the gate; the breast of Matilda now beat high with trembling expectation, when Andrew, entering the apartment, acquainted his lord that they had searched every avenue of the forest in vain, and had proceeded to the vale, where there was no signs of any combat having been fought that day.

Bosmora now felt convinced, by Matilda's conjectures, that Donald had doubtless fallen into some snare laid for him by his deceitful enemy: summoning Venella, he ordered her to conduct her sorrowing mistress to her chamber; then turning to Andrew, bade him prepare his arms, and summon the vassals—"As," said he, "at the break of day, I myself will march against Duncaethal, and demand the youth, whom, I have no doubt, he unlawfully detains."

Andrew retired, with a heavy heart, to obey his lord's commands; and ere sunrise, the loud clang of arms gave notice to the baron that his faithful clan stood ready to attend him; and, buckling on his armour, he proceeded to bid his daughter farewell, who offered to the Virgin prayers for her dear father's safety and speedy return. The baron, tenderly taking her in his arms, kissed her faded cheek, and bidding her trust in the all-ruling power of Heaven, tore himself from her embrace. Andrew now informed him all was ready for his departure; and mounting his black steed, he moved towards the residence of the foe.

Towards evening they came within sight of the castle, which, to the astonishment of the baron, wore the smooth appearance of peaceful serenity. "What!" exclaimed he angrily, "did this haughty lord suppose Bosmora would fail to resent the injury done him, that he thus hugs himself in fancied peaceful security!" Then spurring forth his courser, he quickly arrived at the foot of the drawbridge, which was raised, and ordering his squire to strike loudly upon the shield, he demanded of a domestic who appeared to answer the summons an immediate interview with his lord. The servant retired, and, in a few moments, Duncaethal appeared upon the parapet, and demanded the cause of this warlike appearance; adding—"Is it possible the lord Bosmora has so little honour as seemingly to consent to my condescending proposal, in offering to terminate the breach by single combat with the peasant Donald, to save the lives of your vassals?—was this the mean subterfuge, that he might attack me unprepared? Say! was it well done, baron, to accept my challenge, and then, when I arrived at the appointed spot, to find no foe, who, from cowardice or policy, failed to meet me?"

Bosmora was thunderstruck; but in a moment recovering himself, he thought it was an artful evasion of the speaker to disguise his knowledge of Donald's disappearance; and again addressing him, he said—"Dost thou then pretend to me the brave Donald did not meet thee, thou stain of knighthood?—it is on his account I now appear;—where is he, and by what black treachery has he been prevented returning to Bosmora?"

"My lord," replied Duncaethal, "you are too hot—let your better judgment," continued he, with apparent calmness, "gain the preponderance for a moment, and you will soon perceive the fallacy of your accusation. If I had so far forgot my honour as to make use of stratagem to secure the person of Donald, think you I should have failed to have had my castle filled with soldiers, to repulse the attempt you would, no doubt, make to free the captive?—but I am unprepared—no armed vassals appear upon my walls—and will Bosmora attack a chieftain with such unequal numbers?"

The baron was loath to admit a thought which conveyed with

it the bare suspicion of an action disgraceful or derogatory to the dignity of a knight; and the deep sophistry of Duncaethal confounded him; nor could he fail to admit the plausibility of his reasoning—when once more turning to him, he said—"My lord Duncaethal, dare you swear by your sword you met not Donald in the field?"

"I dare, my lord!" then directly unsheathing it, raised it to his lips with great solemnity. "Now, my lord Bosmora, should you still retain an idea of my having used deceit, I refer you to earl Malcolm of Ross, who attended me to the spot, and is a witness I waited upwards of three hours in vain, and at length returned, accompanied by him, to Duncaethal."

If the baron failed to be convinced, even by the asseveration of the former, this ready reference to earl Malcolm, whom he knew to be a man of strict honour and undoubted veracity, at once brought with it a painful conviction; and turning round his horse, he, followed by his faithful clan, bent his way back to Bosmora, and communicated this distressing intelligence to his wretched daughter.

We will now leave them, and return to Donald and his squire. Soon after his departure from the castle, he reached the outskirts of the forest; a loud shout close to his heels affrighted his proud mettled steed, when being restrained by the reins, and eagerly struggling to be free, he stumbled, and, by the violence of the motion, precipitated his master from the saddle, who was preparing to rise, when he found himself surrounded by a troop of armed men, who, seizing him and confining his arms, conveyed both him and his squire, whom they had bound in the same manner, to a carriage, which had been hitherto concealed by a thick clump of trees. During this action, which was all executed in the space of a minute, Donald was so confounded, that he had not power to utter a word; but recovering a little from his surprise, he demanded the reason of this cavalier treatment; but not a word did they deign to answer, though he repeatedly interrogated them; nor could he gain the least glimpse of their faces, their visors being kept continually closed.

He was now silent, and waited patiently for the conclusion of this strange adventure, as all efforts of resistance would be fruit-less: they had taken the necessary precaution of disarming him; at last he thought total silence would be the best policy.

Not so his squire, for he loudly clamoured forth his com-plaints in the following words—"Here's a pretty end to a battle, indeed! to be seized and cooped up in this rumbling thing, just like a couple of wild-geese in a market-woman's basket! and then to interrupt me too, just as I was composing a long speech which I intended to speak to Dargo, the squire of my lord Duncaethal, when you should have disarmed his master, which I plainly foresaw, my lord, you of course would do—'Dargo,' says I to myself, 'you see it was a mighty foolish whim of your lord, to suppose he was sure of gaining a victory over my master, sir Donald—Ah! ah! Dargo,' says I, 'I plainly foresaw he was playing a losing game; for though he has fought many more combats than my master, yet my master was in the right cause, and conse-quently our patron, St. Andrew, would aid him in the fight, and make him the conqueror; for I foresaw——"

Donald now impatiently interrupted him, by saying—"I wish the wonderful foreknowledge you so abundantly seem to possess had caused you to foresee this strange conclusion to our enterprise."

"Ah! sir Donald," answered Robert, "Saint Andrew grant that I had! then would not I have helped to dissuade the good lord Bosmora from accompanying us. Ah! what will the lady Matilda say? and what will Venella, her ladyship's maid, say? ah! how dis-appointed will she be! good lack! good lack! for," said I, to her, 'Venella,' says I, 'when we return, and while my master is giving your lady an account of the fight, you and I, Venella,' says I, 'will have a cup of good wine comfortably together; and while we drink their healths, I will,' says I, 'tell you the share I took in the encounter; what my lord said to the lord Duncaethal, which,' says I, 'I plainly foresee he will, when he, after disarming him, returns him his sword; then,' says I, 'what a graceful bow he will make to the lord Duncaethal, who will, of course, look fierce and malicious at being overcome! and how I should crow and strut over Dargo, because we had got the day! Now, instead of all this, sir—instead of my eating ragout and drinking wine with Venella, perhaps some of these clumsy-fisted fellows which surround the carriage may make mince-meat of me! Oh that I was once more safe at home in the castle of Bosmora! Oh that I could again taste those happy joyous days we enjoyed, before lord Duncaethal took it into his mad head to demand our sweet young lady for his wife! Now 'tis very strange these bandits never rummaged our pockets, to see if we had a purse for them, or anything worth their taking. Good lack! now it strikes me, I should not be at all surprised if they acted by the command of some lady who has taken a fancy to our persons—what do you think, sir Donald?"

"Think! why that thou art an ass to suppose any such thing."

"Nay, my lord," replied the mortified squire, who imagined that Donald was offended at his ranking himself as an object to be seized by violence, "I did not mean to insinuate that I thought I was so comely and handsome as you are, my lord; but yet, you know, my lord, if they had not been ordered to bring me too, why you know they might have let me gone home again about my business, which I should soon have done, in spite of the honour intended me by the fair one, whoever she is. Venella has often told me that I had a pretty smirking face, but really I never had the vanity to suppose I was so handsome, that any woman would ever proceed to violence to obtain me."

Donald now, in spite of his great chagrin, burst into a loud fit of laughter, at the conclusions made by the simple vanity of his foolish squire, at the same time saying—"Robert, does not thy miraculous foresight inform thee we are in the power of Duncaethal, who, by this treacherous conduct, has us completely in his clutches?" Then pausing a moment, he continued—"Cannot thy shallow brain perceive he will now attack the castle, and carry off the angelic Matilda, now I am absent, and our noble lord is unprepared for his reception? Oh! villainous traitor! Oh that I had some method of escape! but, alas! there's none!—the carriage is surrounded, and the most distant hope is vain!"

The simple squire now being convinced of the truth of his master's suspicions, sunk into a profound silence, and thought no more of amorous ladies or love-sick damsels; nor did he ever once disturb the painful reverie into which Donald had fallen.

Their taciturnity was, at length, interrupted by the sudden stopping of the vehicle, and a demand from one of the men who opened the door, if they would alight and take some refreshment? Donald was on the point of refusing, when an imploring look from Robert, who, with all the misfortunes and disappointments of the day, could not resist the powerful attacks of hunger, made him comply; and alighting, a wallet of cold provisions, and a keg of liquor, were spread upon the grass, of which they were rudely invited to partake; it was immediately accepted by Robert, without the least hesitation, who did ample justice to the viands and keg of liquor. Donald refused tasting either, till one of the men, producing a bottle of wine, which, he said, was of a most excellent quality, earnestly pressed him to take a cup; then offering the same to Robert, who, nothing loth to refuse, drained it to the bottom; and turning round to present the empty goblet, he fixed his eyes on the face of a man who sat at some distance, and, after a moment of surprise, exclaimed—"What, Dargo! ah! it is Dargo!" and directly approaching him, said—"Do, good Dargo, tell us where we are going?"

A morose reply from the latter to command silence, prevented Donald, who was going to make the same question, from speaking; but Robert, not regarding him, continued—"Ah! little did I think, when I was regaling you at the castle with some of my lord Bosmora's best wine—little did I then dream of your playing me and my master such a scurvy trick as this! Ah, Dargo! I cannot help saying that you are a confounded great rogue!" The enraged Dargo, now drawing forth his sword, presented it to the breast of the terrified squire, who stammered out—"Nay, nay, I did not mean to say that you, good Dargo, was a rogue, for you only act by the orders of your lord, as every good servant, you know, ought; though, I must confess, when you was drinking to my success, and calling me your dear friend, I never thought you would turn out such a villain!—I beg your pardon, I mean I little supposed that your master would command you to hold a sword to my throat; but we poor servants must obey orders, and if my master was to bid me cut your's, why I should do it with pleasure—No! I did not mean that, dear, dear Dargo—only meant, my good friend, I should be obliged to fulfil his commands."

They were now rudely bid to re-enter the carriage; and soon after, loud snores from Robert gave notice to his master he had now sought repose in the arms of Somnus; and a heavy drowsiness, which he, at the same time, felt creeping over his own senses, convinced him that there had been infused some powerful soporific mixture into the wine which he so incautiously had swallowed; and, after a long struggle with its influence, which proved vain, he was compelled to submit to its potency; and when, at length, he opened his eyes, he beheld a sight that horrified every faculty; suspended from the top of a loathsome dungeon, in which, on a truss of straw, he found himself reclining, was a rusty iron lamp, from which arose a glimmering flame, whose feeble rays were nearly obscured by the unwholesome damps which exhaled from its trickling walls. He tried to raise himself, when a stiffness which pervaded his limbs, painfully convinced him he must have slumbered, in that wretched situation, a considerable length of time. "Oh, my dearest Matilda," said he, "shall we never more meet? have I but just possessed the precious knowledge of thy love, to be separated for ever! Alas! too surely it is so! I am destined to meet a horrid lingering death! no more to taste the sweets of liberty, and, what is far dearer, thy delightful society, without which life were not worth retaining!" He again cast himself on his straw, and indulging in the most poignant sorrow, abandoned himself to despair.

A loud rattling now attracted his attention, occasioned by the unbarring of his cell door; and he waited in the horrible expectation of seeing his murderer enter to complete the vengeance of Duncaethal. Dargo now appeared, bearing a basket of provisions, a pitcher of water, and a fresh supply of oil for the lamp, which settling down, and turning to Donald, he inquired if he was ready to receive a visit from his lord?

"I am," replied he, "for fain would I see the wretch who has so far forgot his honour as a knight, and humanity as a Christian."

Dargo, without again speaking, retired, and shortly after

re-entered, preceded by Duncaethal. "Well, valiant sir," said he, tauntingly, "I fancy you little expected this commodious apartment? No! no! you thought to be enfolded in the arms of the love-sick Matilda, and triumph over Duncaethal by recounting his fall! Vain wretch! couldst thou, even for a moment, suppose that I would oppose myself, in fight, with an impostor, the grovelling offspring of Bosmora's vassals? Know, thou weak boy, it was a stratagem to check thy pride, and teach thee to know the difference of a peasant's son, ignobly born, and the dignity of Duncaethal!"

"Yes, thou proud wretch! I know thee well, a stranger alike to honour or to valour—thy heart cowardly as it is treacherous! Rapacious, cruel, and bold, amidst thy villanies——"

"Rail on, disappointed boy! 'tis all thou canst now do; yet know I am come to prove to thee I am not cruel; consent to what I shall propose, and thou shalt have safe conduct from the castle."

"Name your terms," said Donald; "but, mark me, I will consent to nothing that will, in the least, sully my fair name, or cast the slightest stain upon my hitherto unimpeached honour."

"Nothing which I propose shall wound the name you now possess," said he, equivocally: "The first condition is, that you quit Scotland, never to return; the second, that you resign all claim to Bosmora's heiress; and the third, that you signify the same by returning that scarf which now adorns you, by a messenger of my providing, and in a manner that I shall direct."

"I disdain the terms," said the indignant youth. "Did not thou say, thou wouldst propose nothing that might stain the fairness of my name?"

"Nor have I," returned the other. "The name you now bear is that of a base coward, who first accepted of the fair challenge that I gave, and then, with ignoble fear, fled, not daring to face me; and such, Bosmora is informed thou art, for he has been here already to demand thee; but being convinced thou art no longer worthy the high honour which he intended thee, has returned with the intention of forgetting you for ever; therefore, by consenting to my propositions, you will not only save your life and regain thy liberty, but might, in return, forget Matilda."

Donald, no longer being able to contain his resentment, exclaimed—"Oh! thou vile traitor! that dares thus, with unblushing front, stand before the victim of thy base insidious arts! Had I but my sword, I would prove, on thy coward head, the falsehood of thy damned insinuations! but threats are vain; and, since my fair fame, by black deceit, is gone, I defy thy utmost power, for I will die in the full assurance of my honour being unstained."

The enraged Duncaethal, now turning to depart, said he gave him to the following night to consider of it, when, if he still refused, he might expect his fulfilling his utmost vengeance; then quitted the dungeon, followed by Dargo; the latter, placing a bar of massy iron against the door to keep it secure, once more left him to indulge his thoughts uninterrupted.

CHAP. VII.

The foe came on like a stream! the mingled sound of death arose! man took man—shield met shield—steel mixed its beams with steel—darts hiss through the air—spears ring on mails—swords on broken bucklers bound! As the noise of an aged grove beneath the roaring wind, when a thousand ghosts break the trees by night, such was the din of arms!

OSSIAN.*

MATILDA had retired to her chamber with a heavy heart; it was now the third night since the departure of Donald; no clue had yet been obtained to the cause of his extraordinary disappearance, and the baron had, for farther conviction, rode to the castle of Ross, to interrogate sir Malcolm, who corroborated the account made by Duncaethal; yet she could not believe but he had been the victim of treachery; that cowardice was the cause, she banished the ignoble thought; nor would she, for a moment, give room to an idea so basely injurious to the honour of her heart's beloved.—"Ah!" said she, "he is too surely in the power of the wily villain Duncaethal! Holy Virgin protect and deliver him from his remorseless enemy!"

Her prayer was interrupted by the sound of a tremendous

crash, and a moment after, by the entrance of Venella, who, pale, agitated, and breathless, seemed unable to recount the dreadful subject which laboured for utterance. "Oh! my lady, my lady! we are lost! we are lost!"

"What dost thou mean?" asked the trembling Matilda.

"Oh, my lady! the castle is attacked by the clan of Duncaethal!—hark! my lady, how their arms clash on the walls! Oh, the Virgin protect us! we shall be all killed!" Now the dreadful bursting of the castle gates caused a noise still more terrible than the first. "Oh, my lady! they are in the castle! oh! let us fly!"

"Alas, whither?" said her mistress. "Oh, my father! my dear father! perhaps thou art, at this moment, breathing thy last! Oh, let me haste to save *thee*, and resign myself into the power of Duncaethal!" She now essayed to leave the chamber, when she sunk down in a swoon upon the ground, occasioned by the fright that now had overpowered her before agitated spirits.

Loud terrific shouts sounded through the lofty halls of Bosmora, as the ferocious besiegers followed their flying victims through the various apartments of the castle; the gleam of wildfire that was thrown in by the dreadful foe, gave a partial light, at intervals, of the accumulating horrors which, at every turn, met the terror-struck eye of the besieged, who had been surprised unawares, at a time they were, for the greatest part, buried in profound sleep, little dreaming of the enemy's black treachery. Loud piercing shrieks from the terrified female domestics, that sought, in vain, for refuge, rent the air, and bursting the caverns of night, told the dangers with which they were surrounded. Horrid War, with rapid and gigantic strides, rushed forth, marking his fatal track with murder! bloody, remorseless, sanguinary murder!— man against man, breast to breast, fought dreadful, tugging hard for victory! Bravely did the faithful but unprepared clan of Bosmora defend their lord; till at length, overpowered by the superior number of the foe, they sealed their fidelity with their lives. Bosmora dealt death around him, but, at last, being surrounded, a blow laid him prostrate on the earth at the feet of his ferocious enemy, who now went to seek the lovely object which had caused this dreadful havoc. He directed his course to the apartments of the unoffending and beauteous victim, leaving his remorseless crew dealing ruin and devastation to all around them. Finding her chamber vacant, imprecations burst from the lips of the disappointed chief; and, on meeting the frightened Venella, he loudly demanded her mistress, and threatened instant death, if she refused to tell him the place of her concealment; in vain did she endeavour to convince him she knew nothing of her—terror preventing her speech; while Duncaethal, thinking her stammering a stratagem to delay time for her further escape, proceeded again to threats, when Venella exclaimed—"Indeed, my lord, you terrify me so, that you prevent me telling the truth."

"Well, then, proceed," said he, more mildly, hoping, by gentle means, to gain that information which passion in vain endeavoured to extort.

She now said—"Indeed, my lord, I was almost frightened out of my wits, when I saw my lady fall into a swoon, and I ran to get some water to sprinkle her face; but when I returned, she was gone, my lord."

"Impossible! how could she leave the apartment if she was in a swoon?"

"Why, my lord," said Venella, "somebody has carried her away, I dare say."

Duncaethal now supposed some of his party, during the battle, had conveyed her to a place of security, as he commanded them all to strict care she did not escape. Summoning them to his presence, he inquired if any had secured her; but not one could give the least account. He then ordered a strict search to be made through the castle, and took himself an active and vigilant part for the recovery of his devoted victim.

Matilda, on recovering from the insensibility into which she had fallen, found herself in the arms of a man, who hurried her on with an amazing rapidity; a scream burst from her lips, when a poniard, which he presented to her breast, made her silent, and caused her again to relapse into forgetfulness. At length, when recollection again visited her, she found herself in a subterraneous apartment; over her stood a tall figure, gazing upon her most stedfastly; his dark scrutinizing eye was fixed full upon her face, with an expression gloomy and terrific, which caused a shuddering throughout her whole frame; scarcely could she consider his dress, which was altogether strange as himself; on his head he wore a casque of polished steel, the crown of which supported a large plume of blood-red feathers; a heavy cuirass, and cuish of iron, defended his breast and the lower parts of his body; a broad leather belt girted his waist, and contained various weapons of destruction; gauntlets clothed his hands, in one of which he held a lighted flambeau, whose glare, reflecting on his arms, gave him an appearance most horribly terrific.—"Matilda," said he, in a sepulchral sounding voice, "arise, and follow me!"

"Alas!" said the wretched girl, "where am I, and whither would you convey me?"

"To safety!" replied he.

"How can I be assured of that?" returned she; "thy appearance is not calculated to inspire confidence; and the mysterious manner in which I have been conducted hither, convinces me that thou art an agent of the tyrant Duncaethal. Oh, Donald! why art thou not here to protect thy unhappy ill-fated Matilda!"

A frown passed across the features of the unknown, as he pronounced—"Lady, your unjust suspicions wrong me—we are not yet without the walls of Bosmora; I repaired here, amidst the confusion of the fight, to save you, and sought your chamber for that purpose, when your insensible state prevented me explaining my intentions; I took you in my arms, and, by a private passage, brought you to this place, which is a subterranean of the castle, and through which I intended to make our escape, but was obliged to rest, till you recovered and became able to proceed."

A loud noise now resounding through the vaults alarmed the stranger, and seizing a long plaid cloak which he had cast off on his entering the cavern, hastily threw it around him; then exclaiming—"Farewell—it is too late! by your foolish scruples you have prevented my intentions of securing you from the tyranny of Duncaethal, whose agents now indeed approach;— bitterly will you repent refusing the proffered kindness of the bandit Darthalgo!"

He retreated through a passage on the right, leaving the hapless Matilda in the power of her remorseless pursuers. Duncaethal at that moment entering, ordered them to convey their wretched victim to a carriage, which was in waiting on the outside of the castle, when sinking on her knees, she begged to see her father ere she departed. The ferocious chief, who did not wish her to be made acquainted with his fall, answered evasively, she should behold him at the end of her journey.

"Ah," shrieked she, "he's murdered! avaunt, thou *homicide!* off! touch me not—thy hands are stained with blood! the life-current of my venerable father now encrusts thy dagger's point; but heavily shall the vengeance of Omnipotence revenge his death, while the never-ceasing remorse of a guilty conscience shall make thee curse thyself, in bitterness of despair and misery of soul!"

"Seize her!" cried the enraged Duncaethal to his followers; "do the ravings of a weak girl intimidate you, that you all stand aloof, gaping like lifeless statues? Instantly lay hold of her, or this sword shall enforce my commands!"

The soldiers now rushed forward, and conveying her through the court-yard, forced her into a carriage, in which Venella was already confined, who sat wringing her hands, and loudly expressing her sorrows; and when her mistress was seated by her, she cried—"Ah! my dear lady, then they have found you at last!—oh! the Virgin! how earnestly did I pray that you might have fled beyond their reach! for then this surly centinel who guards the carriage perhaps would have let me go home to my father and mother. Ah! woeful was the time I left our happy cottage for Bosmora! Ah! never shall I see my dear parents again, nor dance on the green before the door to the sweet-sounding pipe! Oh that I was once out of this carriage, that is now conveying us I know not whither! for I suppose my lord Duncaethal will do just as he pleases with us, now sir Donald is lost, and the good baron is no more."

"No more!" shrieked Matilda, with horror at the truth of what she already feared; "art thou sure my father is no more?"

"No, no! not quite sure," replied the incautious Venella; "I only saw him stretched out on the hall floor; but you know, my lady, he might only have swooned like yourself."

Matilda heard not the conclusion of this speech, but sunk down insensible at the foot of the carriage. All the screams for assistance made by Venella failed of effect, for the unfeeling wretches who guarded them never once offered to stop, thinking her cries were only intended to attract the attention of any traveller who might aid their escape; therefore, instead of lending the least help, they threatened to stop her mouth, unless she was instantly quiet.

At length she had the pleasure of seeing returning animation visit the form of her wretched mistress; and a heavy shower of tears, which, in a torrent, flowed from her lachrymal eyes, chased each other down her sorrowing cheek, gave some relief to her bursting heart; and with an earnest prayer to Heaven for her safety, endeavoured to compose herself, and was patiently resigned to the wretched fate which, she had no doubt, awaited her; and, at last, sunk into a profound silence, which Venella, at intervals, interrupted, by declaring the jolting of the carriage would kill her before she reached the end of her journey: but at last they came in view of the castle of Duncaethal, and passing over the drawbridge, which was lowered for that purpose, the vehicle stopped, and they were handed out by Dargo, on whom she discharged a volley of reproaches; nor could she scarcely be silenced by her lady, who endeavoured to convince her that he acted only by the orders of his lord.

They were now conducted to an elegant apartment, where they found a table spread with a rich collation of the choicest viands, of which they were invited to partake by Dargo, who, in a moment after, left the room. When Venella saw the magnificence of the place, she could not contain her joy, and, in ecstasy, exclaimed—"Oh, what gay furniture, and what a rich supper!—well, how comfortable! instead of being conducted to a gloomy prison, which I thought we should, to find ourselves in the grandest place I ever saw in my life!—Oh! do, my lady, taste of this nice cake or this wine," at the same time taking a glass herself; but Matilda heard her not, for, regardless of surrounding objects, she was plunged in a train of melancholy thoughts, and recalled to herself the dreadful horrors of the late scene, in which she had borne a principal part. The mysterious being who would have saved her, his terrific appearance, and his evident knowledge of Bosmora Castle, what motive could he have for the interest he took in her fate? he who had called himself, and whose person corroborated his words, a bandit! how could he know what was to take place that very night, and why wish to save her, when a person of his calling might have so easily seized on the valuables which, in the confusion, lay neglected?

All these ideas rapidly crossed her recollection, and she earnestly wished she had accepted his proffered kindness;—"for," thought she, "I could not have fallen into the hands of a greater ruffian than Duncaethal, even in those of a professed bravo."

She was interrupted by the opening of the door, and the entrance of an old woman, who, approaching with a low curtsey, asked if she should shew her to those apartments which were expressly designed for her sole use? Matilda answered that she was ready to attend; and arising, followed the old woman to an antique but elegant bed-chamber, ornamented with many portraits of knights and ladies; one of the latter, arrayed in a white robe, particularly attracted her attention. "Whose likeness is that?" asked she.

"Ah, my lady!" answered her conductor, "that was the bonny Agnes Maclean; ah, sweet good lady! she was lost on the outskirts of the forest; her horse taking fright, plunged her in the river that flows near, and she was never more heard of: but see, madam, that young knight next to her, that looks so handsome, is the brave Alexander, the noble heir of Duncaethal, who was slain in the wars, and, by that means, broke the heart of our good old lord. Ah, my lady! the bonny Agnes loved him, and he loved her too—but our dear old lord would never consent to their union;—ah! her death was a relief to her sorrows; for when she was left in the castle with old Peter the steward and myself, she used to mope about just like a ghost, and would sit gazing at this picture of our young lord for days together: at last Peter thought she injured her health, by giving way so much to grief, and prevailed on her to ride in the adjacent valleys, which she did: Peter, at first, attended her, but on her wishing to be alone, and he not supposing any danger would happen, let her go out by herself. Ah, wretched day! the steed on which she rode returned neighing to the castle, but we never saw the bonny Agnes more." The affectionate Gertrude now wiped the tears from her eyes, and directing the attention of Matilda to the opposite side, said— "Look, lady, there is the peerless Mabel Duncaethal."

"Merciful powers, my mother!" said she.

"Your mother, lady!" inquired the astonished Gertrude; "are you the daughter of lord Bosmora?"

"I am that wretched orphan," said she.

"Orphan!" reiterated Gertrude; "is the noble baron dead?"

"Alas, yes!" sighed forth Matilda; "he was last night inhumanly murdered by the tyrant Duncaethal!"

"What!" screamed Gertrude, "did Duncaethal murder the husband of his cousin? Ah! little did I think, when I saw the beautiful Mabel leave this castle for that of her lord, your father—ah! little did I think that I, so old even then, should ever live to hear of his murder—and that too by a descendant of her own family. Ah! when I was ordered to prepare the apartments of the late lady Margaret, for one who was coming to be my lord's bride— ah! little did I think it was the daughter of the sweet Mabel; and is it indeed, my lady, true that you are to be his bride?"

"Bride! thinkst thou," said Matilda, "this breast shall ever receive the murderer of my father? No! sooner would I bare it to meet that dagger's point which pierced his honoured breast, than Matilda Bosmora should become the wife of the murderer Duncaethal, that ferocious homicide!"

"Ah! my dear lady, but will you be able to escape from his power?" asked the other.

"Ah! good Gertrude, could not you assist me?" inquired Matilda; "and I will fly to my sovereign, fall at his feet, and implore protection from your tyrannic master."

"Alas, my lady, 'tis not in my power; old Peter is dead; and Dargo, who keeps the keys, is no friend of mine."

"Then I have no resource," cried the miserable Matilda, "but to trust in that Providence whose attribute is to watch over unprotected innocence!" and turning to Gertrude, continued— "Did you not say these were the apartments of lady Margaret?"

"Ah, Madam," said she, "here, on this very bed, she breathed her last; I saw her myself when she was dead she was a handsome lady, but not the sweet temper of bonny Agnes;—my lord and she had often high words, and when she died, I think he did not mourn for her so much as he would have it believed he did."

"I fancy not," said Venella, who, for a long time, had, much against her inclination, been silent; "he never cared much for her, and I am sure there was no love lost, for when she was first at Bosmora, she——"

"Silence, Venella," cried Matilda, "what are you thinking of?"

"Oh! I beg pardon, my lady," answered the other; "she is dead, and they say you should never speak ill of the dead; and as I cannot say any good of her, why I'll e'en hold my tongue."

"Aye, pray do," returned her mistress; "and don't allow yourself so much freedom."

"Dear heart, my lady, I am sure I spoke no harm!" and then addressing herself to Gertrude, Venella inquired if she was to sleep in the same room with her mistress?

"No," answered the other; "there is a bed prepared for you in the antichamber."

"Oh lord! I dare not sleep there by myself."

"Why not?" said Gertrude; "I have slept there many nights, for, unconscious of ever having injured any one, I thank the Virgin I possess a quiet conscience."

"Marry, indeed!" said Venella, pertly; "I dare say I am as righteous as yourself;" and she was now determined to assume a degree of courage she did not possess.

The clock now proclaiming a late hour, Gertrude, with a low curtsey, left the apartment, wishing a good repose to Matilda, who, shortly after, dismissed Venella for the night; then being by herself, with weeping eyes, fell on her knees before the picture of her mother, and gave utterance to the following words—"Oh thou, whose beatified spirit now dwelleth in realms of eternal glory, regardless of this terraqueous globe of misery and woe, if it be so permitted, look down upon thy unhappy unprotected child; and when the unrelenting hand of cruelty is raised to end my wretched being, step forth, and, by thy presence, strike terror to the heart of my dear father's cruel *murderer!*"

At this moment a hollow groan seemed to proceed from the picture, and Matilda, fixing on the canvas a gaze of terror, each moment expected to see it move; but all was still, and casting a look of fear and wonder round the apartment, all remained as before. She now fancied she had been deceived, and it could be nothing more than the moaning of the hollow blast forcing its entrance into some chasm of the castle; and yet the sound seemed so distinct—so like what they say breaks from the troubled spirit, who, wandering, expiates the crimes done in the days of its mortality, she once more raised her eyes to the portrait, whose mild countenance seemed irradiated with maternal love—"Ah, my mother, thy child never experienced thy tender care; yet she had a father!—oh, Heavens!"——Her voice now became convulsed as she recollected she had not now left one parent, and casting herself on the bed, gave way to the most poignant and unrestrained sorrow. At length nature being entirely exhausted by incessant fatigue, she sunk into repose.

CHAP. VIII.

DUNCAETHAL, on the evening he had quitted the dungeon of Donald, proceeded to an apartment with his trusty minister Dargo, to consult how they might induce the former to resign his claim to Matilda.—"Might I be allowed to speak," said Dargo, "I think I have hit upon an expedient."

"Say on, my trusty fellow," replied Duncaethal; "and if thou canst devise any method, propose it, if it will aid me in gaining Matilda, and disposing of that minion who has presumed to rival Duncaethal."

"If your lordship would be ruled by me," answered the villanous Dargo, "I would seize on the lady Matilda by force; and as to Donald, your lordship already knows I have a dagger very much at his service; and I defy him ever to escape from his prison without my permission."

"Your counsel in regard to the latter likes me well; but by what means can I seize the former and convey her here, for she never suffers herself, even for a moment, without the walls of Bosmora?" said Duncaethal.

"My lord," returned Dargo, "your faithful vassals, by my persuasions, convinced that you have been vilely insulted, in being refused by the baron the hand of Matilda, burn with impatience to revenge your cause; now, my lord, as you treated Bosmora so seemingly fair when he was here to-day, and as you made no mention of his daughter, he will, of course, conclude you have given up the pursuit, and, by that means, will grow remiss in his wonted vigilance, consequently somewhat off his guard: now, my lord, I would have you secretly march your clan to the forest near Bosmora, and there ambush till darkness obscures our motions—then suddenly attacking the castle, when the greatest part of its inhabitants are buried in sleep, then will Matilda become your's by certain conquest, for what can avail the few unprepared domestics, opposed against our numerous party?"

The counsel of this wily wretch met the approbation of his villanous lord, who immediately put his infernal advice in practice, by communicating his intentions to the misled vassals, whose alacrity and eagerness exceeded his most sanguine expectations.

Dargo, previous to their leaving the castle, proceeded to the cell of Donald, taking with him a large basket of provisions; and informing him he should not return to him again for the space of two days, bade him husband them out.

Donald, in a gentle voice, begged him to tell him what had become of his squire?

"He is safe enough," said Dargo, smiling maliciously.

"Is he alive?" asked Donald, earnestly.

"Alive!" returned Dargo; "ah, that he is; the empty basket that stands at the door of his cell will answer for his being alive; this is the third morning he has been here, and, notwithstanding he is in a dungeon, he has eaten more than any one in the castle. I have often heard that sorrow made folks dry, but I never knew before that it made them hungry; however, he has evinced that it sometimes is the case, for I really think the more he moans, the more he eats."

"The third day, did you say?" inquired Donald; "surely I have been here but two mornings," said he, musing.

"Oh, sir," said Dargo, smiling, "you took such a long sleep, and, by that means, the first day past more agreeably than the next."

The cool satirical manner in which the knave spoke, provoked Donald to such a degree, that he angrily bade him quit his presence.

"Ah, that I will," said Dargo; "for I promise you, this gloomy apartment suits not with my elevated notions and aspiring ideas;" and ironically bowing, with a look of the utmost effrontery, withdrew, closing the door on the outside.

Donald now paced his dungeon with agitated steps, ruminating on his dreadful fate; then reclining on his straw, considered within himself, if there was a possibility of devising any method of escape; then arising, anxiously looking round his prison for some chasm through which he might extricate himself—but in vain; at one corner was a small arched door, thickly covered with iron bars closely rivetted, and seemingly fastened on the outside by means of a bar; often had he examined this entrance, with an earnest wish of being able, by some means, to unfasten it—often had he exerted his utmost strength to force it; it now struck him, that probably the dungeon might contain some secret trap, and moving the straw which composed his bed, commenced a strict search; a cold iron ring that met his hand, gave him hopes, and exerting his strength to the utmost, endeavoured to raise it; but not being able to succeed, he took the lamp and examined it more closely, when his disappointment was unequalled by discovering several links of a chain, by which he concluded some unhappy wretch had been fastened to the ground; his spirits, which a few moments before had been raised by hope, with this new disappointment entirely forsook him; and quickly throwing the straw again on the place, he cast himself upon it in all the bitterness of despair; till at length sleep kindly sealed up his eyes, and gave a short respite to his misery.

He had not long remained in this state, ere a sudden noise awoke him, and caused him to look round, and to his utter astonishment, the door which he had so long vainly endeavoured to force stood wide open; at first he could scarcely believe but that he was in a dream, till he heard a rustling on the outside, when, by a sudden impulse, he started up, and rushing forward, passed through the entrance; a glimmering light and receding steps convinced him some one fled his approach; he, swiftly as the winding of the passage would permit, pursued, and caught sight of a figure bearing a lamp; he was on the point of overtaking it, when staggering over a step, it stumbled, and the lamp was extinguished; Donald fell over the prostrate stranger, and seizing him by the throat, with a firm grasp, demanded who he was?

"Oh, St. Andrew save me! mighty sir, I shall be choaked; release me, and I will tell you all, sir!"

Donald instantly quitted his hold, for, to his great surprise, he recognised the voice of his faithful Robert.—"Robert," said he, "for mercy's sake tell me how you came here?"

"Why is that you, my dear master?" eagerly inquired he.

"It is," said Donald; "but where are we?—can we escape from the castle?"

"Alas! not that I know of," returned the other; "for I don't even know the way back to my dungeon, now the lamp is out, for it is dark as pitch."

"Hush!" said his master; "let us endeavour to grope our way back to mine, where there is a lamp burning."

They now felt their way, Donald going first. After many stumbles, he caught a glimpse of the flame which the lamp emitted; it enabled them, at length, to gain the cell, when, immediately upon their entrance, Donald requested Robert to tell him for what purpose he had sought him, and why then fled?

"Alas! sir," said the poor terrified squire, "I thought I would try and give my friend Dargo the slip, as I chanced to find a small door behind an old chest which stood at the head of my miserable couch; and taking an opportunity to raise it when he was gone, I found that I could easily pass through; and when I thought all was still, I took my lamp, and cautiously quitting my cell, endeavoured to find some outlet, that might favour my escape;

when, after turning a long passage to the right, and another to the left, came to this door, and, after removing the heavy bar that fastened it, threw it open, when a light burning, and the noise you made in starting, led me to suppose I had broke in upon some enemy, and I fled, with a view of gaining my prison ere I might be perceived; for I never supposed, in the least, my lord Duncaethal would confine you in such a miserable place as this!"

Donald now proposed that they should both reconnoitre the passage, which being agreed to, they left the dungeon once more, in hopes of emancipation; they recovered the lamp of Robert, and trimming it, they proceeded down a turning on the right, examining it on both sides with great care, hoping to find some door, which, at length, to their great joy, they discovered, with a key in it; this made them conjecture it might be a prison like their own, but, at all events, they were determined to open it: for a long time their united efforts proved fruitless, for, with their utmost strength, they were unable to turn it; till at last Robert bethought himself of a project that flattered them with hope; he took the oily wick from one of the lamps, and thrusting it into the keyhole, softened by that means the cankerous rust which prevented it from moving; success crowned their endeavours; and cautiously opening it, for the hinges loudly grated, to their great joy they discovered a steep flight of stone steps, which seemed to terminate with the upper part of the castle; they gained their summit, and found themselves in a spacious passage leading to a suite of apartments, the dilapidated appearance of which plainly evinced that they had not been inhabited for a considerable length of time: they set down the lamp, as the painted windows admitted the glorious rays of the sun, which, at first, dazzled their sight; but a short time reconciled their eyes to its golden beams, and, from its meridian splendour, proved it to be about the hour of noon. They were on the point of entering a chamber on the right, when a distant sound of footsteps which resounded through the arched ceiling caused them to look up, and, at the extremity of the passage, they beheld Dargo! Donald instantly slipped behind a friendly buttress, and his example was followed by the trembling Robert, who feared that he had been

discovered. Dargo passed the very spot where they were concealed; they expected he would instantly perceive the lamp, and,
by that means, discover their hiding-place; but as it was, by the
projection of a pillar, half-concealed, and nearly extinguished by
the sunbeams darting fully upon its feeble flame, it escaped his
notice, and he went carelessly on.

Soon as he was out of sight, they stole from their hiding-place
to the stairs, and making their way down them, turned the key of
the door; they then consulted how they should proceed. Donald
proposed returning to their cells, and waiting till the inhabitants
of the castle had retired to rest, ere they should again venture
to explore the several apartments they had perceived at the end
of the passage. Robert agreed, and raising the wick of the lamp,
they returned to the cell of Donald.

Robert now proposed remaining with his master till night,
but the latter reminding him Dargo had not yet left the castle
as he had hinted, requested him to go back to his dungeon, lest
their jailor should return in the course of the day, which, in all
probability, he might. Robert could not but admit the truth of sir
Donald's remark, and prepared to leave him; when it was farther
agreed between them, that, when the latter thought it a fit time
for their enterprise, he should repair to the trap door, and give
a signal by striking it with his hand thrice; and Donald stepped
with him through the passage, to ascertain the exact spot it was
placed in. After satisfying himself in this particular, he left his
attendant, and entering his own dungeon, pulled to the door, and
reclining on his straw, anxiously waited the evening's approach.

"Oh, my beloved! could I but once again behold thee, that I
might be able to clear my fame, I should die content! but to be
thought a base coward, and die, conscious of the foul aspersion,
is more than I can bear!" Thus did he soliloquize. The words
of Duncaethal now recurred to his recollection, who said he
should return that night to hear his final determination to what
he had proposed. This had escaped him in his interview with
Robert, and he feared he must forego his enterprize till another
opportunity. Bitterly did he reproach himself for not remembering this, previous to the departure of the latter; and dreading

the consequence of a discovery, he sallied forth to acquaint him with the circumstance; he succeeded in finding the place, and briefly told him his apprehensions, should they venture forth that evening. Robert acquiesced in the prudence of Donald's objections, and they determined to keep in their respective cells till the time mentioned by the latter, which was to be, as near as they could possibly guess, about the hour of midnight. Donald once more retraced his steps to his dreary abode, with intention of waiting patiently for the appointed hour.

Time moved on with leaden and sluggish steps; tediously did he wait in expectation of Duncaethal's appearance; but he came not; and on Donald's awaking from a heavy slumber, which he had imperceptibly fallen into from intense watching, he concluded it was morning; and that, from some unaccountable motive, his enemy had failed to torment him with his presence, so hateful now to his sight. Happily he did not know, that, during the hours which he had slept, his benefactor had fallen a victim to his unrelenting cruelty, or that his beloved Matilda was safe in his power. He arose from his bed of straw, with a determination of making his way to the passage, to judge, by the sun, how far the day had advanced, and proceeded to the friendly door with that intention, when the jingling of keys announced the approach of some one; instantly throwing himself down, he awaited, with all the composure he could assume, for the appearance of this unwelcome visitor.

The door was now opened, and, to his surprise, he beheld Dargo.—"Ah," said he, "I did not expect to see you this morning."

"This morning!" returned the other; "marry, time must pass merrily with you, I think, that you take it for morning!—why 'tis now near twelve o'clock at night!"

Donald felt convinced it must have been near day before he had fallen asleep, and turning to his gaoler, replied—"Why I thought you said you should not visit me again for a day or two."

"So I did," returned the other; "but I come for the purpose of bringing you glad tidings;—the fair Matilda is now in the castle."

"Here!" said Donald, starting; "to what purpose?"

"Why," returned the other, with an ironical look; "why to become the bride of my lord, to be sure."

"Thou liest, villain!" exclaimed Donald, in wrath; "the baron would never consent to it."

"He silently consented," said Dargo.

"Impossible!" returned his agitated prisoner.

"Ah, but he did," replied the other, "for a very good reason."

"What reason?" eagerly demanded the other.

"Why because he could not say anything against it."

"Could not! what dost thou mean?"

"Why because he had not a word to say for himself—he's dead!"

A cold shivering rushed throughout the frame of the horror-struck Donald; as he exclaimed—"Then he is murdered!—inhumanly murdered!"

"Not he," replied the other, with great seeming coolness; "he fell by the chance of war. Last night we attacked Bosmora; the victory was ours, and the lady Matilda became the lawful prize of our lord; I conducted her here myself, and scarcely an hour has elapsed since we arrived."

Donald now became almost frantic, but, after a pause, it, for the first time, struck him, that, perhaps, by the power of a bribe, he might gain over his gaoler to suffer his escape;—then addressing him, said—"Dargo, you cannot be ignorant of the baron's intentions when living to make me the husband of Matilda; and I flatter myself, if I was once at liberty, I should directly be united to her, and, consequently, be equal in power with your lord; if, therefore, you suffer me to gain my freedom, and aid me in procuring Matilda's also, I swear to you, by the honour of a knight, to reward you amply, and place you in a much superior situation than ever you will be by Duncaethal."

"Why," returned Dargo, "you promise greatly."

"Nay," replied the other, "I will perform—I swear it! and, as an earnest of my future favour, accept this," taking from his neck the rich cross presented him by the lady Margaret, which he constantly wore, "which is the only valuable I now possess."

"Sir," said Dargo, "you are very complaisant, and there is no withstanding your offer; so I must, perforce, accept it;" then receiving the ornament from the hand of Donald, made a low bow, and conveyed it to his pocket, at the same time saying—"I am much beholden to your liberality, and shall never forget the obligation; but as to freedom, never let that trouble you, for I have it not in my power, even if I was inclined to grant it."

"Why, wretch! didst thou not say thou accepted my offer?" said Donald.

"And so, sir, I do; believe me, I am truly grateful for this mark of your favour," said the other sarcastically bowing, "and, in return, I have the pleasure to inform you, that you will have the felicity of ending your days in this agreeable place, where it could not possibly be of any service to you; so if you had not good-naturedly made me a present of it, why perhaps I might have been tempted to help myself; for it really is too pretty, and a great deal too valuable, to be buried beneath the surface of the earth, so long as there remains any one above to make use of it."

"Why, villain!" said Donald, "will you break your promise?"

"Promise!" returned the other; "I break no promise; I only said I accepted your proffered kindness; beside, you promised me more than you would ever be able to perform; so I think that you ought to thank me for preventing you from ever having the very disagreeable reflection of forfeiting your word; for when the lady Matilda becomes the bride of my lord Duncaethal, all your hopes will have an end, and so would your promises too."

"Wretch!" returned the other, "torture me no longer with thy hated presence and detested falsehoods! Quit my sight!"

"Oh, sir," coolly replied the other, "don't be in a rage, for really I don't want to force my conversation; so, sir, a good rest to you."

The villain now withdrew, and closing the door, left the miserable Donald cursing his folly, for suffering himself to become the dupe of such an unfeeling monster; and throwing himself upon his straw, once more gave up to despair.

CHAP. IX.

Sure 'tis
The echo of some yawning grave,
That teems with an untimely ghost!

....

Take any shape but that, and my firm nerves
Shall never tremble.

SHAKESPEARE.*

MATILDA, after a night's sleep, disturbed by frightful and horrific dreams, arose, feverish and unrefreshed; then summoning Venella to assist her in dressing, which, after finishing, they repaired to the apartment they had left on the preceding night, where an elegant breakfast had been set forth by Gertrude, who, shortly after, made her appearance.

"Ah, lady," said she, in a tone of sympathy, "those pretty eyes plainly tell me that you have had but an indifferent night's rest: ah! I am sorry for it, lady—indeed I am!—but do try and eat something—do, my dear lady! I have prepared the best breakfast for you that the castle could afford."

"I am very much obliged to you for your kind attention," said Matilda; "but I am really very ill, and feel it utterly impossible to avail myself of it."

"Ah, dear lady," answered Gertrude, "I am sorry for it, very sorry, and I fear I bring you news but little calculated to restore your health—my lord Duncaethal bade me inform you he intended to visit you in the evening, if you would grant him permission."

"If I would permit him!" exclaimed Matilda; "why does he thus insult the wretchedness he has himself caused, by this mockery of complaisance? He can, no doubt, if he chuses, visit his miserable prisoner without her consent; then why thus seemingly request it?—but you may tell him I am ready to receive him, if he has the boldness to meet the indignant eye of the unhappy daughter of the murdered Bosmora."

"Alas, madam," said Gertrude, "I dare not tell him what you have said, for the world."

"Well then, you may deliver to him what message you think fit to that purport," said Matilda, mildly.

Gertrude, making a low curtsey, withdrew, followed by Venella. Matilda, striking the chords of lady Margaret's harp, which never, since her demise, had once been removed, but still remained in all its pristine excellence, sought to compose her agitated spirits by music; sweetly did the enchanting sounds float upon the air; and tuning her syren's voice, she began a melodious strain, but had not proceeded far, ere she recollected that it was the same that had so often charmed the ears of her father and Donald, in those days of happiness spent at Bosmora. This recalled to her perturbed mind her father's dreadful fate, with a train of horrid ideas that tortured her to madness; in frantic accents she called upon Donald to rescue her from the power of the murderous Duncaethal, until, exhausted by the violence of her ravings, she sunk upon the floor in a state of total insensibility. Venella then luckily coming into the room, conveyed her unhappy mistress to bed. The poppy influence of Morpheus once more visited her weary eyelids; and, after a few hours of undisturbed repose, she awoke, much recovered, and returned to the apartment, tranquillized and composed; she inquired of Venella, if Duncaethal had been to pay his visit, or if he was acquainted with her sudden indisposition? Venella replied, Gertrude had informed him, and he intended to postpone his visit till the evening.

Matilda now, for the first time since her arrival, took some refreshment, and dismissing her attendant, with an order of being within call if wanted, seated herself at a large gothic window, and waited reluctantly for the dread approach of Duncaethal. It was rather late in the evening; the sun had already sunk beneath the distant horizon, and the gentle zephyrs played upon her pale cheek. Darkness was swiftly approaching, when closing the casement, and arising to summon Venella for a taper, she heard her name pronounced, and quickly turning round, beheld at her elbow the mysterious figure which she encountered in the subterranean of Bosmora. A loud shriek was just bursting from her lips, when raising his hand, he motioned her to silence, and, in a low tone, thus addressed her—"Matilda, fear not! thou shalt not fall a victim to Duncaethal:—thou art reserved for another fate! I tell thee so—I, the bandit Darthalgo! Hadst thou accepted my proffered protection, long ere this, thou wouldst have been free from sorrow—but I perceive my appearance offends you; girl, trust not to that! for I could so far change myself, that, in some eyes, I might even appear prepossessing—I am not what I seem!"

"Indeed!" said the terrified Matilda, who now, for the first time, had recovered the use of speech, of which his sudden and terrific appearance had deprived her, "indeed!"

"Nay, I swear I am not, lady! I will save you; to-morrow I will return, and, in the mean time——" A voice in the antichamber interrupted him, and instantly snatching a mantle from the shoulder of Matilda, he cast it over her face; and ere she could remove it, not the least trace remained of her mysterious visitor.

Duncaethal now entered the apartment, and, in a voice of studied complacency, asked if she was better? at the same time remarking that her cheek retained all the lovely carnation, as when first she enslaved his heart.

"Monster!" said Matilda; "if that colour does indeed appear in my face, it is to express the indignation which I feel at beholding the murderer of my father. Would I could arm those eyes with avenging lightning, to strike thee dead!"

"Lady, spare your rage," said Duncaethal, coolly; "it will not avail thee half so much as gentleness. If thou wilt hear me patiently, I may remember the respect and dignity due to your sex and rank; but if, by ill timed rage, you scorn my offers, it will but hasten the fate prepared for stubbornness." Then kneeling before her, he thus continued—"Lovely Matilda, behold me at your feet!—me whom you have for ever enslaved, to beg for your pity, which can alone make me happy! 'Twas for the great felicity of calling you mine, that I rushed into fatal war, to gain that prize which courtesy solicited for in vain!"

"And didst thou, mistaken wretch, think the heart of Matilda was to be won by imbruing thy hands with the blood of my father? Hear me, Heaven, as I hope for mercy at thy great judgment-seat, never will I become the wife of a homicide!—never will I call the murderer of my father, husband!"

"'Tis well, madam," said Duncaethal, while rage shot from his fierce dark eye, "'tis vastly well; but if you care not for your own life, I have yet another hold on you—your minion, Donald, he is in my power, and amply will I revenge myself in his death, for your scorn and haughtiness!"

Duncaethal had attained his point. Matilda, who feared not for herself, when she heard her heart's beloved was within his grasp, all the woman's tenderness arose, and sinking on her knees at the feet of her remorseless tyrant, in piteous accents, implored him to save the life of the unoffending Donald.

"What!" said he, exultingly, "can the proud imperious Matilda descend so far as to prostrate herself before a murderer, whom her eyes would fain strike dead! and, in humiliating language, can plead for the life of a wretch beneath her regard!—but I pity your weakness, and will spare his life, if you will consent to become mine; but if you still reject me, I will wreak on his head my utmost vengeance, in which I am irrevocably fixed."

The agitation of Matilda almost amounted to madness, as she struggled between fear for herself, and dread for the life of Donald, which, to preserve, she was nearly on the point of consenting to his wishes, when suddenly she recollected the words of the bandit—"Thou shalt not fall a victim to Duncaethal—I will save you!" "If," thought she, "he can rescue me, he might also be able to preserve Donald." Gathering courage at this idea, she hastily arose, and exclaimed—"Never, never will I become the wife of the murderer Duncaethal!"

"Indeed!" said he, instantly seizing her in his arms; "you have now, haughty madam, signed the fiat of your own destruction; I will not again sue for the happiness which is already mine by right of conquest, and force shall procure for me what I have so long solicited in vain."

A loud shriek burst from the lips of Matilda, as she endeavoured to extricate herself from his loathsome kisses and rude embrace, when a dismal and hollow groan, sounding through the apartment, caused him instantly to quit his hold, and a voice, in sepulchral tones, cried—"Murderer, forbear!" The room, which, till now, had been almost dark, was instantly illuminated by a flaming lamp, that was borne in the hand of a tall spectral figure; a deep wound appeared in her breast, from which the sanguinary stream still seemed to flow, while, in hollow accents, it thus addressed the terror-stricken Duncaethal—"Behold me, thou homicide! long shalt thou not flourish amidst thy horrid crimes; thou shalt fall by the hand of one, who, by thy blood, must give peace to the suffering spirit of the murdered Margaret!"

The conscience-smitten Duncaethal sunk to the floor, as the figure, approaching him, uttering a dismal groan, slowly disappeared. Matilda fell upon a couch, in a state of total insensibility, for she beheld, in the pale countenance of the spectre, the features of the departed lady Duncaethal.

Venella, who was, with great anxiety, longing to know the result of the interview, and not being able longer to resist, advanced to the door of her lady's apartment, and placing her ear to the key-hole, as was her usual custom, when she wished to gratify her ardent and irresistible curiosity, she was greatly surprised at not hearing any one, and, after waiting a considerable time, was tempted to open the door, and, to her great surprise, beheld them both in the state already described; she loudly called for assistance, and, in a moment after, Gertrude made her appearance, followed by Dargo, who, with looks of astonishment, beheld the prostrate situation of his lord, and summoning another domestic to his aid, conveyed him from the apartment, while Venella and Gertrude were both endeavouring, by all possible methods, to recover Matilda, who, on opening her eyes, uttered many incoherent expressions relative to the strange sight which she had so lately witnessed, not a word of which was understood by her hearers, who concluded she was delirious. After a pause, she asked Gertrude if she had ever beheld the ghost of the departed lady Margaret?

"Who, I, my lady? No, the Virgin forbid! why have you, madam?"

Matilda then recounted the cause of her fainting; and minutely described the figure she had beheld; when she mentioned the wound in her breast, Gertrude shook her head, and said—"Ah! I fear that there has been sad doings, in some respects; but I do really think it could not be the ghost of lady Margaret, for I saw her lie dead, with my own eyes."

Matilda was surprised, and yet she felt convinced it bore her likeness; and the words she uttered striking so forcibly on Duncaethal's guilty conscience, corroborated her suspicion of Margaret's having been basely murdered; but not being able to develop the mystery, she endeavoured to change the subject, inwardly blessing that Providence which had, by its heavenly interference, saved her from a fate worse than death.

She now interrogated Gertrude respecting what prisoners there were in the castle, and if the person of a young knight was amongst the number? hoping that Duncaethal had only made use of artifice, by saying Donald was in his power, to intimidate her with the fear of his vengeance falling upon him, which she now began somewhat to suspect.

Gertrude replied—"Alas, my lady, I know not indeed! but I suppose there are several confined in the dungeon, for Dargo frequently carries several baskets of provisions from the hall, which I know not how he disposes of, except for the use of prisoners: I once had the curiosity to inquire, but he surlily bade me mind my own business, and not question him. Ah, madam! this castle is not like what it was in the time of our good old lord, your noble grandsire! Ah! he little supposed this old mansion, which was the seat of benevolence and hospitality, would ever be converted into a prison! but when our present lord came to be possessor, he dismissed a great many of the ancient domestics and bards, who had, for many years, eaten the bread of our good old baron; but when he returned from his travels, and brought home his bride, lady Margaret Monteith; it became again enlivened by the resort of company, for she was never easy but when having revels and masks; and I believe, by her extravagance, wasted much of my lord's substance; and since her death, the castle has been solitary enough, for my lord seemed to make amends for her profusion by his parsimony, my lady:—but, lack-a-day! I am talking away my time, when I ought to be in the hall; and so, my dear lady, if you are better, I will leave you with your maid."

Matilda assured her that she was perfectly recovered; the kind old woman, making a low curtsey, and desiring she might be called if her illness should return, modestly withdrew, leaving her to the care of Venella, who was terrified to death at the idea of ghosts and apparitions, declaring she should never be able to remain alone after dark, or sleep again by herself, long as she lived, for fear of being visited by some supernatural intruder.

Matilda now recurred to the words of the mysterious Darthalgo—"I am not what I seem, and could appear prepossessing." She thought it might be a friend in disguise, who had some particular motive for his strange conduct, and offers for her service. Then formed the resolution of trusting herself under his protection, if ever another opportunity should occur; and after earnestly returning her thanks again to that Providence who had, in such a mysterious manner, delivered her, she offered to Heaven a petition for the safety of Donald; but feeling no inclination for sleep, she took up a book which lay in the room, and sought to beguile her time by reading; she accidentally opened it at the commencement of the following tale:—

"Deep in a glen, obscure and lowly, dwelt the lovely and innocent Mora; sweetly glided her days till she was seen by Rothma, lord of the castle, which, in proud majesty, frowned upon her clay-built cottage. Loudly had the horn of the hunters sounded through the winding of the vale, as the fleet hounds swept away the pearly dew-drops from the grass, when the proud-mettled steed threw his lord near the gate of Mora. Her father, with a ready hand, assisted him to their dwelling, and he departed not for several days, but, like the fiend, lingered, with many evasive excuses, until he triumphed over the virtue of the innocent Mora. The poor deserted one pined in secret, till the damask hue which had once blushed upon her cheek changed to a death-like paleness, as, with rapid steps, she was hastening to hide her shame under the green sod which covered her heart-broken father.

"Not so the proud Rothma; he forgot the daughter of Carlina;

and his bridal day, in all the pomp of lordly pride, quickly followed the destruction of Mora. Loudly sounded the harp in his halls, and the banquet board sunk under the weight of the rich viands which composed the feast. In the midst of the revels, a wandering minstrel approached, and bowing gracefully to the bride, skilfully struck the lyre, and, with a melodious voice, sung the following legend:—

> 'List, sweet lady, to my ditty—
>   'Tis of Mora fair I sing;
> Prythee drop a tear of sorrow,
>   While I gently touch the string.
>
> 'Lovely Mora, in a cottage,
>   Sweetly pass'd each fleeting day;
> 'Till lord Carril, like a canker,
>   Crop'd this flow'r and fled away.
>
> 'Many days, in silent anguish,
>   Gentle Mora pass'd away;
> Many tears of briny sorrow
>   Damp'd the pillow where she lay.
>
> 'Now the merry bells are ringing
>   Through the vale with clamour wide,
> Tell poor Mora, the deluder
>   Basely has receiv'd a bride!
>
> 'Mora now, in strange attire,
>   Seeks the castle where he dwells,
> And, as in a minstrel's legend,
>   To the bride her story tells.
>
> 'Yes, fair lady, that is Carril!
>   I am Mora the betray'd!
> Thou'rt the bride that have with patience,
>   Listen'd to the ruin'd maid!'

"She was silent, while all within the hall cast their eyes upon the proud Rothma, who in vain endeavoured to hide the stings of guilt, as the minstrel earnestly fixed on him her penetrating gaze; when, at length, endeavouring to recollect his scattered spirits, he loudly exclaimed—'Seize that vile impostor, and bear him instantly to a dungeon!' The domestics approached, and the minstrel in a moment vanished, when, in his place, stood a *meagre spectre!* All started aghast, and Rothma gazed in wild afright, while the spirit of the deserted Mora thus addressed him—'Rothma, my bridegroom, haste! quit that form, and come away!' In a moment the flesh faded, and the noble person of Rothma sunk into a loathsome skeleton! loud thunders shook the battlements, as, enclasping him in her arms, they both disappeared from the view of the astonished assembly!

"The castle was deserted for ever! and as the hind nightly seeks his peaceful cot, he hies him swiftly by the gate; for as the bleak wind whistles past him, he hears, or fancies he hears, the sigh of Mora borne on the shrilly breeze."

CHAP. X.

She lives; but wastes her life in constant woe—
Weeping her husband slain—her infant, lost!

HOME.*

D ONALD, after in vain reproaching himself for resigning the jewel, and his tumultuous passions had somewhat subsided, endeavoured to rally his subdued spirits, and resolved to make another attempt, if possible, to procure his emancipation. He cautiously proceeded to the door of Robert's cell, and giving the appointed signal, the latter gently raised the friendly trap, and, in a moment after, joined his master. They both repaired to the staircase, and opening the door slowly, found themselves once more in the passage or corridor. Donald, with great precaution, entered the chamber on the right, whose ruinous state proved that it had long been uninhabited; and, after searching in vain for some outlet, returned to Robert, who remained in the passage, to give a signal if any person should approach.

They now perceived a flight of stairs, which had escaped their notice on their first entrance, and, with renewed hopes, both ascended them; but to their disappointment, found they communicated with the roof, and had been erected for the purpose of a quick ascent to the parapet; but the top was closed up. Being dejected with this disappointment, they descended, and were debating whether they should return to their cells, as there seemed to be no chance of success; but Donald was determined to search every cranny, ere he quietly resigned himself to his fate.

At this moment a voice, seemingly in earnest supplication, attracted his attention, and motioning to Robert for silence, he followed the sound through a chamber to a door at the end of it, which was barred on the outside; he proceeded to unfasten it, in spite of the fears of Robert, who sought to deter him, by saying they possibly might break in upon some of the ministers of Duncaethal. His master felt convinced it was some poor captive, or else, for what reason should the entrance be secured? He soon succeeded in his attempts to remove the bar, and opening the door, found it was the antichamber of another apartment. An earnest prayer, which a female voice was offering up to the Virgin, encouraged them to proceed; their approach did not alarm the supplicant, and gave time, ere she perceived them, to contemplate her strange appearance. A long black vest was fastened round her waist, from the girdle of which hung a rosary; her long hair waved negligently on her shoulders, and her arms were crossed upon her bosom, in the posture of adoration; her fine blue eyes seemed irradiated with pious fervency, forgetful of all sublunary objects.

Donald knew not whether to advance or recede, so fearful was he of disturbing the devotions of this mysterious recluse. She now arose, and turning, beheld the two intruders—"Ah!" she exclaimed, "is my tyrant, at last, determined to extirpate my wretched existence? but I am prepared—so, murderers, advance, and execute his bloody purpose."

Donald, gracefully bowing, said—"Lady, you are deceived; we are not assassins, but almost strangers here."

"Ah!" exclaimed she, "by what happy chance come ye?" and falling at their feet, continued—"I beseech ye, for Heaven's sake, to conduct me from this prison. Not for myself I sue, but I would learn the fate of a being far more dear to me than my wretched life."

"Alas, madam," replied Donald, "I regret 'tis not in my power, for, like yourself, I am but a prisoner; and it was in hopes of gaining my liberty that brought me here."

"Are you then in the power of Duncaethal?" said she, sympathetically.

"I am," returned Donald.

"Then, stranger, I pity you; for you are in the fangs of a lion, from whom escape is impossible. Many years have I wretchedly lingered here; yet bless my fate that I have not, ere this, fallen a victim to his rage, and still remain in this world of woe."

She now inquired of Donald how he had contrived to leave his dungeon? He informed her briefly as possible, at the same time saying he must return, lest his gaoler should, by chance, visit his prison and find it vacant. The lady agreed with his obser-vation, and bidding him farewell, added—"Stranger, if you could again contrive to visit me to-morrow night, you shall be made acquainted with the sad events of my wretched life; and if you should ever escape, may seek out one I shall mention, and inform him of my hapless fate."

The castle clock at this moment proclaimed the hour of two; and supposing the inhabitants were all buried in sleep, he said— "Madam, the interest I feel for your wretched situation, together with the hope I may, by the help of Heaven, have it in my power to serve you, makes me resolved to seize the present opportu-nity, lest another should not occur, to know in what manner I can effect it."

She pointed to a bench, when being seated, she began her wretched narrative.

"In me you behold the sad remains of Agnes Maclean."

Donald started; she marked his emotion, and said—"Why start you, stranger?"

"I had heard," Donald replied, "she perished in a flood, and was never heard of more; but I beg pardon, lady—proceed."

She continued.—"My father, on his deathbed, entrusted

me to the care of the former baron of Duncaethal, who acted the part of a tender guardian, and reared me with his own son and daughter. For the lovely Mabel I felt all the affection of a sister; but the youthful Alexander won my virgin heart, and he returned my affection by a passion amounting to adoration. He disclosed his love to his father, without hopes of success, for family pride cast a shade upon a character otherwise generous and benevolent.

"About this period lord Bosmora visited the castle, and being smitten with the beauty of Mabel, married her, and bore her away from Duncaethal. 'Twas now that her brother's flame for me burst forth, and pleading his passion in the most glowing terms, urged me to consent to the solemnization of a private marriage. This I constantly declined till he was on the point of going forth to terminate a feud, existing between his father and a neighbouring chieftain; when, won by his parting solicitations, I gave him my hand, and consented to his making me his wife, ere he quitted Duncaethal. We concerted that I should walk out alone, as was my custom, and he should meet me at an appointed spot. Every thing succeeded to our wishes, and we repaired together to a neighbouring monastery, where my beloved lord bribed a father of the place secretly to unite us. A woman who had attended me from my infancy, was a witness and confidant of this inauspicious marriage. Two days after he left me, to meet his death, for never did he return until his eyes were closed in lasting sleep. Wretched woman as I am, how did I ever survive this blow, as fatal to my peace! but, alas! my cup of misery was not yet full.

"The news of his son's death smote the old baron to the heart's core, and he speedily closed his sorrows in the grave. Oh, would that his fate had been mine! Mabel came to close the eyes of her father, and would fain have conducted me to the castle of her lord, which I was on the point of consenting to, when the present possessor of this castle arrived, to invest himself with the rights of possession; but on his saying he should leave the place for a few weeks, I requested of Mabel permission to remain for a short time, and wear off the poignancy of my grief in solitude.

She consented, and I saw her depart, with a promise of my following shortly after.

"One day, as I was riding in the adjacent forest for the benefit of the air, I recalled to my afflicted mind how often I had, in that very spot, accompanied my departed lord. The tears unbidden rushed in torrents down my cheeks, when turning my steed, I was about to quit the place; but the reins were suddenly seized by a ruffian, who commanded me immediately to dismount and follow; I was forced to comply, and another fierce-looking man assisted me in so doing. They now proceeded into the thickest part of the forest, and seating me under a tree, waited for approaching evening. Resistance was in vain, for they threatened me, on their first appearance, with instant death, if I attempted to make the least noise.

"When they thought it sufficiently dark, they reseated me, but on another horse, (for they had left mine to retrace its way back to the castle, and, by that means, to cause its inhabitants to suppose I had perished,) and placing a bandage over my eyes, swore, if I uttered a single word, that moment should be my last. We now proceeded, and, after an hour's riding, near as I could guess, they stopped, and lifting me from the horse, conveyed me up some steps, where being unbound, and the bandage taken from my eyes, I found myself in the adjoining chamber to this: I knew not then that it was the castle of Duncaethal, for this wing being in a ruined state, the old baron had always kept it closed up.

"I now inquired for what purpose I had been brought hither? They replied I should soon be informed, and left the room, closing the door, and securing it on the outside. When left to myself, I revolved within my mind the strange motives for this unaccountable procedure. That they were not robbers was evident, for they neither demanded my purse, or any valuable about me, or offered the least violence to my person; what could they be?

"My ruminations were interrupted by the appearance of no other person then Duncaethal himself. Surprise bereft me of the power of speech, while he thus addressed me—'Lovely Agnes, behold before you the man whom the power of your charms has compelled to act thus forcibly against his inclinations; but consent to be mine, and you shall reign in this spacious and noble domain with unbounded sway. 'Tis not in my power to espouse you, but, as my mistress, you shall command a heart that pants with adoration.' Then kneeling at my feet, he continued—'My soul's idol, let me only call you mine, and my happiness will be complete.'

"I now interrupted him by saying—'Arise, lord Duncaethal, and insult not mine ears by your detested passion, but instantly tell me where I am, and by what authority you have dared to seize my person, and convey me from my friends?'"

'I have no authority,' said he, 'but love: I must also be so free as to tell you, that, unless you consent to my wishes, you have tasted liberty for the last time. You are in my power, and the whole world shall not compel me to resign you. My plans are securely laid; no one but my trusty emissaries knows of your being here; the old stupid servants of the castle are lamenting you as lost, by supposing that you were thrown into the flood near the forest; and every precaution has been made to prevent your escape. You can only impute all that I have done to the effects of passion, ardent and irresistible. I have loved you from the moment I first saw you, which was at the death of the baron; and my pretence of leaving Duncaethal was a stratagem to get you into my power. I have beheld you when you thought your-self in solitude, and every glimpse I caught of that lovely countenance served only to rivet my chains, that were already galling, and I found it was in vain to resist the force of charms ordained to enslave my heart—therefore, lovely Agnes, consent to my happiness, and, in a distant land, we'll enjoy the bliss of love, uncloyed by the trammels of the canting priest.'

"He now paused, and I replied—'My lord, I have heard you with patience, but am at a loss to account for the motive of this insult, or what part of my conduct could ever induce you to suppose that I should listen to the offer of an illicit connexion; nor can I imagine how you could so far insult the unstained honour of a descendant of the house of Maclean—of one who, though poor, has the claim of noble birth. That I possess not riches, is my fault, not my misfortune; for know, thou insulting wretch, I have a legal right to those which you enjoy, and it was only with a view to forget my sorrows that I withheld my claim; and may it strike terror to thy soul, as I now inform you that I am the lawful wife of Alexander, the deceased heir of Duncaethal!'

"These words, for a short time, seemed to petrify the wretch; the pale cheek was blanched with fear and surprise; but recovering himself, he said—'Well, if it really is so, why I have a double cause then to retain you: but fear not, for I shall no longer persecute thee with my passion;—my heart, which burnt to possess the virgin, is cold towards the widowed wife.'

"He now, coldly bowing, left the room, regardless of the entreaties which I made for liberty.

"On the following morning he returned, leading in Peter and my woman; I fell upon my knees before the old steward, and besought him to rescue me from this wretched place. I was rudely raised from the floor by Duncaethal, who told me prayers were in vain; and if I made such ill use of his indulgence in allowing me servants, he should find means to make me wait upon myself. He then left the room, when old Peter informed me the tyrant had returned to the castle on the evening that I was missing, and pretended to take an active part in the vain search that was made for my recovery; but finding my mantle, which, it seems, had been purposely left in the forest, asserted that I had been thrown into the river, and caused Peter to send a messenger to that effect unto Mabel. He then visited me, in hopes of gaining my consent to his infamous proposal, when making a discovery so little expected, his love was converted into fear, and he determined to make this place my eternal prison. Upon leaving me, he summoned Peter, and Beatrice, my woman, from whom he extorted a dreadful vow never to divulge what he should disclose to them, at the peril of their lives; at the same time insinuating to them, that if they acted faithfully, they should be rewarded amply. They had no resource but compliance; and after administering to them the oath of fidelity, which, in its form, was truly horrid, as he acquainted them with his securing me, and his purpose in so doing, until a recent discovery had caused him to alter his project, which required their service to perform, in attending me and preventing my escape. To this, with reluctant hearts, they were compelled; then giving them notice that he should be absent for a considerable length of time, he renewed his threats and promises, as their conduct might merit; and departed from the castle, accompanied by the ruffians whom he calls his domestics.

"I had not been long imprisoned, ere I found that I was fast approaching to that period when I should produce a living pledge of the unhappy loves of Alexander and myself. I implored Beatrice and Peter that, if they could not save me, they might my child, as their oath extended no further than to myself. Both of them consented to my request of placing my infant beyond the power of Duncaethal, should the time of my accouchement arrive before his return, who, happily for me, had not suspected my pregnancy.

"At length the important moment approached; and here, imprisoned and unknown, I gave birth to the rightful heir of these rich domains. The very day after, Peter received notice from his master, that he should return in about five weeks. They suffered me to retain my babe the space of a month; when deeming it no longer safe, lest his lord should come unaware, Peter prevailed on me to resign it to him, for the purpose of conveying it to some safe retreat. With a breaking heart I was forced to comply with his prudent advice; and, with many tears, I kissed his infant cheek, and consigned the precious charge to his care.

"I now recollected that I was entirely bereft of money, and knew of no person that, without reward, would receive an unknown child, when the good old Peter, producing a purse of gold which contained nearly half of what he possessed, quieted my fears in that respect; and again embracing, for the last time, my darling infant, I fastened round his lovely neck the only valuable in my possession, which was a string of small pearls, from which was suspended this cross;" at the same time drawing from her bosom the exact counterpart of the jewel given to Donald by lady Margaret, and which he had that night resigned to the villain Dargo.

"God of mercies!" exclaimed he, soon as it met his astonished

sight; and thrusting his hand into his breast, drew forth the necklace given him by Allen; he said, in broken accents—"Ah! it is!
the pearls—the cross!" and sinking on his knee, exclaimed—"Oh,
mother! mother!—bless your child!" But she spoke not; surprise
and joy overcame her, and she sunk senseless into the arms of
the agitated Donald.

Robert, who had been a silent spectator of this moving scene,
wept with joy, and jumping frantically about the room, cried—
"My dear master is a true baron! oh dear, how glad I am!"

"Hush," said the youth; "your noise will betray us. Calm your
transports, and assist me to recover my mother:—mother! oh
thou name revered! but that it should be my unfortunate lot to
discover my parent in a prison, damps the joy I feel. Oh, mother!
dear mother!"

The name seemed to bear with it a powerful charm, for the
poor Agnes once more felt returning life; and once more falling
on his neck, crying—"It is—it is my long-lost child!—my dearest
Alexander!" she now endeavoured to tranquillize her much-agi-
tated frame, and addressing him, said—"Tell me, my son, how
thou hast fared since the fatal day when Peter saw you for the last
time?"

Donald, with all the brevity possible, gave her a sketch of his
eventful history; which concluding, begged her to proceed with
her wonderful narrative, which she did as follows:—

"Peter, on his return, informed me that he had, with safety
and great secrecy, consigned you to the care of an honest well-
meaning peasant; at the same time returning me the cross which
I had fastened round your neck, gently reproved me for risking a
discovery, by so remarkable an ornament: it had been presented
me by your father, who, on the departure of Mabel, gave her one
also, that bore, in every respect, a resemblance and caused the
mistake of the good old peasant Allen.

"Shortly after my painful separation from you, the usurping
tyrant once more shocked me by his hated presence; but finding
I bore my confinement with seeming fortitude and resignation,
expressed his approbation of the care of Peter and Beatrice, and
seldom troubled me.

"About a year after his return, the good and faithful Peter acquainted me with the death of Mabel, who had left an infant daughter. He had learned these tidings from old Allen, whom he had persuaded to retire to a cottage near the castle of Bosmora, to whom he presented a second purse, containing all that he possessed in the world, promising a renewal of his visit at the end of another year; but ere the expiration of that period, I lost both my faithful servants; and since that time have been attended by the villain Dargo, who inhumanly prevented both old Peter and Beatrice from obtaining a confessor, fearing, I suppose, lest, on their deathbeds, they should disclose the place of my confinement. Duncaethal never supposed that I had ever given birth to a child; and since the deaths of my attendants, I only have mentioned your name in my orisons, imploring for you the protection of Heaven.

"A long series of years have I now passed, without seeing a human being, except Dargo, whom his cruel master left to guard his hapless prisoner, who every week generally brings me a supply of food, during his travels. Upon his return from them, he brought with him a bride, as I was told by my unfeeling gaoler; nor since that time have I ever heard of him; and when I to-night saw you in my prison, I supposed he was agitated by some new fear of discovery, and had employed you to put an end to my then wretched experience. Little did I suppose I then beheld my son!—that son for whose safety I had daily offered up my constant prayer!" and again embracing, said—"We are now both in the villain's power; but fear not, my child—the omniscient Being who has been graciously pleased to let me once more behold you, will still preserve you from the murderer's poniard, to add lustre to the name and virtues of your noble sire."

The hour of four now loudly sounded, and the streaks of approaching day warned them to separate, lest a discovery should take place by a visit from Dargo. Robert now relighted the lamp; and ere Donald left his mother, she earnestly besought him, however he might be incensed by Duncaethal, not to let drop a hint relative to his real name or title. This he promised;

and repeatedly embracing her, tore himself away, after agreeing to a proposal of his venturing to return on the following night.

Robert then assisted him in fastening the door as they at first found it; then repairing to their separate cells, Donald again beheld himself in a place now become doubly disgusting, by his knowledge of the real claim he possessed to an elevated rank, by being the rightful heir to the castle of Duncaethal.

END OF VOL. I.

THE

Caledonian Bandit;

OR,

THE HEIR OF DUNCAETHAL.

A ROMANCE

OF THE THIRTEENTH CENTURY.

TWO VOLUMES IN ONE.

BY

MRS. SMITH,

OF THE THEATRE-ROYAL HAYMARKET.

A Tale of the times of old.

OSSIAN.

VOL. II.

LONDON:

PRINTED AT THE

Minerva-Press,

FOR A. K. NEWMAN AND CO.

(Successors to Lane, Newman, and Co.)

LEADENHALL-STREET.

1811.

THE

CALEDONIAN BANDIT.

CHAP. I.

Oh that my head were laid, my sad eyes clos'd
And my cold corse wound in my shroud to rest!
My painful heart will cease to beat,
Will never know a moment's peace till then.

HOME.*

MATILDA, the night she had witnessed the strange appearance that had struck terror to the guilty soul of Duncaethal, undisturbed by the remorseless pangs of the latter, slept tranquil and secure until the late hour the following day. Gertrude then made her appearance, and informed her, among other circumstances, of the severe indisposition of her master, who, she said, was unable to leave his chamber. That day heavily passed on, unmarked by any change favourable to the lovely captive; but on the evening of the second, as she was reclining on her couch, a loud sigh, seemingly close to her, caused her to start, and at her elbow she again beheld the mysterious bandit!

"Well, lady," said he, "once more chance has given me an opportunity of serving you; will you avail yourself of it, or must I again deprive myself of the satisfaction of conveying you to a safe retreat?"

"Alas!" said Matilda, "your appearance is doubtful, not to add forbidding; therefore be not offended at my objections; for how am I certain but that I may, perhaps, change my miserable situation for a still worse?"

"Worse!" exclaimed the bandit; "thinkst thou there can be a worse wretch in existence than Duncaethal, or dost thou entertain suspicions of my injuring thee? If that were my motive, have I not now an opportunity? and if thy life was my object, have I not the power now to take it?"

As he spoke he presented a poniard to the breast of the terrified Matilda; then, instantly replacing it, continued—"Foolish girl, are you now convinced? If so, banish your timid fears, and say whether I shall depart alone, or will you confide in the honour of the bandit Darthalgo?"

"I will entrust myself to your care," said she, tremblingly, "for you seem to take great interest in the wretched fate I endure, and will place myself under your protection."

"You are right, lady; no one living takes a greater interest in the fate of Matilda than myself."

An indefinable expression crossed his features as she uttered—"Mysterious being! what art thou?"

"Lady, I repeat to you that I am not what I seem; follow me, and, ere this hour to-morrow, you will be convinced of the truth of my assertion."

He now seized her half-reluctant hand, and pressing a secret spring at the side of her mother's picture, it flew back and discovered a large aperture, through the cavity of which they proceeded, when Matilda found herself in a dark narrow passage (the manner of their escape from the room fully explained to her the method by which the bravo had made his nocturnal visit, and accounted for his sudden appearance): at the end was a door, where taking up a lamp that had been left burning, and shading the flame, they moved slowly on: at length they arrived at a trap in the floor, so cunningly contrived, that not the least appearance of such a device could be detected by any one unacquainted with its construction; The bravo placed his feet on a particular board which composed it, when he instantly sunk from the sight of the wondering Matilda; but, in a moment after lifting up his head, bade her act as he had done, and she would soon find herself in the under apartment. The trap now arose, when she, with a palpitating heart, followed his directions, and found herself, after safely descending, in a spacious room; the damp air instantly chilled her whole frame. The bandit now seemed to think himself beyond the reach of detection, and, with a ghastly smile of exultation, he proceeded with a quick pace, leading by the hand his trembling fugitive, through the intricacies of a winding passage, when arriving at the extremity, and striking with his hand three distinct times upon a small door, he was answered, in a rough voice, by a signal of "Liberty and Darthalgo!" He now withdrew a bolt and threw it open, and pulling Matilda along, entered a small cavern, where three rough-looking men appeared to be in waiting.

One of them, in a discordant voice, said—"Darthalgo, we have tarried for you a long time; if we are not speedy, day will break ere we arrive at the end of our journey."

"Fear not," replied Matilda's incomprehensible conductor; "here is the lady, and our horses are swift of foot."

She was unable to conceal any longer the fear which the sight of these ferocious men had excited, and falling upon her knees, she besought Darthalgo to inform her whither he intended to convey her.

"Rise, madam," said he, in a voice more stern than what he ever before addressed her in; "have I not sworn to free you from your troubles, and yet still do you fear. Cannot you confide in my oath?—Are our horses ready?" said he, to one of the men.

"They are," answered another; "all is prepared."

"'Tis well," said Darthalgo, "and we will make no longer delay."

"Lady, you must consent to my placing this bandage over your eyes, a ceremony which we never omit when a stranger is admitted into our dwelling."

Matilda tremblingly consented to this strange request, which being performed, she felt herself in the arms of a man, who bore her a considerable distance, and placing her on a horse, mounted himself, without speaking a word to his companions, whose horses feet she could plainly hear. He now spurred on his courser, and riding briskly for a long time, a voice cried out— "Halt!" in a tone she recognized for the bandit's, and another gave the signal, by saying, "Liberty and Darthalgo!" which was answered by "'Tis well! all is in readiness!"

Matilda was lifted from off the horse, and being desired to stoop, was conducted through a very narrow aperture; then descending several steps, and turning into a winding passage, proceeded onwards, when a door, which grated on its rusty hinges, was opened; and the bandage being removed, she found herself in a large dismal apartment, hung round with various weapons; a lamp burning on the table, round which were seated a group of men, discovered to her their savage features and uncouth appearance, which plainly spoke their dreadful calling.

"Oh Heavens!" mentally ejaculated she, "Darthalgo has betrayed me!"

She was that very moment addressed by him, saying—"Lady Matilda, be seated and partake of our cheer; we shall shortly have breakfast."

She declined the invitation; when one of the men at the table said—"Don't be alarmed; you need not fear us, my pretty dear."

"No, no," said a second; "we have too much respect for the fair sex, to offer them any injury."

"Aye, aye," said a third; "we love a pretty girl as well as other people, who call themselves honest—don't we, my boys?"

"Aye, aye, that we do," returned the others.

"But," said the first, "the lady don't seem to relish our freedom; mayhap she's weary. Call old Peg, and let her conduct her to bed."

Darthalgo till now had been silent, when, in an authoritative tone, he said—"Go, one of you, and desire that old grumbling harridan to come here."

Matilda felt somewhat easy when she heard that a female was in this strange habitation, as she hoped to experience from her some small commiseration; but her hopes vanished when she beheld the entrance of an old withered hag, whose wrinkled features betrayed evident marks of ill humour, as, in a harsh voice, she demanded their business with her.

"Here," said Darthalgo, "take this lady, and conduct her to a couch."

"Marry," said she, eyeing Matilda with looks of great dislike, "her fine tender joints will rest ill enough upon any couch of ours; she has been used to sleep upon down, I have no doubt. What does she do here, I wonder?"

"What's that to you," returned the former; "go, prepare the best apartment you have, and never ask questions about what you have no business."

"Marry but I have business," said she, "and will have business, let me tell you. You take too much upon yourself, Darthalgo; our chief, Morven, never gave himself any such airs—no, never. Heaven send that he was once more amongst us! I should have cured his wounds long before this, had he entrusted me; but he must suffer himself to be advised to stay among a parcel of strangers, quotha! and invest his command upon one, the newest of our gang. Why did he not appoint Hugh or Gilbert? for I promise you, I care not for Darthalgo; and when Morven returns, I will tell him how you have endangered our community, by bringing among us this young strange minx. She, marry, must have attendance; she is not like me."

"No, no," said one of the band, "that she is not; we can see that with half an eye."

"Don't mind her, my pretty dear," said another; "she hates the sight of any one young or handsome; for it reminds her that it is not her happy lot. Does it not, old Peg?"

"Wretch!" muttered the hag, "I defy——"

"Peace! No more of this jangling," said Darthalgo; "get a bed ready for the lady, or, by St. Andrew, I'll punish this audacity."

"You punish!" returned the hag, "I should like to see you—ha, ha, ha! But come, my fine madam, follow me."

She then quitted the cavern, and Matilda, at any rate willing to leave the company she was in, patiently measured her steps after her, and arriving at a flight of steps, which on ascending, she found herself in a spacious room, tolerably decent. An old arched painted window, through which the moonbeams gleamed, made her suppose it was the ruins of an old monastery, which this banditti had converted into a rendezvous. She now sunk upon a couch, to which the old woman pointed, and, muttering, left the room.

Matilda, when alone, was bewildered by painful conjectures what strange motives the mysterious Darthlago could have in rescuing her from the power of Duncaethal, only to expose her to the insolence she endured from a rude band of robbers; till at last she gave herself up as lost. "He has deceived me!" thought she; "his conduct is at once inexplicable and dangerous!"

The door was at this instant opened, and the object of her thoughts made his appearance. She started hastily from the couch, and, in a dignified tone, demanded the reason of this intrusion?

"Intrusion, lady! I hoped that the conduct of Darthalgo had merited permission to break in upon your solitude at any hour."

As he spoke, a dark meaning lurked in his eye; and now, for the first time, the horrid idea was suggested by Matilda, that he entertained for her a wicked passion. Her heart sickened at the thought; a sigh burst from her agitated bosom; and the tears rushed down her pale cheek, as she uttered, in broken accents— "Mysterious being! I implore, I beseech you, to tell me what the motives are for your incomprehensible conduct?"

He seemed for a moment a loss for a reply, and after a short pause, said—"The motive that first urged me to act as I have done, was love."

"Oh, Heaven!" exclaimed she, "Love! You love me! A bandit!—the outcast of society! Oh God! for what dreadful fate am I reserved? Thou base deceiver, didst thou not say thou wert not what thou seemest?"

"I did," said he, "nor did I speak false; for I appeared *disinterested*, but I was not; and know, thou weak girl, though I am determined to make you mine, 'tis not so much to gratify my love, as it is my revenge!"

"Revenge! revenge on whom?" said Matilda.

"On one whom I hate; on one who is the bane of my life—Donald!"

"Oh, Heavens!" shrieked she, "how has he offended thee?"

"How offend me! Has he not given the worst cause of offense—deprived me of my love?"

"Deprived *thee!* Dost think, vain man, Matilda Bosmora would have ever listened to a bandit?"

"Matilda's credulity confided in the honour of a bandit," said he, scornfully, "to gain your freedom; but know, shallow girl, I did only free you from Duncaethal, to be the more able to gratify that passion which preys upon my very vitals. Here will I refine upon cruelty, and vainly shall my victim seek for help; for revenge, that so long lay smothered, shall break forth in flames, and deal destruction on thy head, thou puny lovesick girl!"

A loud shriek burst from the lips of the terrified Matilda, as Darthalgo, unsheathing a poniard, pointed it to her bosom; but suddenly returning it, he cried—"No! by this my vengeance will be but half complete; I could long since have had thy life; I must glut on revenge, by making Donald witness thy death!"

He left the room, and the undone, the deceived Matilda, bitterly reproached herself for her credulity, in trusting herself to the power of a remorseless bandit. At length, thought she, "I might very well suppose that a wretch, whose business it is to live by rapine and plunder, could be no protector to a helpless girl." His threatening words still rang in her ear—"Here will I refine upon cruelty!" "Who is he, or what can he be? A robber he acknowledges himself; but where can he ever have seen me, that he should entertain in his breast such horrid passions? for never did I behold him until the fatal night when Bosmora fell a prey to a treacherous foe. Oh, Donald! art thou too in his remorseless power? Has he beguiled thy unwary feet into the snare? Alas, it too surely is so! For did he not say thou should behold me perish? Wretched, wretched Matilda! but six months since, and I was the happiest of the happy. A beloved father anticipated my most distant wishes, while Donald existed but upon my smiles. Days, weeks, and months, fled away, unmarked by the slightest anguish, till the villainous Duncaethal, like a devouring, desolating fiend, appeared, and blighted all my happy blissful prospects. A horrid, dreadful contrast has succeeded to my joys, and I shall at last resign my wretched life beneath the murderous knife of a cruel bandit! Oh, horror, horror! But let me not thus despair; there is an Omniscient Power, who rules all; in him I'll put my trust. Oh, thou all-seeing Providence! who before was most graciously pleased to rescue me from a wretched fate, again step forth and interpose thy all-powerful arm, to deliver me from a dreadful death! My father! my dear father! thou sleepest in peace, unconscious of thy wretched daughter's fate; soon now shall we meet in a better world, to live in realms of eternal bliss! Donald, beloved Donald, farewell! Long, long have I struggled with my cruel destiny, but now methinks the chilling hand of death is upon me, and the roscid* sweat, trickling from my forehead, warns me of my premature exit from this transitory scene of woe, which will save Darthalgo's guilty soul from one more horrid crime. Donald, beloved Donald——!"

Her eyes now closed, a heavy stupor benumbed her faculties, and she sunk into a state of total insensibility, from which she at length awoke, raving in all the fever of delirium. Many times did she, in frantic accents, rave for liberty, and accusing Darthalgo of treachery, exclaimed—"But Heaven will avenge my wrongs, and strike the murderer with his hottest lightnings!"

Thus did she rave, till exhausted nature sunk into sleep, and when recollection again visited her, she beheld the terrific bandit hanging over her couch. When he found that she was sensible of his presence, he withdrew. Feeble and languid was the frame of Matilda, as she now endeavoured to recall the occurrences of the two or three last days; and, as remembrance struck upon her fancy, the torturing reality appeared in all its gloomy colours; then, closing her eyes, she wished again for that insensibility which happily deprived her of the sad conviction of her wretched condition.

CHAP. II.

> Had I one grain of faith
> In holy legends and religious tales,
> I should conclude there was an arm above
> That fought against me.
>
> HOME.*

DONALD, on the morning he had left his mother, remained in his dungeon undisturbed for several hours; but at last his gaoler appeared, to whom he remarked that his visit was rather more than usually late.

Dargo morosely replied—"Perhaps it is, but I have other affairs to mind besides attending to you; and then there's the other; but it seems he wished to save me further trouble—he thought to escape; but I have clipp'd his wings. For him to escape from me, quotha!"

Donald, fearing that their nightly rambles had been discovered, with some degree of tremor, said—"What do you mean?"

"Mean, quotha! why that the hungry elf, in the other dungeon, thought to give me the slip. I caught him in the very fact of trying to raise a trap door; but a padlock, which I have placed upon it, will prevent him for the future; he must be a cunning fellow, indeed, that escapes from confinement, when Dargo is his keeper."

The feelings of Donald during this recital, may be better imagined than described; and he, every moment, expected his wary gaoler would try the security of the friendly door, but, with all his self-boasted precaution, it seems it escaped his notice, for he shortly after left the dungeon. Donald mourned the fate of his faithful servant, whom he concluded would no more be able to leave his dungeon, and, perhaps, at last might perish by the hand of his remorseless keeper. He determined to visit alone his mother once again, when he thought he might venture unseen. The day seemed to drag heavily on, and when night at length arrived, long before the hour he intended to venture forth, a confused sound of voices, murmuring through the passage leading to his cell, struck upon his astonished ear; he had not ceased wondering at this unusual noise, ere his door was burst open, and Duncaethal, with his eyes darting fury, in a voice broken by passion, said—"What then, thou art safe? I thought thou too hadst escaped like the fugitive Matilda!"

"What!" said Donald, "has she escaped? Great Heaven, I thank thee! I now indeed rejoice!"

"Indeed!" returned Duncaethal; "but thy triumph shall be short; for when I return from the pursuit I shall make to recover her, which if I fail in; thy life shall recompense my vengeance for her loss!" He now withdrew, leaving Dargo to secure the door.

The noise which at different times he heard in the subterraneous parts of the castle, made him deem it unsafe to put his resolution in practice. Not for himself did he fear, but for his revered parent; for should Duncaethal discover, by any means, their consanguinity, he would, most assuredly, exterminate them both. After deliberately weighing the hazard which he must run, he wisely concluded to remain in his cell.

Venella, on the evening of her mistress's strange disappearance, entered the room, to inquire whether she intended to take her evening's repast, but finding it vacant, proceeded to the bedchamber, when finding her not there, she could scarcely believe her senses; and, after waiting a considerable time without her appearing, at last conjectured that she had escaped. She dreaded alarming the inhabitants of the castle, till she found it would be useless to remain longer silent, and running down stairs, exclaimed—"My lady is gone! She's gone, she's gone!"

"Gone!" said Dargo, "where to?"

"Why," said Venella, "I know not indeed, but she's not in her apartment."

He ran up stairs, and searching the apartments, found them in their usual state, but entirely evacuated. "Yes," says he, "she's surely escaped, but by what means I cannot conjecture." Then hastening to his master, who had not left his room since he had been conveyed senseless from the apartment of Matilda, he acquainted him with the event.

Duncaethal in a moment forgot his illness, and the remorse which at first preyed upon his conscience, in his anxiety to recover his victim. "What, has she escaped, and is her minion Donald a companion in her flight?" eagerly inquired he.

"My lord, he was safe at noon," said Dargo.

"Follow me," said his master; "I will myself see if he is secure!"

Being satisfied as to that, he proceeded to search every apartment in the castle, followed by a train of attendants; but their efforts were fruitless. He then ordered his horses, exclaiming—"Ere I will now lose, I will pursue her to the extremity of the globe!"

He ordered a party to scour the mazes of the forest, where, if they found her not, to meet him on an appointed spot; then bidding Dargo prepare to go with him, he retired to deliberate how or by what manner she had effected her escape; for at the time of her flight, his minister, the villainous Dargo, had the keys of the castle in his own possession; and after numberless conjectures, which only served to puzzle him still more, he could only suppose that she must have been aided by some one of his domestics, as it was evident it was somebody well acquainted with the different entrances of the castle; "which," thought he, "if I could detect him, he should dearly repent it; but I wrong my trusty servants by such suppositions. She's gone, but how? 'Tis fate that seems to snatch her from me! Fool that I was, not to seize upon my happiness when it offered! Fool that I was, to let an idle vision overthrow my purpose! But if my search proves abortive, I will revenge myself by the death of Donald; to-morrow shall he breathe his last!"

He now mounted his horse, and followed by Dargo, hastened to the place where he appointed to meet his attendants, who had not been able to procure the least trace of the fugitive Matilda. Foaming with disappointed rage, he returned to the castle, with the full intent of fulfilling his horrid purpose. At night he repaired to the cell of his intended victim, and throwing open the door, beheld his prisoner in a tranquil slumber. "Ah!" said he, "does sleep then visit the eyes of my captive on this bed of straw, while I in vain do court its influence upon my downy couch? 'Tis even so; but he now shall close his eyes." Then, in a loud voice, he cried—"Donald, awake, and look upon thy death!"

He started, and beheld the glimmering poniard up-raised, ready to pierce his heart; by a natural impulse he swiftly arose from his recumbent position and suddenly caught the arm of his foe, which he held with a sinewy grasp; then each tugging with the other, breast to breast, the conflict long was doubtful, for fierce as lions did they encounter, each striving to gain the superiority of the other, but neither yet the conqueror or the vanquished. The natural hope for life stimulated Donald, and exerting his utmost strength into one great effort, pressed forcibly on his enemy, who must inevitably have fallen beneath the shock, had not Donald's foot struck against the iron ring on the floor, which caused him to stagger. The other instantly availed himself of this, and rallying his almost exhausted strength, by a sudden exertion overthrew him. Donald now sunk, and his exulting foe raised his arm to give the fatal blow, when a person rushed like lightning between them, and, in a voice of thunder, cried—"Duncaethal, hold!" who instantly exclaimed—"Who art thou?"

"Thine enemy!" said the other; "thy bitter enemy, the bandit Darthalgo!" at the same time aiming a dagger at his breast, which in the hurry failed, and only pierced his uplifted arm.

Duncaethal, with horror and surprise, fell senseless to the earth, in all appearance dead; when the bandit, beckoning to Donald, cried—"Follow me, youth!"

He instantly obeyed, and in a short time found himself in a cavern—the very cavern into which the night before the deceived Matilda had been decoyed by this wily bandit. They now ascended the steps which conducted them to the passage that terminated upon the edge of the forest, where was waiting several of the bravo's comrades, who motioning to Donald to mount behind one of them, and then mounting himself upon his own horse, when clapping spurs to their nimble-footed steeds, they made for their rendezvous.

They had proceeded a considerable distance from the castle, when Donald inquired whither they were conducting him?

Darthalgo answered—"To safety! but if sir Donald doubts our honour, why he is at liberty to go wherever he thinks fit; only, at the same time, I must inform him, if he chooses to go with us, we will conduct him to the presence of Matilda."

"Gracious Heaven!" ejaculated he, "is it possible? Can she be indebted to you for her escape?"

"If there is any obligation," returned the bandit, "she certainly owes it to us; but, sir, I had motives for acting as I have done, which shall be explained to you when we arrive at our place of destination. Comrades, let us on!"

They again proceeded, till halting at the spot where Matilda had been blindfolded, they used the same ceremony with Donald, who, submitting, was conducted through the secret entrance, when the bandage being taken from his eyes, he found himself in the midst of the banditti, who sat regaling themselves over some flasks of wine.

They desired him to be seated, and partake of their jollity; he thought refusal might give offence—he complied. Darthalgo, saying that he would acquaint Matilda with his arrival, withdrew, and immediately seeking out the old woman, inquired how the fair captive fared?

"Dying!" said she; "a high fever has caused her to be delirious ever since you last saw her."

He now proceeded to her chamber, where he earnestly contemplated the dreadful ravages which decaying illness had caused in her once beautiful countenance. Her lovely form was now emaciated, while a hectic glow, which suffused her cheek, bespoke approaching dissolution.

A fiend-like smile passed across the features of the exulting wretch, as he exclaimed—"Oh, vengeance, how sweet thou art to injured souls! This beautiful ruin, this havoc of love, is a grateful cordial to my long-thirsting heart! Fain would I exterminate the hated name of Bosmora! But where is my other victim, that minion Donald, the bane of my peace? Let him come, and by the exquisite torture of his feelings, gladden mine!"

At this moment Matilda opened her eyes, when the bravo left the room, and in a few minutes returned, leading in Donald, who rushing to the side of the couch, started back, for he could scarcely recognize the once blooming heiress of Bosmora, in the sad object which now met his anguished sight.

She at this moment cast her eyes towards the spot on which he stood, when a loud shriek bespoke her remembrance of him, and, in almost inarticulate accents, she uttered—"What, Donald, art thou then here, and has the wily wretch caught thee in his toils?"

"Alas! what dost thou mean, my beloved?" said he; "we have escaped from the power of Duncaethal."

"Alas, yes!" returned she, "we have indeed exchanged his chains for those of a worse villain—the villain Darthalgo! that cruel fiend, who, under the mask of friendship and protection, beguiles his unsuspecting victims to certain ruin."

A cold shiver ran through the frame of Donald, as he turned to examine the bravo, who stood in a distant part of the room, the fierce expression of whose dark eye, where gratified revenge seemed to glisten, convinced him of the dreadful truth, as he uttered—"Is it possible?"

"It is!" said the wretch, advancing. "Didst thou think, weak youth, that I rescued thee from the power of Duncaethal, actuated by motives of friendship? No! I had more powerful reasons for my conduct—love, jealousy, and revenge!"

"Love!" said Donald.

"Yes, love!" reiterated the bandit; "love, disappointed love! Is it then a wonder that I should feel keen jealousy for my hated, damned rival? and my great revenge can only be appeased by the destruction of you both! Thou, boy, shouldst have perished beneath the dagger of Duncaethal, had it not been for the desire of gratifying my great revenge; for by thy death it would only have been half complete, and I should have lost the joyful rapture I feel in restoring thee to the sight of Matilda, and doubling both of your pangs by separation!"

He now shrilly sounded the whistle, which he wore at his breast, when two ruffians made their appearance, whom he motioned to secure Donald; they obeyed, and rushed upon the defenceless youth. The heart-rending shrieks of Matilda made him repel them by force, and long he struggled vainly, like a lion in the hunters' toils; but being unarmed, and finding every effort fruitless, was at last compelled to submit. The ruffians enfettered and conveyed him to a dungeon, where he was left in all the bitter anguish of disappointment, and dread for the fate of his hapless Matilda. He now endeavoured to recal to his memory whether he had ever before seen this new and formidable foe; he thought that the sound of his voice was familiar to his ear, but, after fruitless pondering, he could not recollect that he ever saw any one that in the least bore any resemblance to the cruel, bloody Darthalgo!

"My beloved!" mentally said he, "hast thou escaped the power of the fierce Duncaethal, only to fall a victim to a remorseless bandit, sanguinary as mysterious?"

He now revolved in his mind by what miracle he entered his cell at that critical juncture. "Ah! he, no doubt, contrived to extricate me from Duncaethal's power, that I might the more easily fall in the gin laid to entrap my unwary steps! Oh, my mother! my revered parent! who now shall save thee? Alas! my parent, and my heart's beloved, are both in the power of villains, capable of the vilest measures! The chaste, the beautiful heiress of Bosmora will fall a wretched victim to the unlawful desires of a murderous bravo!" He was frantic at the idea, and smote his head with the enfrenzied action of a maniac.

In the intermediate time, Matilda's fever returned with redoubled force, and her loud ravings echoed through the decaying arched vaults of the old abbey, till the banditti, fearful that her shrieks might attract the notice of passengers, at length bound a handkerchief across her mouth, when the suppressed respiration deadened all her faculties, and she lay scarcely breathing, till Darthalgo every minute expected death would deprive him of his victim, ere he had completed his dire revenge; but in a few days her disorder took a favourable turn, and restored, with her own anguish, the hopes of the cruel, merciless bravo. Earnestly did she wish for the moment of her dissolution, to release her from her endless sorrows; but the awful minister of death shrunk from the eager grasp of the truly wretched, to visit the happy and the affluent, and our heroine was yet reserved to taste still more misery.

CHAP. III.

Techy and wayward was thy infancy;
Thy prime of manhood daring, bold, and stubborn;
Thy age confirm'd, most subtle, proud, and bloody.
SHAKESPEARE.*

WHEN Duncaethal sunk to the earth, apparently dead, it was not from the effect of the wound he had received, but from the sudden sound and terror of the words which so unexpectedly struck upon his ear—"I am thine enemy! The brave Darthalgo!"

He had most potent reasons for remembering the name of this mysterious robber, for the explanation of which we must turn back to his early days. His parents were noble, and of an ancient race, but not wealthy; they were remarked for their virtues, which added lustre to the name they bore. By a study to render each other happy, their days glided in happiness, when their bliss was augmented by the birth of a son, the subject of these memoirs; dearly did they love him, and sought to rear him in those virtues which characterized themselves; but vain and abortive were their anxious and maternal cares; for in his early youth he betrayed a predilection for vice, with a disposition morose, ungovernable, and ferocious; and ere he had arrived to manhood, committed actions so very atrocious, that induced his parents to send him on his travels to a distant land, hoping that time and absence might effect more than reproofs or admonitions.

Italy was fixed upon for the place of his destination; and after fixing upon a good venerable priest as his mentor, to guide him in the path of honour, he set forth for that land of harmony and pleasure. There, unrestrained by the presence of his parents, and regardless of the exhortations which the good father never failed to use, he plunged into every species of extravagance and libertinism that could tend to ruin his future health and character—gaming with all the dissipated youths into whose company he fell, until he had contracted debts to a larger amount than what he possibly could discharge.

At this period, luckily, a summons arrived from his father, commanding his return, as he felt himself fast approaching to his end. This served him for a sufficient plea to his companions for his departure, whom he satisfied by promises of a speedy return, with a fresh supply of cash. "For," added he, "should my father die, which probably he will, I will make myself full amends for his niggard allowance during his life."

His profligate companions highly applauded his intentions, and wished him a speedy succession to the estates of his father.

Then, bidding farewell to Venice, he embarked, and prosperous gales soon wafted him to the shores of Caledonia; but ere his arrival, his father had fallen a victim to his disorder, a malignant fever; and his mother, who, regardless of herself, had attended him during his illness, caught the infection, and shortly after followed him to the tomb. Their loss was not deeply regretted by their unfeeling son, for he never made a return of that tenderness which they so strongly evinced for him.

Now free from controul, he collected the greatest part of his patrimony, with an intention of returning to those scenes of debauchery that he had but just quitted; but, on the very eve of his departure, he learned the death of Alexander. This to him was joyful news—"For," thought he, "if the old baron should have no more children, and it is unlikely that he should marry again, I must, of course, succeed to the honours and dignity of Duncaethal;" for, by his mother's side, he was the next relation, and to whose children, in default of the baron's male issue, the honours of the family were to devolve.

His wishes were propitious, and the subsequent demise of the baron crowned his sanguine hopes. He now repaired to the castle of Duncaethal, to take possession of the wealthy inheritance, and invest himself with the titles and dignities which now became his, when he became deeply enamoured of the beauty of Agnes; and despairing of her ever consenting to gratify his unlawful desires, he disclosed his secret passion to his minister Dargo, a knave who attended him, and assisted his libertinism when in Venice; they both concerted a diabolical scheme to obtain her, which was executed in the manner already known.

The first journey he made after her confinement, exhausted his well-stocked purse; and, nearly at the period of Donald's birth, he returned once more to Duncaethal. But the unvaried life of a gloomy castle suited not a mind that had been foremost in scenes of gaiety and pleasure. He panted for the joys of carnivals, and the riotous scenes of gaming-houses; and entrusting the conduct of his affairs to the vigilance of Dargo, he once more set forward to the shores of Italy, and again plunged into every species of dissipation.

In the many of his acquaintance, he contracted an intimacy with a celebrated courtesan, who enslaved his heart, even beyond the power of freedom; her house was the resort of a set of the vilest wretches, for the black purpose of gaming, and often enticed the unwary to their ruin. Duncaethal fell a victim to their artifices; and when they had fleeced him of his fortune, he joined the desperate gang, who initiated him in their villanous arts, for the purpose of betraying other dupes, as he himself had been betrayed.

His rank gave him frequent opportunities of inveigling unsuspecting youths, upon whose credulity he and his associates enriched themselves. One of these deluded victims he pretended to profess a particular regard and friendship for; this youth was the nephew of a rich old signor, upon whose benevolence he was a dependant, and to whose liberality he was indebted for the sums which he daily squandered, till at length wearied out by repeated applications, the old signor refused all further supplies, and severely rebuked his nephew for his extravagance. The youth, being greatly embarrassed, applied to Duncaethal for the loan of a small sum, which was granted, in the hopes of securing him for his prey.

Valando, in a burst of gratitude, seized Duncaethal by the hand, and said—"Oh, my friend, 'tis not for myself I would become your debtor! No! but I have another cause—my repeated losses has deprived me of the means of procuring sustenance for my beloved wife!"

"Wife!" reiterated Duncaethal.

"Yes!" returned Valando; "I have married a lovely girl, a peasant, unknown to my uncle, or the world; but your goodness has merited my utmost confidence. Come this way, and you shall hear the history of my Paulina." Then, taking Duncaethal by the arm, and leading him to a retired part of the grove in which they were walking, thus began—

"One evening, as I was rambling near the vineyards, east of the city, a neat white cottage attracted my attention; the flowers which adorned a garden, laid out with excellent taste, convinced me it was the dwelling of some one superior to a common peasant; I leaned over the little gate, and was viewing it with attention, till the lovely mistress of this fairy mansion made her appearance, and was approaching down the walk, which terminated in the place where I stood rapturously gazing on her; but, raising her eyes, a slight exclamation of surprise escaped her, and she swiftly retraced her steps back to the house. I followed, and in a gentle manner apologized for thus surprising her; she curtsied, and modestly requested I would leave her; adding—'Signor, I every moment expect the return of my father, and, should he see you here, I know not what might be the consequence, as he has always charged me to avoid the sight of strangers.' I sought to obey her, but her enchanting simplicity rivetted me to the spot, when, for the purpose of prolonging my stay, I asked her who was her father? 'Delphine Roviria," replied she. 'And what is your appellation, sweet maid?' 'Paulina, signor,' again answered she. 'Paulina!' I shall never forget it, thought I. At that moment I rivetted my eyes on her lovely countenance—her's eloquently met mine; love instantly took possession of my heart, and never since that period has its ardour abated.

'Where is your father, sweet Paulina?' She innocently answered—'He is gone to attend our little vineyard in the valley, but I momentarily expect his return; pray begone, signor.' I was on the point of retiring, when a thought entered my mind of again seeing her, and I earnestly requested another interview; she, blushing, refused me; but her countenance betrayed that it was more proceeding from the idea of shame, in being thought too forward, than from any inclination to deny me. I urged my request with redoubled ardour, and obtained from the beautiful girl a half-reluctant consent. I now took my leave, and made my way to the city, but Paulina still remained before my sight, in all the charms of unsophisticated innocence.

"Earnestly did I long for the time of the appointed interview, not that I had resolved upon any plan in regard to her, and therefore ought to have shunned, not have sought her acquaintance. I was not villain sufficient to think of seducing the innocence of this unsuspecting child of nature, and marry her I could not; as my uncle, on whom I solely depended, I was well assured, would never forgive a step so seemingly rash. What infatuation then could possess me to further our intimacy? But to be brief—I repeated my visits several times to the cottage, and at last, in an unguarded moment, triumphed over the virtue of the hapless Paulina. I then avoided her; not that my passion was abated; no! Heaven is my witness, it was not! but I dreaded the reproach of her mild blue eyes, which affected me much more than words, as they silently conveyed the keenest signs of melancholy and despair. She at last appeared to be in a situation which forbad all further concealment; and, urged by my love, I sought her father, when throwing myself at his feet, confessed the dishonourable act, but offered to make what reparation was in my power, by immediately uniting myself to his injured daughter.

"He was at first struck dumb with amazement, for he had not in the least suspected our intercourse; but recovering the use of speech, he vowed vengeance on my head, and bitterly reproached his child for her clandestine proceeding; till at last, passion getting the better, in a paroxysm of rage burst a blood-vessel, and in a few hours expired.

The miserable Paulina now became frantic, and, in despairing heart-rending accents, besought his forgiveness, which he bestowed, in accents almost inarticulate, ere death closed his eyes for ever. Paulina would not be removed from the inanimate corpse, but continued—'Oh, my parent, hear your wretched child! oh, bitterly do I repent deceiving you, but you have forgiven me! Yes, with your dying breath you have sealed my pardon—miserable else indeed must my lot have been!' Thus, in frantic accents, she continued, till I was at last obliged to have her removed by force; and as soon as serenity once more visited the fair form of my beloved, I united myself to her by the most sacred bonds.

"She still resides in the cottage, which she cannot be prevailed upon to quit, and every day do I expect that she will become a mother; but to-morrow you shall see her, and she shall thank you for your present friendly aid, as my late extravagance and losses at the house of the courtesan Viola, have incapacitated me from supplying her with money, which her present wants demand."

Duncaethal now parted from Valando, promising to meet him at an appointed spot the next day, for the purpose of visiting Paulina. When the time arrived, they proceeded together to the humble residence, where the fair inhabitant welcomed Valando with all the joy demonstrative of a pure affection; he then introduced his friend, and explained to her his obligations to him. Her manner of acknowledgment sealed her destruction, for he inwardly resolved to betray Valando, and possess the beautiful person of the amiable Paulina.

He was already grown weary of the artful Viola, and this simple unsuspecting girl gave new ardour, and a fresh scope to his long dormant machinations. He had resided in Venice for several years, hearing occasionally from Dargo, and sometimes obtaining a supply to his finances; but this was only on particular occasions, for he generally found dupes sufficient to support his unbounded extravagance. He hoped to bear away the lovely Paulina, to enliven the dreary residence of Duncaethal, to which he was on the point of returning, and commenced his horrid plans in the following manner:—By his orders, Valando was seized for the debt, and conveyed to prison; then, in a few days, he repaired to the cottage of Paulina, when he gave her to understand she was basely deceived by Valando, who was on the point of marrying another lady of great fortune; and, after expressing pity for her helpless situation, offered to render her every assistance in his power.

She regarded not his proffered help, but said—"I will see you, my lord, to-morrow."

He took his leave, hoping to bear her away from her home at the next interview; and, lest his plans should be frustrated by the wretched husband, he wrote and informed the old signor of his degrading marriage, well knowing he would not then assist him in regaining his liberty. Every thing succeeded to the villain's wish, and the next night, with a heart triumphing in the success of his deep-laid scheme, he sought the dwelling of his victim; when all around seemed silent, he opened the door—no voice greeted him on his entrance. The moon, glimmering through the humble lattice, fell full upon the face of the wretched Paulina, stretched lifeless upon a couch—having, by poison, put a period to her existence. The wretch retreated as his eye viewed the desolation he had caused, and in all the agonies of guilt sought his abode, where remorse, for the first time, touched his guilty soul.

On the evening preceding this, Paulina had, on the departure of Duncaethal, composed a billet, which she had conveyed to the wretched Valando, who had left orders where any letters, at any time, might be forwarded to him, as, by the law then existing, he might receive, but could not send any one, without their being first inspected by his gaoler; he therefore did not dare write to his hapless wife, for fear of discovering his connexions, but wrote, with great persistence, to his uncle; when the answer he received simply contained these words—"Release yourself with the dowry of Paulina!"

He now found that Duncaethal was completely a villain; concealment was therefore no longer necessary, and to ease the anxiety of his dearly beloved wife, he took up a pen to explain the reasons of his absence, when, at that instant, the billet from Paulina was put into his hands; tremblingly he tore it open, and read the following words:—

"VALANDO, I do not accuse thee of cruelty, and yet I think the sorrows which our fated connexion has cost me ought to have merited your love. Oh, my dear father, bitterly do I feel the effects of my disobedience! The signor whom you brought home the other day, has acquainted me with your desertion, and your intended marriage with another, which your non-appearance corroborates. I shall not attempt to prove my legality to the rights of a wife, but will leave you to the full enjoyment of the happiness which a perjured heart will allow, while I seek for peace in the silent grave. The fatal potion is now in my hand! I lift it to my lips! Farewell! In drinking this oblivious draught, I free you from those galling fetters which bind the husband and the father! Sometimes think on me, and always remember that your future bride will not love you with a more pure undisguised affection, than her, whose heart, when you peruse this, will have ceased to beat! My life is near a close! Farewell, Valando!—a name still dear but cruel; and my last breath shall pronounce Valando! oh, Valando!"

The wretched youth was almost petrified with horror at the perusal of this, and he franticly exclaimed—"Oh that I could but fly to save her! I would give my life for one hour's freedom!"

The gaoler now entered, whom he, on his knees, besought, in piteous sounds, to permit him to visit his wretched wife, pledging his honour to return. The unfeeling Cerberus was deaf to entreaties—accustomed to scenes of horror, his heart was inflexible; when, armed by desperation, he plunged a stiletto, which he had concealed, into his side, and instantly fled. Swift as lightning he sought the once happy peaceful cot. It was just after the departure of the vile Duncaethal, and he beheld the woeful scene, which had already met the eye of the author of this horrid catastrophe.

The billet had been entrusted to a village girl, who, not thinking it of any import, retained it till noon the following day. Though Paulina had procured her messenger after swallowing the fatal draught, yet so well did she conceal her pangs, that not the least suspicion of any rash attempt was ever dreamt of; and long ere it reached her wretched husband, the affectionate and faithful Paulina was no more! Valando called loudly upon her name, and his piteous moans attracted to the spot some of the vintagers, who were returning from their daily toil; when, imagining they were in pursuit of him for the murder of his gaoler, he fled, and never afterwards returned to Venice. Large rewards were offered for his apprehension, but in vain; and some time after Duncaethal received a billet, containing the following words:—

————

"BASE wretch! I have seen the murdered Paulina, whose blood calls aloud for vengeance on thy destroying head; and if I dared to appear in the city, thy life should answer for thy perfidy; but as it is, I am hunted from society, to herd with outlaws; therefore dread to meet me, for thy arts have made me familiar with scenes of blood! If thou shouldst hear the name of Valando, may it strike thy conscience! but if ever thou hearest the name I have now assumed, expect my dagger to strike thy guilty treacherous heart.   THE BRAVO DARTHALGO."

———

Duncaethal thought it prudent, for his safety, to hasten his departure, and in a few days he embarked, to return to his native clime; but he nearly met the reward of his crimes in a watery grave. A dreadful tempest drove the vessel on the isle of Orkney, and the seamen being unable to combat with the dreadful storm, it split upon a rock, and only himself and one mariner escaped upon a part of the wreck, the strong tide washing them over-board, and drove them upon the neighbouring shores, near to the castle of Monteith; they were both conveyed to this hospitable mansion, where, by great attention, they were restored to life. Duncaethal here, for the first time, beheld Margaret; her person enslaved his inconstant heart, and her fortune was sufficient to gratify his avarice. He offered her his hand in marriage, and when he quitted Monteith, bore her away as the lady Duncaethal.

They soon after visited Bosmora, where the wavering baron beheld the peerless Matilda; he burned to possess her, and his love for variety caused him earnestly to wish he had first seen Bosmora's beautiful heiress. The subsequent death of Margaret released him from his galling chains of bondage, and he was again free to offer himself to the beautiful Matilda. He never sup-posed a refusal, and when his offers were rejected, it aroused the revenge of his vindictive malevolent heart, and he resolved to stop at nothing till he had gratified his passion.

On the evening when he thought to stain his hands in the blood of the youthful Donald, when the mysterious bandit inter-posing, and uttering the name of Darthalgo, struck terror to his soul, and aroused all his long-hushed fears; for he never supposed in the least that the bravo would pursue him for revenge even to his very castle; when he a little recovered from his surprise and agitation, with his arm still bleeding, he sought Dargo, to whom he unfolded the manner of the youth's escape.

"Ah!" said he, after musing a moment, "then the man you have this night seen is, no doubt, a member of the desperate banditti, which infest the old abbey ruins, some miles distant, in the forest."

"Indeed!" said his master; "art thou sure that a band of robbers inhabit there?"

Dargo answered—"Report says so, and our sovereign has several times offered rewards for their apprehension; but nobody ever yet had the courage to effect it."

"Indeed!" said Duncaethal; "a thought strikes me! Muster our soldiers; we will proceed against this banditti, when, perhaps, we may secure our victim, and at the same time I shall be able to ingratiate myself in the favour of our king."

He had his wounded arm bound up, and, followed by Dargo, descended to the lower apartments of the castle, to discover, if possible, the means which the bravo had made use of to gain entrance. They proceeded to the cell in which Donald had been confined, where they at last perceived the entrance through which Darthalgo had conducted him; it was fastened on the outside, but being by Duncaethal's order broke open, they continued their search through the subterranean, and arrived at last to the cavern, which, unknown to them, communicated with the castle, and at a distance opened to the forest.

The mystery now was developed; and having the door properly secured on the inside, to prevent future intrusion, he gave notice to summon his clan, and bade them make preparation for a march in two days, for the purpose of attacking the banditti.

CHAP. IV.

Revenge, impatience, all that mads the soul,
All that despair and frenzy's flame inspires,
Shown by the tapers, in his eyes did roll,
Hot meteors they amid the lesser fires.

RICHARD PLANTAGENET.*

MATILDA was scarcely restored to a state of convalescence, when Donald was conducted to her apartment by Darthalgo, who said—"There, youth, take thy last farewell; for, by all my wrongs, she shall die, and ere to-morrow she shall breathe her last!"

"Monster!" said Donald, "wouldst thou dare to imbrue thy hands in the innocent blood of that lovely maid?"

"I dare, and will!" said the sanguinary wretch.

At this moment the old woman rushed in breathless, and, fast as her fears would permit, she cried out—"The abbey is attacked! Haste, Darthalgo, and head our band!"

He instantly left the chamber, followed by the trembling hag, when Donald, seizing a sword, which the bandit in his haste had let fall, took the hand of Matilda, and said—"Come, my love, now is our only time; Heaven favours our escape. I know the way to the caverns; let us seek out the private entrance of this den of horrors, and make a bold effort for freedom."

He bore the trembling girl in one arm, and with his sword explored his way to the subterranean, which he found was totally deserted by the band, who were defending themselves in an outer part of the ruin. With anxious eye he sought the concealed entrance, but in vain; and the sound of voices indicated the approach of some one, but whether friend or foe they knew not, and he expected each moment to be surprised. Desperation seized him as he swiftly hurried Matilda into a large natural cavity of the subterranean.

Soldiers now entered, bearing lighted torches, and discovered their hiding-place, and seizing upon Donald, who defended himself with great magnanimity, till he was disarmed, conducted him and the wretched Matilda to the chamber they had so lately quitted, where, to their great surprise, they beheld Duncaethal, giving orders for the disposal of the bravoes, who lay bound beside him.

When he beheld our poor hero and heroine, he exultingly and tauntingly said—"Now, my runaways, have I once again, by fortune's kindness, got you into my power, now dearly will I revenge myself!"

A soldier of his clan entered the room at that instant, and said—"My lord, a force, superior to our's, advances swiftly towards the ruin, for what purpose I know not."

Duncaethal stepped towards the window, and said—"If I can aright distinguish, they are the king's troops, coming, I suppose, to subdue this daring band; but we have already obtained the honour of victory."

They now entered, and Duncaethal was proceeding to harangue the commanding officer on the important service, when the other cried—"Seize him!" and in a moment he was surrounded and made prisoner, with the banditti already subdued.

"What means this outrage and violence of my person?" demanded Duncaethal; when a voice exclaimed—"Thou treacherous miscreant, where is my daughter?"

"Here! here!" shrieked the joyful Matilda, and in a moment fell senseless in the arms of her father, who, kissing her pallid cheek, by his fond embrace restored her senses; nor was Donald forgotten. Bosmora, turning to him, said—"Thou much-injured youth, receive from my hand this sword, and head the troops which shall convey that tyrant to a dungeon, where he must remain, till, by proper trial, he is sentenced to a punishment adequate to his crimes."

"Ah! who dares accuse me of crimes which authorize this vile treatment?" said the fallen chieftain, while fear shook his guilty frame.

"Agnes, the lady of Duncaethal!—Well mayst thou start, thou vile usurper of the rights which, by thy villainy, thou hast dared to possess! Bow, proud wretch, to the lawful heir!—Donald, the son of Alexander, and Agnes, thy wretched captive, who for more than twenty years has been held a prisoner in her own domains. Matilda, my dearest child, greet your future husband—once the humble peasant, but now the noble baron Duncaethal! And you, the misled clan of this vile usurper, I promise a free pardon to all who shall acknowledge this youth, who is the lawful son of your late lord Alexander, for your laird."

They in a moment fell on their knees, and with one voice, unanimous, they loudly greeted their young laird, and besought him to forgive their late behaviour, which proceeded from the fidelity of their supposed laird, whom they now reviled.

"Hold!" said the villain, "do not suffer yourselves to be deceived; do not let a tale like this delude your senses; Agnes never gave birth to a son."

"'Tis false, villain!" said the baron Bosmora; "Donald was born in the very prison she was released from this day, and was conveyed secretly, by the humanity of old Peter, the steward, to the cottage of Allen: and what could it avail thee, even if she had not borne a child? As wife of Alexander (and the holy priest who joined their hands still lives to prove their legal union), she is mistress of the domains, long as she exists; of this thou canst not be ignorant, or else thou wouldst not so carefully have concealed her from the world; but your villanies are laid open—we have traced you through all your wicked schemes of guilt—and thy minister Dargo, who is seized, has confessed the manifold crimes of which thou art guilty. But why do we thus delay, by parleying with this monster? Donald, let us haste, and glad thy fond parent by our presence."

He was on the point of following Bosmora, when he, for the first time, bethought himself that he had not among the prisoners beheld Darthalgo. He briefly explained the conduct of this mysterious bandit to the baron, who immediately ordered a strict search to be made throughout the ruin; but it proved fruitless, and they were obliged to depart, with the conviction of his having effected his escape.

Matilda was seated on a horse, between the one her father

and that on which Donald rode, when, addressing the former, she said—"My dear father, what wondrous act of Providence has restored thee to me at a moment so critical, when I have long lamented thee as dead? do, my dear parent, explain this mystery, which has caused thy daughter so many hours of sorrow."

Donald requested the same, when the baron proceeded as follows—"On the fatal night when the castle of Bosmora was in the most treacherous manner subdued, I was left by my enemy for dead; and as soon as the place was deserted by the conquerors, the remaining few of my faithful servants, together with old Allen, came to remove the corses of those brave, zealous, and trusty men, who fell in the conflict. Among the rest whom they examined, to see if life yet remained, was myself; a slight pulsation convinced the affectionate Andrew that the vital spark was not yet extinguished; he called to the good old Allen, who hastened to his assistance, and together they conveyed me to the cottage of the latter, when old Jannet, by attentive and unremitting care, restored me to life. Several days passed ere I was able to quit my bed, and then I learnt the dreadful tidings of thy loss, my child. With a heart almost broken, I sent Andrew to a neighbouring baron, with my solicitations for his aid of troops to recover thee, which was immediately granted; and mustering up my remaining clan, we marched for the purpose of, jointly with our forces, attacking Duncaethal, where I had no doubt but you was held a prisoner. When we arrived at the walls of the castle, without demanding an audience, I ordered the soldiers to burst open the gates, and then entering, in the hall I was met by Dargo, who informed me that you had escaped, and that his lord at that time was absent. I, imagining it was only a stratagem to deceive me, ordered the rascal to be secured, and commenced a strict search, even in that part of the castle I knew long had been uninhabited. There it was my good fortune to find the poor imprisoned Agnes; she recognized me instantly, and I learned from her the villainous conduct which had been practiced against you, my son—and she added that you was confined in one of the subterraneous dungeons. Procuring the keys from the villanous Dargo, whom we forced, at the peril of his life, to conduct us, we examined each of them; in one I discovered poor Robert, who was overjoyed at beholding me and Venella; and the good old Gertrude informed me that you both had really escaped, and that you were among banditti, whom her master had gone against, for the purpose of subduing, and once more getting you in his power. While she was speaking, Agnes entered the room, when the old woman was terrified out of her wits, supposing it was her ghost, till your mother affectionately convinced her to the contrary. I left Agnes in her care, and gave orders to proceed instantly towards the ruin, to which we were conducted by a peasant, where the search has answered to our utmost wish. The base usurper shall be confined in the dungeon from which you are so lately liberated, until a jury of barons can sit in judgment, and condemn him to that sentence which his various and manifold crimes may deserve. But, my dearest Matilda, hast thou, at any time, ever before seen that fearful bandit?"

"Never, my dear father," said she; "the first time he ever met my sight was on the dreadful night I thought you had perished; he has often expressed hatred for our very existence, for what cause I know not, and his malice is extended equally to Donald as to myself."

"Indeed!" said the baron; "'tis strange, but we must leave the discovery to that Providence, who, by his great interference in this last wonderful discovery, has convinced us that the day of retribution must at last arrive."

They now came within view of the high turrets of Duncaethal, and Donald was soon clasped in the arms of his affectionate mother. "Oh, my son!" said she, "Heaven has heard my prayers! Oh, never let despair enter thy heart! After so many years, thou art at last restored, with my long-lost liberty!"

She now took the hand of Matilda, saying—"Thy father, maiden, has informed me of your mutual loves; take her, my son; she adds lustre to the noble name of Duncaethal! Heaven will repay you both for your many sufferings, by numberless days of conjugal bliss and domestic happiness!"

They now were joined by Robert and Venella, who, with warm congratulations and tears of joy, welcomed the return of

Donald and Matilda. The joyous shouts of the clan, late their enemies, now the most loyal and zealous defenders of their rights, rent the air, while with bursts of acclamations they made the vaulted roof and arched halls resound the name of their new laird Duncaethal; and in flowing goblets they quaffed to the health of his destined bride. The neighbouring peasantry caught the glad tidings, when, forgetting all their toils, they thronged in the court-yard to behold the happy sight, till warmed by wine, and roused by the sweet brisk enlivening pipe, they sought each his favourite lass, and led forth the festive dance.

The late gloomy castle, so long a stranger to the sound of mirth, was now converted into a universal scene of joy; every heart beat with rapture in the light bosoms of its inhabitants, save alone in the guilty breast of the usurper, who was manacled, and thrown into the dungeon, where he so malignantly sought the life of Donald. Dargo too was now a prisoner, in the very cell so lately occupied by Robert. Thus, in a short time, what a strange reverse of fortune was experienced by both lord and servant! The latter seemed to bear his fate by sullen insensibility; not so in the guilty tyrant's breast. Conscience! that never-erring monitor, told him he deserved not mercy here, nor could he hope for forgiveness hereafter! The shades of Paulina, Margaret, and all who through his damned machinations fell, seemed to flit before his tortured sight within the gloomy cell, till, in bitterness of soul, he cursed the hour which gave him birth; and had he possessed the means, of which he was carefully deprived, he would, by horrid suicide, have ended the career of his wretched, miserable, and guilty life.

CHAP. V.

When rugged March o'errules the growing year,
  Have we not seen the morn with treach'rous ray,
Shine out awhile, then instant disappear,
  And leave to damp and gloom the future day?

So dawn'd my fate, and so deceiv'd my heart,
  Nor wean'd me from my hopes, but cruel tore,
In one unlook'd for moment, bade me part
  From all my comforts, to return no more.

RICHARD PLANTAGENET'S TALE.*

D AYS passed away in happiness to our heroine, and the most
    blissful prospects to Donald, till the day preceding the trial
of Duncaethal, when, on his going to Venella, to inquire for her
mistress, he found they were both absent, and, after many efforts
to find her, he sought Bosmora, and recounted his fears. A strict
search was then set on foot, which not availing, they were at last
forced to conclude that, by some unknown means, she was spir-
ited away from the castle.

Who could be the perpetrator of this daring outrage was the
next subject of debate. "Ah!" said Donald, "'tis doubtless, the
villain Darthalgo! Fool that I was, to reckon on happiness, while
that fiend had escaped from our power."

"Patience, my son!—patience!" cried the baron.

"Oh, my gracious lord!" returned Donald, "have I not the cup
of happiness again snatcht from my lips, when I was on the point
of quaffing the nectareous draught, the beverage of bliss, which
gods might envy me the taste? Order my horses; instantly will I
pursue my search."

"Alas! whither?" said the sorrowing Bosmora.

"No matter! The abbey ruins; and if she is not there, why
fortune must be my guide; for never will I return without my
dearest, best-beloved Matilda!"

His frantic accents of grief attracted the attention of his mother, who, feelingly alive to the happiness of her long-lost son, inquired the cause of his sorrow.

"Alas! my dear mother," sad he, "our sweet Matilda is gone!"

"Gone! Where?" asked she.

"Alas! I know not; but I suppose the wretch Darthalgo, I fear, has once more got her in his power! Where is Robert? I will leave the castle this night in quest of her. She cannot be conveyed to a great distance as yet, for she was here at noon."

Robert now attended, and in a few minutes they bade adieu to Duncaethal; and, applying the spurs to their light-footed steeds, posted towards the ruined abbey. The shrill sound of the bleak wind whistling through the trees, gave notice of an approaching storm, and in a few minutes large drops of rain fell upon their armour. Robert exclaimed—"Sir, do let us seek some cover, to shield us from the tempest, for I fear it will be terrible!" At that instant a loud crash shook the earth to its foundation, while the vivid lightning gave a partial light to our wanderers.

Donald dismounted, and ordered his squire to do the same, as it was become dangerous to keep longer on their horses, whose feet every moment slipped, owing to the wetness of the grass. They gently led them by the reins, while with anxious eyes they sought for some hospitable cottage, whose brisk blazing hearth might dry their garments, and warm their chilled limbs, which already began to stiffen with cold; however, no such friendly habitation appeared, and as they feared they had missed their way, they proposed to stand still till the light of day should gladden their sight. Long had they not remained in this situation, before a glimmering light, through the trees, gave a renewal to their hopes; they set forward, but finding they gained not upon it, Robert, by his master's orders, loudly shouted, when the light, which before seemed to recede, became stationary, and a few moments brought them within view of the figure who bore it.

By his dress he appeared a hermit. His long beard almost reached to his waist, and the large rosary of beads, which was suspended by a cord from his girdle, add to which the placidity of his countenance, convinced Donald that he was right in his conjecture, and addressing him by the name of holy father, he said—"We are poor benighted travellers, who have missed our way; can you direct us to any dwelling where we may obtain shelter till the day's approach?"

He answered—"Strangers, I know of none which you can reach in haste, but if you will follow me to my humble cell, you shall be welcome to all it affords, and it will at least shelter you from the inclemency of the storm."

"Ten thousand thanks, father!" said Donald. "Come on, Robert, and lead the horses."

The drenched squire speedily obeyed this welcome command, uttering to himself—"If ever there was an angel with a long beard, this is he! Methinks I hear the faggot crackling on the hearth, with a cold pasty and a flaggon of wine on the table, which I have often heard these holy men like as well as their neighbours; perhaps a good couch too, to rest a body's bones on, after we have satisfied our appetites. 'Tis very hard my master could not keep Lady Matilda when he had her; and as for our going to the ruins, why 'tis all nonsense. Darthalgo knows better than to go where he is sure to be searched for; but, however, as I told Dargo, we poor servants must do as we are bid, so I must e'en jog on with him in this wild-goose chase."

He was interrupted from this soliloquy, by his master loudly calling him to come on.

"Oh, my dear lord, I cannot make the steeds walk any faster; they have not half the appetite I have, or else they would feel for a fellow-sufferer; but they keep slipping down every minute, and don't seem to mind anything but the fear of breaking their legs. How much further is it, holy stranger?"

"We are within sight of it," said the hermit.

"Oh, St. Andrew be praised! Is that the little chimney that smokes so merrily?"

"It is," said the conductor, the lightning now, at intervals, being so vivid, that they could plainly discern the dwelling of this venerable anchorite. "So, please you, sir knight," added he, "you must fasten your horses to one of these trees, as I have no accommodation for them, though I will do my best for you."

They did as he desired, and following his steps, soon found themselves in a spacious cave, in which stood an antique oaken table, with some fruit, the remains of what had composed his repast; to these he added a fresh supply; and going to a kind of recess, brought forth a flaggon of wine, saying "You see, son, though I live as it were from the world, I am not without some of the good things thereof. Come, be seated, and eat and drink heartily."

"Aye, that we will," said Robert. "Oh, how comfortable it is, after one thought of passing the night under an old tree, to find one's self by a blazing fire, with a cup of good wine to cheer one's spirits! Egad, I think I will turn hermit myself, if they always live so merrily! But do hermits, father, ever marry? For, notwithstanding every other comfort, I should, I think, like to solace myself with a wife."

"Silence, Robert!" said his master; then addressing the friendly anchorite, he said—"Venerable father, have you long inhabited this retreat?"

"Some years, my son," answered he; "but if you are not inclined to sleep, to beguile time, I will recount to you the sad events of my life, which caused me to abjure the world, and seek retirement in this humble cell."

Donald expressed the gratification it would give him, and said that he was all attention, when the other began—"First, 'tis necessary to give you some account of my family, ere I proceed to relate my own unfortunate history. My father, whose real name I shall conceal under that of Flodiardo, was a noble Venetian; he was his parents' only child, who, by too much indulgence, spoilt his temper, which was naturally good; but, by such ill-timed lenity, made his disposition, as he advanced in life, rather ungovernable; and at his parents' death, being possessed of a handsome fortune, he fell into the destructive company of the libertine youths of the city which gave him birth. A courtezan squandered his substance, to which he greatly contributed by gaming. He had attained his twenty-fifth year, when one evening, as he was walking in a grove near to the suburbs of the city, the loud cries of a female sounded in his ear, and, ever ready to lend assistance to the distressed, he fled towards the spot from whence the cries proceeded, where he beheld a lovely young girl in vain endeavouring to extricate herself from the arms of a man, who, with brutal force, dragged her towards a horse, seemingly for the purpose of bearing her away. My father rushed directly to him, and commanded him to desist, when, drawing a stiletto, the stranger wounded him in the arm, and swiftly mounting the steed, fled precipitately towards the city. The lady he had so fortunately rescued, perceiving the blood flow from the wound he had received, expressed her sorrow for the accident, and lending her arm, endeavoured to assist him in reaching the dwelling of her father, which, she said, was not above half a mile distant; he accepted of her offer, and they slowly proceeded through the windings of the grove. At length they came within sight of an elegant residence, which, she said, belonged to signor Rivolti, her father, and, stepping forward, she rapped at the gate, which was opened by a female servant. She conducted Flodiardo to a room, the elegant simplicity of which bespoke the dignity of the inhabitants.

"At that moment the owner of the mansion made his appearance, when, on seeing his daughter's companion, he exclaimed—'Rosalie, my child! where is Vallentia?'—'Ah, my dear father!' said she, 'Vallentia is a wretch! and it is owing to this stranger's interposition that I did not fall a victim to his villainy. See, my dear father, my brave deliverer is wounded in my defence!'—'Good Heavens, signor, you bleed!' said he. 'Here, Albertini, instantly fetch a surgeon.'—'You need not,' said Flodiardo; 'it is only trifling. Suffer your servant to bind it up, and I will have it dressed when I reach the city.'

"Rosalie now left the apartment, to summon an ancient domestic, who, she said, understood something of surgery: when he appeared, with a look of skill he said it must not be disturbed by motion, and declared that it demanded immediate rest. Signor Rivolti insisted upon his not leaving the house till he was recovered, and offered to dispatch a messenger to acquaint his friends of what had transpired. 'It is unnecessary,' said my father, 'for it is what often occurs, and will cause no alarm in

my being absent for the night.' In fact, Flodiardo was rejoiced at
this invitation, for the fair Rosalie had made a deep impression
upon his heart, and virtuous love, for the first time, reigned in
his breast triumphant. 'May I presume to ask,' said he, addressing
himself to Rivolti, 'who that ruffian is, from whose violence I had
the good fortune to rescue the fair Rosalie?'—'Alas, it is a grief to
me to say!—but I had intended Vallentia for the husband of my
daughter, and by his vile conduct, the son of my friend has not
only rendered himself hateful to her, but has forfeited my esteem
for ever. I will recount to you the circumstances which led to
this proposed union:—The father of Vallentia and myself were
schoolfellows and soldiers together; we both married nearly at
the same period, and this young man was born in the same year
with my son. We often, previous to their birth, said, should the
children prove of different sexes, we would betroth them to each
other: we, however, were disappointed in our intentions by their
both proving males; but in two years after my Rosalie was born,
and we hoped at a future day to see our families united by her
marriage with Vallentia. Rosalie, as she advanced in life, improved
in beauty and accomplishments; but ere she had attained her fifteenth year, both the parents of Vallentia were carried off by a
fever, first expressing their wishes that he should take in marriage
my daughter, which he faithfully promised. He now visited our
residence at Venice, as my future son, and I thought he loved my
child with a passion beyond the power of fortune to diminish;
but his conduct to-night has proved the base motives of his selfish
heart. A few months since I lost the principal part of my fortune
by fire, which destroyed bills to a large amount; and since that
time I have, with the residue of my wealth, procured this dwelling, with an intention of ending my days in it; as, by economy,
I have still sufficient to support me with credit, though not with
the splendour I was wont to enjoy. Vallentia still continued his
visits, and now it appears he wished to obtain her as a mistress,
who it had long been his pride to seek as his wife. Oh, stranger!
I know not how to requite you for preserving her virtue, and
restoring her to me! For had Vallentia succeeded in his diabolical schemes, the shame of Rosalie would too surely have broken

the heart of her wretched father.'—'Did Rosalie love Vallentia?' eagerly inquired Flodiardo.—'Alas! I think so, signor; but she has been from childhood accustomed to regard him as her destined husband, and she never expressed the least repugnance for him, though certainly I sometimes thought she treated him more as a brother than a lover.' The heart of Flodiardo leapt with joy at the conclusion of this speech; and, during the few days he remained with them, he ingratiated himself so far into the favour of both child and parent, that he was the declared and accepted lover of Rosalie.

"Sometime after, when business had required his presence at Venice, previous to his return to the villa, which he intended to do in the evening, a messenger arrived, informing him that signor Rivolti was taken suddenly and dangerously ill, and was scarcely expected to survive till his arrival; he instantly followed the messenger, mounted on a swift horse, and speedily reached the residence, where he beheld his loved Rosalie weeping beside the couch of her dying parent. His disorder was a sudden fit of apoplexy, which deprived him of speech; but taking the hand of Flodiardo and that of his daughter, he joined them together in his; then, murmuring a blessing on them, expired. I will not dwell upon this, but let it suffice to say, that, soon as decency permitted, my father made Rosalie his wife; he took her to a grand chateau which he possessed in Venice, where, in due time, she gave birth to the unfortunate being who now addresses you. My father, whom the novelty of marriage had made domestic, for the first two years was scarcely ever from her side; but at length growing palled with the chaste beauties of my mother, his inconstant heart sought for variety in the arms of courtesans. Often did poor Rosalie drop tears of anguish on my infant face, as she saw my inheritance wasted by gamblers and sharpers. She expostulated with my father, but he was deaf to her apprehensions, and laughed at her fears; however, one fatal night, when wine had got master of his senses, and fortune declared against him, he betted deeply—the dice betrayed him—he grew desperate, and staked the whole of his property on one fatal cast—it was decided against him, and he arose from the board a beggar.

'Twas now he sought my mother, and from her pious resignation learned to bear his lot with some degree of fortitude. The villa still was her's, and there they sought for tranquility; but, alas! my father was not formed for happiness. One fatal night, returning from the city, he slowly entered the apartment level with the garden, and was making his intention of surprising his wife by his quick return, when, passing a door which led to another room, he beheld my mother in the close embrace of a man of noble appearance; he stole behind the couch on which they both sat, when he saw his wife kiss the stranger, and exclaim—'Flodiardo is in the city, beloved Orsino!' 'Thou liest, base strumpet!' said he; 'he is here to reward thy perfidy!' Thus saying, he plunged his stiletto to the heart of my mother, who sunk weltering in her blood.

'Oh God! my sister!' said the stranger; 'look up and speak to me, my sweet Rosalie!' My father uttered not a word, being struck dumb with horror; for he now conjectured this must be the brother of his murdered wife, who had been absent many years. In frantic accents he called upon her to forgive him—'Oh, slaughtered saint, look up one moment, or I will follow you.' Alas! she was already dead! My father, in despair, took the stiletto, still reeking with my mother's blood, and plunged it deep into his breast, ere he could be prevented by the horror-struck Orsino. He kissed the pale cheek of Rosalie, and told my uncle he left a wretched orphan to his care, who now had no claims of kindred to any but himself. My uncle promised to protect me, and my father soon bade adieu to this world for ever. I was at this period about four years of age, and my foster-parent took me with him to Venice, where he bestowed on me every accomplishment which money could procure. When I had attained my eighteenth year, a very distant relation of my uncle's died, and as he was next in ties of blood, left him an immense fortune, providing that he would forsake the name of Rivolti, for the one which his family bore—of course he consented; at the same time adopting me as his son, with the promise that I should become heir to all he possessed. His unlimited indulgence was my ruin; I followed the footsteps of my father, and was often made the egregious dupe of the fraudulent and designing. At length my unbounded extravagance called forth the serious anger of my relative, who refused to advance me a sous beyond the sum stipulated for my allowance, which was rather liberal; this I soon squandered; and, to complete my disgrace, I married a young woman considerably beneath the rank I bore; but she was beautiful and amiable, and proved truly affectionate; yet I knew my uncle would never be reconciled, so I intended to keep it from him for ever as a secret, when a villain, to whom I confided it, betrayed me, and by his diabolical machinations, caused my innocent unsuspecting wife to end her miserable existence by horrid suicide. A letter, which she had written to me previous to her perpetrating this rash deed, made me frantic, and, in hopes of again beholding her, I plunged my stiletto into the breast of one who detained me from her side: but, alas! I was too late—she had been dead some hours. Her billet had informed me of the base contriver of this dreadful tragedy, and had I dared to venture in the city, his life should have paid the price of his perfidy; but my crime had doomed me to proscription; and, growing desperate from grief, I joined a band of lawless ruffians which infested the neighbouring forest, and subsisted by plunder, when abandoning my own name, I assumed that of the bandit Darthalgo!"

Donald, who till now had listened with the greatest attention, started at the mention of that dread name—"Yet," said he, mentally, "there probably might be two of one name." Robert sat trembling; he had never seen the bravo, and concluded that this was he, in the disguise of a hermit. They neither of them uttered a syllable, but the agitation they both evinced proved to the stranger they had heard the name before.

"What's the meaning of this surprise?" said he to Donald; "have you ever heard of Darthalgo?"

"Oh, yes!" returned he; "this night were we in search of a bravo of that name, but you are not he. Will you favour me by continuing your history?"

"I will," said the astonished stranger. "I wrote to the wretch who was the contriver of my miseries, and threatened vengeance, should we ever meet, upon his wicked head. Upon this information he quitted Venice, to return to his native land, and I have never since beheld him, though I sought these shores for that purpose. The time when I commenced robber was during the period I was frantic with sorrow; but no sooner did reason regain its seat, than honour represented unto me the horrid calling of a bandit, and I was determined to abandon it. One day I made a proposal to our band, to divide what money there was in the hoard, and separate; this met with the approbation of the major-ity; when, on receiving my share, I embarked for this country, with the intention of wreaking my vengeance on the destroyer of Paulina; but several miles distant from this, during a storm, the vessel was wrecked, and I alone of all the numerous crew on board was the only one who survived. The little wealth which I possessed luckily was about me. Long did I wander about the neighbouring shores, undetermined how to proceed or act, when chance brought me to this hermitage; here I found the unburied body of the former inhabitant, who seemed to have departed from this world several days; I dug up the earth with an iron instrument which I found in the cavern, and laid him decently under the green sod, at the back of the cell. In the recess I found some fruits, with which I satiated my hunger, and sinking upon yon couch of rushes, I fell into a profound sleep, during which I beheld a vision, that made me determine to take up my abode here. Methought the spirit of Paulina appeared to me, and said—'Valando seek not revenge; leave to thy great Creator the disposal of thy enemy; but by devoting the remainder of thy sinful life to religion, in seclusion from the world and all its follies, seek to purify thy soul from all the foul crimes thou hast commit-ted—so shall we meet again in those bright realms and regions of peace, where deceit and hypocrisy never again can part us.' I started and awoke from my sleep, resolving to obey the heavenly vision, which, under the form of the spirit of my departed wife, thus converted me. I attired myself in the habit belonging to my predecessor, and have by penance endeavoured to atone for my misspent life. You are the first that have entered this lowly dwell-ing since I have possessed it, except a poor hind, who sometimes purchases for me a few necessaries which nature requires; and it was by going to seek for whatever the storm might cast upon the neighbouring shore, that I this night have had the pleasure of shielding you from its inclemency. And now, my son, if it be not inconsistent with prudence, I prithee unfold to me what thou knowst of Darthalgo?"

"I will, venerable father," said Donald, "and will be equally candid as yourself." He then recounted all the knowledge he possessed of that mysterious bandit, which greatly excited the wonder of the hermit, who could not give the least clue respecting the sameness of names. Daylight now began to appear, and the tempestuous night was succeeded by a serene morning; the sun darted its bright rays into the cell. Robert, who had fallen into a sound sleep, was roused by his master, who sent him forth to search for their horses, which he found quietly grazing beneath a clump of trees, where he had fastened them; he led them towards the cell, where both mounting, after thanking the venerable anchorite for his hospitality, who at parting bestowed on them his benison, they departed, and with some difficulty gaining the right road to the ruins of the abbey, proceeded onwards.

CHAP. VI.

The cloud-capt towers, the gorgeous palaces,
The solemn temples, the great globe itself,
Yea, all which it inherit, shall dissolve,
And, like the baseless fabric of a vision,
Leave not a wreck behind!

SHAKESPEARE.*

"WELL," said the loquacious squire, the first who broke silence, "who would suppose, my lord, to look at the hermit, that he had ever been a bravo? When he called himself Darthalgo I shook in my skin, for I have never seen this famous robber, and I expected every moment that he would eat us both alive."

"Nay," said Donald, "I think he had most reason to fear that you would eat him, for you paid a great deal of respect to his wine and provisions."

"Why as to that, my lord, I like good eating and good drinking, more especially after a storm; for I think, with submission, when one has been well drenched without, we should also be well drenched within."

"A very sound reason indeed," said Donald; "but come, Robert, spur on your horse, and let us press forward."

"Certainly, my lord, I will; but if I might be allowed to speak the sentiments of my mind, I think it is but a wild-goose kind of a chace, as a body may say."

"What do you mean?" said his master.

"Mean, my lord! Why, my lord, I hardly know what I mean. But do you think it very likely that Darthalgo would be fool enough to take my lady to the very place where they were all routed out from but the other day, as a body may say? No! no! I plainly foresee, my lord, that we shall have our trouble for our pains, and very likely we may only be wandering further from lady Matilda and poor Venella, when we ought to rescue them from the power of demi-devils, who, perhaps, ere this have found out a fresh haunt."

"Pshaw! nonsense, Robert; I have reasons, at any rate, for going to the ruin; for I believe there still remains the old hag, whom Bosmora gave liberty to go where she pleased. Now we can inquire of her, if, since the day the rest were subdued, she has ever seen Darthalgo, and by that means judge if it was really him who carried off my dear Matilda."

"And pray, my lord," said Robert, "with all possible deference, do you suppose she would tell you, even if she knew? No, no! I plainly foresee, my lord, she would not let you into the secret; no, she's not fool enough for that."

"Well," said Donald, "however, I am determined, at all events, to proceed; and if you are afraid to accompany me, you are at liberty to return."

"Return!" said Robert; "I return! Well, I never suspected, my lord, you could have uttered such cruel words;" and, with his eyes almost filled with tears, he added, "I am sure I never foresaw that indeed."

"Well, well, my good fellow, I did not mean to offend you," said Donald; "but I am so heart-rent by this second loss of my beloved, that I believe my temper is grown irritable. Robert, I ask pardon for those words spoken in my wrath."

"Oh, that is quite enough!" said the other. "When a lord asks pardon of his squire, I foresee that would content any body as well as myself: and look, my lord, yonder is a high turret; does that belong to the abbey ruin?"

"It does," replied Donald; "Heaven grant that within its walls I may find my beloved Matilda!"

"I hope we may, my lord," answered Robert; "I prayed to St. Andrew to direct us when I was getting the horses ready: and now, my lord, which is the nearest way, for both these roads seem to terminate near its walls, as far as I can guess? Ah, I sadly wanted to accompany my lord the baron, but he would not let me, because I was somewhat debilitated by the long confinement I endured in the dungeon. Which, my lord, is the right road?—do you know?"

"Why," said Donald, "near as I can guess, this branching off to the left."

"Well then, my lord, we shall soon be there. Oh, if we do but find the lady Matilda, how the baron will rejoice, and how glad the lady your mother will be, my lord! and how pleased Venella will be at seeing me! But look, my lord, what black clouds! As sure as I live, there is another storm coming on; let us hasten, and reach the ruin ere it commences. What an unlucky squire am I, that there should be one tempest following another in this manner!"

"Fear not," said Donald; "we shall reach the abbey in a few minutes." He applied his spurs to his proud courser, when, after riding about a quarter of an hour, he stopped, exclaiming, "We must certainly have come the wrong way!"

"There now!" said Robert; "my mind misgave me when you took this road, for I plainly foresaw we should be caught in the shower; the rain begins to patter on my head already. Oh that I could see another angel, in the shape of a hermit, for I have not yet broke my fast!"

"Prythee cease prating," said Donald, "and ascend that tree, and see if by that means you can discover anything of the rain, that we may be able to tell the nearest direction to proceed in."

"I will, my lord, but really I am a poor climber of a tree; for once, when I was a boy, I fell backwards from the top of an elm, and ever since I have had a sort of antipathy to exaltation; but however, my lord, to oblige you I will do my best, and I plainly foresee that it will be the worst imaginable." He had scarcely spoke, when taking hold of a weak branch, it broke; and the unfortunate Robert, without the least foreknowledge, was precipitated into a ditch. "There!" said he, with a rueful countenance, "I knew I should never reach the top." He clambered up the side of the bank, by the assistance of his master, not much worse for his fall, except being covered over with mud, and then, in a peevish tone, continued—"What would Venella say if she saw me now?"

"Prythee cease prating," said the impatient Donald, "and I will see if I cannot succeed better than yourself."

"Then, my lord, do take a fool's advice, and do not get up that same tree. What a blockhead was I, when I foresaw that I should fall, to choose that whose branches hung over a ditch! had I but gone on the other side, I might have tumbled on the soft grass, and avoided being in this confounded pickle."

Ere Robert had finished these wise observations, Donald's agile limbs had reached the highest branch, when quickly descending, he exclaimed—"Let us take the cross path! We cannot be far from the spot; for, as well as I can distinguish through the thick mist, it lies to the right. Come, bustle, Robert, bustle!"

"Indeed, sir, I wish I could bustle this mud off my clothes; but as that seems impossible, why I must e'en remain in my present trim. Heigho! I wish our journey may prove successful, and then I will so eat and drink when I get back to Duncaethal, I should not wonder if I got tipsey."

"Nor I either," said Donald, laughing, in spite of his misfortune.

"Well now, my lord," said Robert, "I am quite ready to set

forward, and I hope this road may prove the proper one, though, under favour, sir, I think we are the first that ever travelled this way on horseback; for if a man be not as short as a dwarf, he will certainly get his head taken off by the boughs of the trees, they grow so near the ground. Now, my lord, my advice is, that we dismount and lead our poor steeds."

Donald acquiesced in this plan of the honest squire's, for it began to be so very foggy, that they could scarcely see a yard before them; and often as the branches of the trees came in contact with the head of Robert, he would cry—"Well, I plainly foresee I shall never return alive to Duncaethal! Do, my dear lord, let us rest till this mist disperses; who knows but we are going wrong all this time."

A large projecting limb of an aged tree at this moment knocking the helmet from off the head of Donald, made him determine to adopt the advice of his squire, and seating themselves at the root of a large oak, they waited for several hours the dispersion of the heavy fog which filled the atmosphere. At last Donald, suspecting the near approach of night, was determined at all events to proceed; and after a great deal of difficulty, and some danger, they found themselves in a beaten road, which he recognized to be the same he had travelled on the night he left the abbey with Bosmora. The mist now was, in a great measure, dissipated, and was succeeded by the sober grey of evening; they pressed forward, but night overtook them by their arrival at the tumbling gates of the abbey. Robert, taking the arm of Donald, pointed to a window, where they perceived a light, borne in the hand of a figure, but whether male or female they could not distinguish, owing to the old dusky windows, whose heavy frames and painted lattices were covered with the accumulated dust of many rolling years. "'Tis well!" said he; "there are yet inhabitants remaining."

"Ah, my lord, too many for us, I fear!" said Robert.

"Hush!" said Donald; "follow me—we must work by stratagem here; I wish to obtain entrance without alarming anyone. Fasten our steeds to this stump, and let us proceed in silence."

Robert obeyed, and Donald, making his way to the entrance,

applied his hand to the fastening, which yielded to the touch; then proceeding together, they found themselves in the ancient halls.

"Oh, my lord, look there at that white figure!" said Robert.

"Where?" said his attentive master.

"Why there, my lord!—as I live it's coming towards us! Oh, it's a ghost, my lord, it's a ghost!"

At this moment the object of Robert's terror sent forth a dismal moan, which convinced his master that it was no other than a harmless owl, which they had disturbed in its nocturnal ramble. He whispered to the simple squire—"Be more careful, Robert; you vociferated so loud at the sight of this poor bird, which your fears transformed into a ghost, that it might have subjected us to a discovery."

"I beg your pardon, my lord," returned he, "but I hate the sight of ghosts; and where is any one so likely to meet them as in an old abbey, where hundreds of monks and friars have been buried? Who knows but they may haunt this place? and though I have all possible respect for priests, yet I can't say I should so very much like to meet one after he was dead. 'Tis dreadful dark, sir! do you know where we are going, sir?"

"Why," said Donald, "as near as I can remember, the caverns lie off to the right, so follow me, and draw your sword, which will serve to explore the way, and we shall be ready in case of a surprise. Come on! By the glimmering of the moon," which now began to shine forth, "I can perceive a door, that I think belongs to the room in which Matilda was confined when the abbey was attacked." He pushed it open, and on a table they beheld a lamp burning; Donald concluded it must have been left there by some one, who would, no doubt, soon return for it, and he resolved to lie perdue* behind the ruins of a kind of altar to wait for their appearance. Robert retired with him, and after waiting about ten minutes, a door, at the extremity of the place, was opened, and, with a small basket on her arm, the old hag made her appearance. The squire was on the point of rushing from his hiding-place, to seize her, but was restrained by his master, who wished to gain that knowledge by stratagem he feared he could not effect by force. Soon as she had taken up the lamp, motioning to Robert to do the same, they followed her through the door-way by which they had entered. She proceeded straight to the hall, till, seemingly through fatigue, she seated herself at the foot of a kind of throne, which had once borne the dignitary of the house, arrayed in the abacot* and purple, on the festival of their patron saint, but was now fast sinking to that oblivion which had long been the lot of its possessors. After resting about two or three minutes, the old beldam got up, mumbling something to herself, and seemed as though she had forgot some article or other; for, leaving the basket on the place where she had just been seated, she retraced her steps back again. Robert now proposed stealing from behind the buttress, where they lay concealed, and helping themselves to its contents, but was reprimanded by Donald, who said—"Would you, for the gratification of your appetite, lose the knowledge of where lady Matilda is concealed? for I have no doubt but she is going to convey those provisions to her, and I am resolved to follow and watch her motions. Hush! she comes."

The old hag returned, bearing in her hand a stone vessel, which they concluded contained water for her captives, when, reaching the basket, she slipped behind the throne, and, opening a secret entrance, disappeared; they quickly followed, and observed her almost at the bottom of a flight of steps; they lost no time in pursuing as quick as they possibly could, without her hearing the sound of their feet. A dark subterranean appeared, through which she advanced, and applying a key to one of the cell-doors, entered, ironically saying—"Well, my fine madams, have you found your appetites? Can your dainty stomachs relish any thing? Here is some good black bread and water as——"

Donald's heart leaped with joy at this address, and his rapture was unbounded at hearing Matilda interrupt her, by saying—"Do you call yourself a woman, that you can have the cruelty to assist a villain like Darthalgo, in the persecution of those who never injured you?" The old hag was about to reply, when Donald, followed by Robert, rushed in and secured her.

Matilda, at the unexpected sight of her beloved, gave a loud shriek, and sunk in a swoon upon her wretched couch, while

Venella, who before was sitting in a corner, clung round the neck of the squire, exclaiming—"Oh, my dear, dear Robert, take us out of this nasty place directly, for I shall die if I stay in it a moment longer. But, lack-a-day, look at my lady!" She took up the stone jug brought by the old woman, and rushing towards Donald, who was in vain endeavouring to recover her, when sprinkling some water on her face, and forcing a little in her mouth, it had the desired effect; and opening her eyes, she perceived what she at first took for a vision was real. She expressed her happiness by tears of joy.

Robert, who had bound the old woman, asked how he should proceed; then turning to the captive, politely said—"Shall we leave you here a prisoner, where you have so lately officiated as a gaoler?"

She replied only by horrid curses and imprecations, and earnestly wished they might be taken by Darthalgo and his party ere they left the place. This was a hint sufficient to hasten their departure; for instantly quitting the ruin, leaving behind the old beldam, and mounting Matilda and Venella behind them, with all possible speed made towards Duncaethal, whose lofty turrets met their anxious sight just as the morn began to dawn, and pressing forward their wearied steeds, shortly reached its walls. Robert dismounted, and knocked loudly at the gate.

Old Andrew, whom the baron had brought with his clan, answered the summons, and demanded—"Who's there?"

"Open, open!—'tis I, Robert! Where is the baron? We have brought back the Lady Matilda."

"Indeed! Marry that is rare news! And is my young lord come too? are they both well?"

"Come, Andrew, you talk so, we shall never get in—make haste and draw back the bolts—my lady is almost fainting!"

"Oh, marry," said he, as the gate flew wide open, "then enter I pray you!"

"Ah, that will I!" said the other. "I little thought one night, as I was groping about this castle to try if I could escape, I should ever be so glad to come into it again when I had once got away; that is, when I was visited by my good friend Dargo, who used to supply me with food and drink, sparingly enough, the saints bear witness, for which I will make ample amends this day."

"La, Robert," said Venella, "how you chatter! why don't you lead me in? Don't you see how tired I am?" said she, exalting her voice.

"Tired!" said the other; "I should like to know if your tongue is ever tired? No, no, I warrant it never is."

"Silence!" said she, "here is my lady; see how nicely my lord leads her over the bridge by the arm, while I was obliged to walk by myself."

"Ah," said Andrew, "my dear young lady is welcome back; and give me leave, my lord, to congratulate your return; and proud am I in the honour of admitting you into your own castle, the rights of which you are to be invested with tomorrow. But let me haste to acquaint the baron with your arrival, and send word to the lady Agnes, who has been almost distracted lest any evil should have befel you. Come in, my dear young lord Alexander, heir of Duncaethal!"

The old man, with tears of joy streaming down his cheeks, conducted the youthful pair into the hall, then hasted fast as possible to acquaint the baron, who had but just retired to rest, for the first time since the departure of Donald, when, worn with watching, sleep overtook him, and he was unconscious of the entrance of the good old steward, who, not wishing to disturb his repose, was on the point of retiring, when hearing his master exclaim—"My daughter! oh, my daughter!" the old man, thinking he was awake, drew back the curtain, and said—"She is arrived, my lord!"

The baron started from his unquiet slumber, and, seeing Andrew, inquired what news of lord Alexander and Matilda?

"They are both returned, my lord!"

"Indeed!" said the baron.

"Yes, my lord; they are both in the hall."

The baron, dropping on his knee, said—"Gracious Heaven, accept my thanks! Come, Andrew, assist me to dress," then hasting down stairs, he found them with Agnes, who had heard of their arrival from Gertrude. She saw them from her window enter the court-yard, and ran directly to her lady, the bonny Agnes, as she called her, with the joyful tidings. They both were alternately pressed to the bosoms of their parents; and after the first flood of joy was past, Bosmora said—"My son, the castle is full of company; numbers of the greatest nobles in Scotland are assembled, to be present at the trial of the usurper, and to-morrow it will take place: yesterday, you know, was the time appointed, but it was obliged to be postponed on account of your absence. Now will you stand forward to crush your deadly foe, and at once revenge the injuries of yourself, your mother, and your elected wife. But say, my child, was you in the power of Darthalgo, that mysterious bandit, who seeks to revenge an injury ignorantly given by us, yet he affirms it was given? Was he the ravisher, my child?

"He was, my dearest father, and I will relate to you the whole proceeding."

"Had not you better rest first?" said Agnes; "and you too, my son? Let us defer it till you have recruited your exhausted strength."

They acquiesced in this necessary arrangement; and after the repose of several hours, they met in the apartment of Bosmora, where Matilda related the event, as recorded in the next chapter.

CHAP. VII.

Oh! I have pass'd a miserable night!
So full of ugly sights, of ghastly dreams—
I would not spend another such a night,
Though 'twere to buy a world of happy days!
So full of dismal terror was the time!

SHAKESPEARE.*

ON the afternoon which Matilda had been forced from Duncaethal, she had, attended by her maid Venella, strolled to the outskirts of the adjacent forest, the day being remarkably fine. "How beautiful is the surrounding scene!" exclaimed she;

"the peasantry appear so clean and healthy, and look so cheerful, while, as they attend to their different occupations, they beguile time, and lighten their labour by merry songs or mirth-inspiring jests. Oh, how much they are to be envied, for they certainly are the happiest race of mortals existing!"

"What!" said Venella, whose ideas of happiness consisted only in riches; "what, madam, a parcel of shepherds the happiest folks? Oh, no! With all possible deference to your ladyship, I think that you are the happiest person in the whole versal* world."

"I!" said Matilda: "by what means," blushing at her maid's allusion, "am I so happy?"

"By what means, madam! why are you not the rich heiress of Bosmora? Is not your enemy a prisoner in the castle? Will you not have the pleasure of seeing him condemned to death, and not the most gentle one, I am sure, if he gets half what he deserves? And is not sir Donald free? I beg pardon, my lady, I mean my lord Alexander. Does he not go down on his knees every day, to pray for the arrival of that period when he may claim you as his lady? Then will not his rich domains be added to your's? Ah, madam, how often have I heard you say that you would sooner die than be the wife of Duncaethal! Ah! little did you then know that sir Donald's real name was Duncaethal, or else I think, my lady, you would have spared your vows on that head!"

"You are too free, Venella," said her mistress.

"Oh, I beg pardon, my lady! but you know you asked me by what means you was so happy, and I was only explaining, my lady, what I thought made you so, my lady."

They had now wandered a considerable distance from the castle, and were just going to return, when a piteous moan, seemingly close to them, caused them to look round, and they beheld a person, in the habit of a pilgrim, under a tree, seemingly in acute pain. Matilda, ever ready to assist the distressed, hastily advanced, and, in a voice of commiseration, asked if she could do anything to serve him?

"Sweet lady, if you will help to raise me up, I should be obliged to you, for I am faint and weary." She stooped for that purpose, when being raised from the earth, he, in a tremulous voice, said—"Alas, alas, I am very feeble! Gentle lady, would you so far extend your charity, as to allow your attendant to lead me to the hollow of the glen? There is a cave which I inhabit, and from which I have wandered so far, I cannot get back in my present state without assistance, and night is coming on; therefore, dear lady——"

"I will attend you, father, but do not exhaust yourself with talking. Venella, take hold of the stranger's other arm. So, father, take your time—we will assist you."

In this manner they slowly walked forward, till stopping, as if to rest, the old man pointed to a thicket, saying—"There, charitable lady, there is my humble dwelling."

"So, so, we shall be there anon."

They reached the spot, when once more stooping, he said— "Oh, I shall sink!" and seemed falling to the ground. Matilda placed her arms round his body, and endeavoured to support him, when, thrusting his hand into his bosom, he drew forth a whistle, which he applied to his mouth, and blew a shrill sound. Two men rushed from the thicket, forcibly seized Matilda and her attendant, while the hypocrite, casting off his disguise, discovered to her maddened sight the countenance of Darthalgo. With a loud shriek she sunk upon her knees, imploring him to save her.

"What," said he, "is the proud Matilda once more before me? Ha! ha! Bring forth the horses, Hugh, and let this fair captive again be conducted to our retreat."

Venella now loudly screamed—"Help! help!" upon which the ruffian gagged her mouth, and confined her hands, the fingers of which she had several times applied to his cheek, and, by the red stream that followed, gave evident proof of her powerful nails. Though she had used him thus scurvily, he told her, if she would be quiet, he would unbind and suffer her to travel comfortably; she bowed her head in assent, inwardly resolving she would call again for help, should she see the least chance of assistance. He set her mouth at liberty, and placing her before him, in the same manner his comrade did Matilda, they set forward, preceded by Darthalgo. They passed the glen, and kept in a circuitous rout through the forest, and after a few hours riding, Matilda once again beheld the hated ruin. They did not, as before, convey her through the cavern, but rode boldly to the gate, which was opened by the old woman.

"Ah!" said she, "welcome! What have you brought the fine madam back again?"

"Aye," said Hugh, "we have brought two ladies."

"Two!" said she, eyeing Venella, who could scarcely refrain serving the old hag's face as she had the ruffian's, "who is this other? Do you suppose, Darthalgo, I can take care of two?—No, not I. You must stay and attend to them yourself."

"Well," said Venella, who, in spite of the perilous situation, could not restrain her natural flippancy, "and pray who wants you to take care of us? we had much rather go about our business, I assure you. Who do you suppose wishes to be attended by an old weather-beaten beldam like yourself? If I was to meet you in the forest, I should take you for a witch, and expect to see you mount a broomstick, and fly away."

"I'll take pretty good care that you don't fly away upon——" growled the other. "Marry come up! weather-beaten indeed!"

"Silence!" said the bandit; "is the apartment of lady Matilda prepared for her reception?"

"It is," answered she; "there is a stone vessel of water, a basket of food, and a clean truss of straw to rest her dainty joints upon."

"Straw!" said Venella, "indeed my lady can't sleep upon straw, nor I either."

"Then her ladyship may stand, and you too," muttered the old hag.

They were now conducted through the secret entrance behind the altar, upon which the hopes of Matilda yielded to despair, and the pellucid drops chased each other down her cheeks, as Darthalgo thus scornfully addressed her—"Madam, you see I am provided against a surprise, should any one come in quest of you. To your care," addressing the old woman, "I commit her; and should any one come to search for her, conduct them through the abbey; fear not the most rigid scrutiny, for

I defy any one, but our band, to discover the entrance of this dungeon, the future residence of Matilda." He now closed the door of this horrid prison, from which she never could have been released, had not Donald luckily followed old Peg, when conveying them provisions.

Darthalgo, after seeing his victims properly secured, returned to the hall, where being joined by his two myrmidons, said— "Come, let us leave the abbey for a short time, as I have no doubt but the love-sick Donald, or Bosmora, will come in search of our captive; therefore we will be absent, while Peg will conduct them through the ruins, when they will conclude it to be deserted by all but herself, and then depart." The storm now began to rage with great fury, but it deterred not the villains from quitting the abbey; and while Donald was listening to the tale of the hermit, they were proceeding to a new haunt, which was inhabited by Morven, chief of the band.

Bitterly did Venella weep when she found herself left in the gloomy cell. "Ah, my dear lady, how differently did we rest last night! Then you had a handsome couch, covered with velvet, and I a nice soft mattress by your side. Ah, but a few hours since I said you was the happiest person in the world, and now you are in a miserable dungeon! Oh dear, I wish we had never ventured out of the castle! Oh dear, who would ever have thought it! But do you think, my lady, they will kill us?"

"Alas! I know not," said Matilda; "perhaps, at least, they may me, for that mysterious bravo seems to bear me the most inveterate malice."

"Ah, my lady, what have you ever done to offend him? If I was in your place, I would ask his pardon, and see if that could induce him to release us."

"Alas! he is deaf to all entreaties," said Matilda, "and my begging pardon would avail nothing; indeed I never did any thing to offend him: often has he terrified me by presenting a poniard to my breast, but some powerful motives has restrained him from becoming my destroyer, though Heaven only knows how long he may be now before he does indeed put a period to my existence. I hope the moment is not far distant, for rather would

I perish beneath his dagger, than linger out a miserable existence, while memory would continually torture me with what I might have been, and what I am."

The tears quick chased each other down her cheeks as she concluded these reflections and, hiding her face in her robe, she fell into a reverie, when all the torturing horrors of her fate passed in rapid succession, till frenzy almost took possession of her brain, and, bitterly weeping, she prayed for instant dissolution. In this manner did the night pass on in silence, save that time they were alarmed by the loud peals of thunder, which shook the ruins to the foundation, and, in awful sounds, re-echoed through the vaults of the subterranean, and they every moment expected to be buried beneath the ruins. The day dragged heavily as the night, when at last hearing a key applied to the door of their prison, they expected the appearance of the bandit; how great then was the surprise of Matilda, in beholding her much-loved Donald, who, by his magnanimity, once more restored her to the arms of her affectionate father!

When Matilda had concluded the recital of her sorrows, the baron again clasped her to his heart, and bade her prepare herself for the banquet, where she was expected by the numerous lords and ladies, who had assembled to congratulate her on her deliverance, and Donald on his newly-acquired dignity. She retired, and, after some time devoted to her toilet, arrayed herself in a plain white robe; she was then led into the banqueting room by the joyful Agnes, who in the other hand conducted Donald, and proceeding forward in an introductory manner, said—"Noble lords and ladies, my son Alexander and the lady Matilda!"

Earl Malcolm, of Ross, now stepped forwards and, after congratulating him, said—"I too have been an innocent enemy of your's, my lord, by corroborating the report of your cowardice, made by the villanous Duncaethal, who, by his diabolical stratagem, caused me to suppose you had failed to meet him; and were he not situated as he is, with his sword should he answer for the stain cast upon my honour, which no man before ever presumed to trifle with."

Donald, whom for the future we shall distinguish by his

proper title, answered—"That he felt fully assured, that had he even suspected the least idea of its being a device to sully his fame, he would have been the last to join in the plot."

These conversations were interrupted by the sounding of a harp, and an aged minstrel accompanying it with a song, expressive of the happy occasion on which the assembly had met. After several hours spent in festivity, they all retired to their respective couches, while the servants prepared the hall for the trial, which was to take place on the following morning, when the base usurper was to be stripped of his ill-acquired dignity, and receive the reward due to a villain.

CHAP. VIII.

> Oh! had I dwelt in the bright beam of my fame, then had my years come on with joy! But I fall in youth! My father shall blush in his hall!
>
> ....
>
> Who on his staff is this? Who is this, whose head is white with age? whose eyes are red with tears? who quakes at every step? It is her father!   OSSIAN.*

THE place of trial was crowded at an early hour, which exhibited an assemblage of the most noble families in Scotland. Bosmora sat as the principal of these impartial judges, for the culprit's numerous crimes would admit of no palliation; yet was he allowed a fair hearing and defence. A signal being given, the door was thrown open, and the once imperious Duncaethal entered that hall, a captive, where he had long reigned the lord. Silence being commanded, the baron arose, and addressed the degraded chief in the following words, while he stood with an unaltered countenance—"Philip, or, as thou hast long called thyself, lord Duncaethal, bitter indeed is it to me to see a noble of Scotland arraigned for so heinous a crime as your's; can you hope for mercy, after basely wronging both the widow and the orphan? What punishment inflicted on you can atone for the lady Agnes of Duncaethal's many years of sorrow and captivity?"

"I ask no mercy!" said the haughty Philip; "but if Donald is indeed so brave, as he would fain have it believed, why did he appeal to the arbitration of those noble barons? why not rather justify his claims by his sword? Nor can you, my lord, say I have intentionally wronged the orphan, being ignorant of his existence."

"Thou hast wronged him," said the baron, "in the unknown Donald, by diabolical machinations and stratagems, disgraceful for a noble to use; but sanguinary and inhuman has always been your conduct. Thinkst thou the youthful lord would again meet him in the field, on equal terms, who had, by so base a fraud, stained his honour as a knight? Nor is it proper the usurper of his father's house should, black with crimes, have equal chance with the virtuous son of the brave Duncaethal."

Alexander now arose, and bowing, requested permission to be heard, which being granted, he addressed the assembly as follows:—"My lords, if it be consistent with the laws, restore to Philip his sword, and I, by force of arms, will prove my rights; my cause is just, so fear not I the victory; nor can there be a more honourable method of revenging my own and my mother's wrongs."

The eyes of Philip flashed with gratification at the thought of his offer being accepted; not so much did he cherish the idea of conquering, as by an honourable end he should escape the degrading sentence he had no doubt would else be passed upon him.

Bosmora, in the meantime, thus addressed his accepted son—"I have no doubt the taunt of cowardice, conveyed in the speech of that wily wretch, hath induced you to rush into the danger that is proposed, with a view of clearing the stain from your honour; I wish not to check your bravery, and if those noble lords thereby are content, you have my consent."

The majority acquiescing, Alexander was on the point of leaving, to arm himself for the occasion, and Philip, the usurper, accompanied by a guard, was about to retire for the same purpose, when Matilda, who sat next to Agnes, unable any longer to restrain her concern, burst into a flood of tears, while a blush of crimson suffused her cheek at the weakness she had thus evinced.

Her lover sunk at her feet, saying—"My beloved Matilda, shake off this depression; shall I not in this combat revenge your wrongs also, and prove myself worthy of being Bosmora's son, when there cannot be the least doubt remain of my courage, even in the breast of my enemy, by accepting his challenge?"

"Why then," a voice loudly exclaimed, "would Alexander stain his dignity by combating with a murderer?"

"Ah!" said the usurper, while the paleness of death succeeded his late exultation, "who dares to accuse me of a crime like that?"

"I!" said a tall figure, rushing forward, and casting off a long cloak by which he was concealed; "I, the bandit Darthalgo!"

Matilda gave a loud shriek when she beheld him, and cried— "My father, 'tis he! 'tis he!"

"Ah!" said Bosmora, "seize him!"

The guard advanced, when waving his arm with dignity, he exclaimed—"I will follow you, when the purpose is answered for which I came hither. My lord Bosmora, thinkst thou, if I feared you, I should thus voluntarily appear before you when surrounded by soldiers?—No! But I come to criminate that murderer!"

"Ah, again!" said Philip, trembling. "Who art thou?—not Valando?"

"Dost thou not know me? I am not indeed Valando, but one still more injured than that unfortunate Venetian!"

"I know you not," said Philip, in trembling accents; "but produce the proof of your injuries."

"I will!" said the bandit. "Here, look in this sun-burnt visage— are there no traces left of your victim? Then come nearer!" said he, drawing close to the usurper: "what, you dare not! then I will advance to you, and whisper in your ear the name of——" Then, drawing near, a poniard at that moment pierced the heart of the guilty Philip, and ere the horror-struck assembly could prevent it, plunged it deeply in his own, at the same instant exclaiming— "Revenge sweetens the pangs of death! Look on me, Alexander, and triumph in my fall! and you, proud Matilda, behold the victim of your beauty!"

She tore off her false hair and counterfeit beard, that had half covered her face; they both rushed towards her, for in the mysterious bandit they beheld the once-lovely *Margaret of Monteith*. The struggles of dissolution convulsed her frame as she continued to address Matilda, whose tears fast trickled down her cheeks, for all her past sufferings were forgotten, in the surprise and pity she felt at beholding this martyr to her ungovernable passions. "Can you forgive me," said the dying Margaret, "for all the sorrows which I have caused you? for, oh, Matilda, you have caused the fatal pangs you now behold! I was made a sacrifice to your superior charms, by that fallen wretch, whose guilty soul has only set forth a few moments before mine, to account for his manifold crimes! Did I, did I not deal the blow? Oh, sweet revenge! how grateful art thou to my——Ah! what horrid fiend is that? Art thou impatient to conduct me to those shades of woe, the just reward of deeds so foul as mine? Duncaethal, we shall meet again! I thought to revenge myself by thy death also, Matilda; but, wretch as I am, my arm was palsied at the idea of murder till this fatal moment! Now have I stained my soul with the blood of Philip!—yet can *that* be called murder? Did he not suppose he had done the same by me? I should have left his punishment to the retributive hand of Heaven, but 'tis now too late; repentant pangs and dire remorse is all in vain! Farewell! Pray for the guilty Margaret! Oh!—oh!—oh!"

A lengthened groan bespoke the final exit of this once beautiful creature, who, beneath the rough disguise of a bandit, had long been the scourge of the innocent Matilda, and the unoffending youth who had excited her deadly hatred by refusing her proffered love. Not the least whisper in the assembly had interrupted this awful tragedy, till Bosmora, now somewhat recovered from the amazement which had enchanted every faculty, led his weeping daughter from the spot, and ordered a courier to proceed immediately to the castle of Monteith, and request the speedy presence of the earl.

The remains of the unhappy Margaret, together with the guilty Philip, were laid in state, with all the mournful magnificence due to their exalted rank; for the generous Alexander forgot his wrongs and pursued not hatred beyond the grave, but bowed himself to that Omnipotent Power, who had taught him vice could only flourish for a time, and must at length sink before the virtues of the innocent. Bosmora would have demanded of Dargo, whom he had no doubt could have given some clue to this wonderful event, but he had the preceding day left the castle with the banditti, who were sent to meet the punishment due to their infamy.

Alexander, on the following day, accompanied by Matilda, sought the apartment where lay the bodies of Margaret and Philip. He approached the bier of the former, and while he contemplated her inanimate countenance, he thus apostrophized— "Are then those eyes for ever closed! those that could once assume the melting tenderness of love, but, being thwarted, flashed forth sparks of ireful vengeance! and will that voice, which thou couldst sink to whispering melody, or raise to the rough-sounding accents of a remorseless bandit, never again will it charm by harmony or terrify by threats—threats which thou hast too well fulfilled! Thou hast indeed oft rended my heart-strings, and in the person of Matilda——"

"What means my lord?" said the latter, who had listened with an attentive ear to his incomprehensible words.

"Oh, my beloved," said he, "that bitter foe, whose sad remains we now behold vowed dire vengeance on thy innocent head, the evening the festival of thy birth was celebrated at Bosmora."

"I pray you, my lord, explain yourself; I have long had an earnest desire to learn what passed during your interview with lady Margaret in her bedchamber."

He started; he knew not that she was acquainted with the circumstance, but on this discovery being made, fearful lest the smallest suspicion should yet remain on her mind, he took her arm, led her to another room, and unfolded the whole affair.

In a day or two the venerable Earl of Monteith arrived, to whom Bosmora, with all the delicacy possible, imparted the late wonderful transaction. The old man clasped his hands in agony, while the drops of bitter anguish stole in torrents down his furrowed cheeks, as, in heart-broken accents, he said—"Lead me to her! let me behold her hapless remains! Great indeed have been her injuries to you, my lord, but you are a father, and can feel with me! Oh, my child!—a robber's disguise!—the heiress of Monteith! Horrid indeed must have been the prelude to this fatal tragedy! Alas, my daughter! Bosmora, I beseech you let me see her!"

"Check these passions, my Lord, and I will instantly conduct you to the apartment," said the baron, while the sight of the old man's tears excited the commiseration and sympathy of his feeling heart, and he was obliged to summon all his fortitude to prevent weeping in unison.

When they entered the room, the sable draperies and funeral ornaments, which by the baron's orders it had been decorated with, caused the venerable Earl to tremble, and supporting himself upon the arm of his conductor, with tottering steps he approached the bier. He started; scarcely could he recognize a single feature, so much was she altered since the time in which he last beheld her. "What!" said he, "is this Margaret, my child— she who was so justly extolled for her great beauty? Can this weather-brown'd visage have taken place of the lily, which once intermixed with the damask tint, that used to charm the eye of every beholder, and was the pride and glory of her old father? Oh, my child, my child!—my beloved, my sweet, my beautiful daughter!—little did thy wretched parent think, when thou didst beguile him with thy infantile prattle, that he should one day see thee engored with blood drawn from thy heart, or sure his own had broke! Let me once again press upon those lips a father's kiss! Happily thy mother is no more, and I shall not long remain to bear this load of sorrow and disgrace which so heavily oppresses me!" He placed one hand upon his breast, and again stooping to the corse of his daughter, he staggered back into the arms of Bosmora; the cordage of his heart was rent asunder, and, without a sigh or groan, he expired.

The terrified baron called loudly for assistance, and the room was presently filled with domestics, who, on seeing the situation of their master, supposed the old earl had only fainted, and bearing him to a couch, some flew for cordials, till Bosmora, in a voice of grief, informed them it was quite useless, for his spirit was for ever fled. Many of the company now assembled unfeignedly mourned his death, for they had known him to be a man of most excellent qualities, and his only failing had been too great an indulgence of his daughter, whom he had loved even to a fault. Time had almost meliorated his sorrow for her supposed death, when this awful renewal of grief, added to the ignominy she had brought upon their illustrious and hitherto unsullied name, proved too great for his exhausted nature to endure, and he sunk beneath the oppressive burden, never more to rise.

"Peace to his departed soul!" said the surrounding spectators.

After some time spent in making necessary arrangements for the funeral solemnity, which shortly after took place, the remains of both the father and daughter were conveyed to Monteith, where all the remembrance of her crimes were buried in the tomb of Margaret.

CHAP. IX.

There's not a wretch, that lives on common charity,
But's happier far than me: For I have known
The luscious sweets of plenty; every night
Have slept with soft content about my head,
And never wak'd but to a joyful morning:
Yet now must fall, like a full ear of corn,
Whose blossom 'scap'd, yet's wither'd in the ripening.
                                             OTWAY.*

MARGARET of Monteith, when she consented to be the bride of Duncaethal, was not inclined so to do from any affectionate motive, but to gratify her ambition, in being united to one of the most powerful nobles in Scotland; and she ardently panted to launch forth into all the unrestrained liberties of a wedded beauty. The masque, the tournament, and revels, delighted her imagination; and though she had never felt the soft interchange of mutual love, yet was her unbounded pride won by the humble adoration of Duncaethal, who seemed to exist only by her smiles, and expire with her frowns; though, to do him justice in this instance, he did not act the hypocrite, but did really feel for her all the passion of an enthusiastic admirer: but was it doomed to be lasting?—No. It was not in the nature of Philip to feel constancy.

That he was enraptured by her commanding dignity of deportment, and her regular symmetry of features, it is true; then her great fortune, added to his own, was sufficient to make him one of the wealthiest, as well as the most powerful barons of his nation: yet had her anxious father, desirous of placing her beyond the power of a husband's caprice, settled this immense fortune upon her, by way of jointure, except a very handsome sum paid down upon her marriage, as her dowry; and in default of an heir, she was at liberty to bequeath it to whom she might think fit. This arrangement did not altogether meet with the approbation of her lord, but he hoped, by indulgence, he should so far be able to win upon her nature, as to induce her to resign her power unto himself; but he was mistaken; for the discerning and political Margaret was fully aware, as she each day witnessed his wavering disposition, that by resigning to him unlimited sway over her fortune, she should lose the superiority which she possessed over himself.

Being convinced of the propriety of this determination, she still retained the first in gaiety and splendour; and one day, when he reproached her for wasting his substance, she tartly replied— "I think, my lord Duncaethal, my father's liberality to you on our marriage is not yet expended; and when it is, I have a resource, which, like that of Crœsus, cannot be exhausted by all the extravagance that your lordship is pleased to complain of."

"Then why not, beloved Margaret," said he, "invest me with that power? It is not well that the baron should look up to his lady for a supply. Would it not have been more proper if your father had entrusted me? Surely I should have proved a better guardian of your fortune than you can possibly be."

"Oh pray, my dear lord, don't alarm yourself," said she, ironically; "I don't wish to give you so much trouble; I can take care of it myself; and give me leave to observe, my lord Duncaethal,

that if you disapproved the arrangements made by the baron
of Monteith, you should have rejected them, ere the priest had
bound us in those trammels, which, I think, from your late
conduct, do not promise to be very agreeable to either party.
In the meantime, my lord, rest assured that I shall never yield
to your covetous nature the unrestrained liberty of disposing
of my fortune to those who, by their conduct, may most merit
my esteem. Not any mortal living shall ever possess the least
command over me during my existence! No, never will I give
the reins out of my own hands; and were I even weak enough to
settle it on you, in case of my decease, your lordship could not be
much the gainer; for, according to the regular course of nature,
there is all likelihood of your first bidding adieu to this transitory
life; but, perhaps, your lordship could remedy that, by removing
me, as you have already done the hapless *Paulina!*"

"Ah! what mean you?" said the conscience-struck wretch.
"Madam, beware, beware what you say! I murdered not Paulina!
What Paulina do you mean?" endeavouring to recover himself;
"who do you mean, madam?"

"I shall leave that to your superior judgment, my lord;" and,
curtseying sarcastically, withdrew, leaving Duncaethal over-
whelmed with surprise and confusion.

Margaret had come at the knowledge of this black affair in
the following manner—by going to a cabinet, to procure something for which she had an occasion, belonging to her lord, when
observing a small desk of curious workmanship, having the key
left in it, prompted by her curiosity she opened it, for the purpose
of examining it more minutely; in one of the drawers she discovered a packet of letters, which, being written in the hand of a
female, she was tempted to peruse the contents. They were from
Viola, the Venetian courtesan, and addressed to Duncaethal; five
of which contained all the seeming fervency of an ardent affection. She was proceeding to unfold the sixth, when the billet of
the unhappy Valando met her eye; horror ran through her veins
as she perused the dreadful words—"I have seen the murdered
Paulina, whose blood calls for vengeance!"

"Oh God!" uttered she, "have I wedded a murderer?" She,

quick as her agitation would permit, replaced the drawers, immediately left the apartment, and retiring to her own, ruminated upon this extraordinary and unexpected discovery. How he could think of retaining a paper of so much danger, was to her a source of the greatest astonishment. In fact, Duncaethal knew not of its being in his possession, for when he received it, it was at a time he was engaged with company, and, after hastily glancing over the contents, he put it in his desk; and fearful lest by any chance it should be seen, he unfolded a letter of Viola's, and enclosed it. This circumstance entirely forsook his memory, so great was his confusion at the time; for shortly after, wishing to peruse it again, he felt for it in his pocket, when missing it, he felt much alarmed, and concluded it to be lost. Upon his departure from Venice he forgot it altogether; and little did he suppose when he was shipwrecked near Monteith, when every thing valuable was lost, save only a pocket-book, containing letters and other papers, which were preserved by being about his person, and among the rest this witness of his infamy; therefore it was to him a matter of the greatest astonishment how she could possibly gain a knowledge of this horrid circumstance.

Margaret would never have betrayed it, had not an incident occurred, which converted the cool indifference she felt for her lord into the deadliest hatred. She had long beheld his neglect towards herself with no little indignation; and one evening, returning somewhat unexpectedly from a walk, she heard voices whispering in the apartment of Duncaethal; and, applying her eye to a crevice in the door, she discovered her own maid, a pretty brunette of seventeen, familiarly seated upon the knee of her inconstant lord. In the greatest mortification she retired, and meditated how she should revenge this wounding insult; after revolving in her mind various modes of vengeance, she concluded it would be wisest to dissemble her knowledge of his incontinency, and come to the determination of dismissing her attendant immediately, who, when she came to assist in undressing that night, she informed that she might return to Monteith, as she had no further occasion for her services.

Guilt flew in her face, and, stammering, she said—"She hoped no part of her conduct had been construed into offence?"

"No matter!" said the indignant Margaret, "'tis my desire!" and was accordingly complied with.

This obstacle removed, she began to adopt measures of retaliation, which seemed to her the most feasible method of revenge; for she could not forgive such a slight of her resplendent beauty, which she most certainly possessed.

A young gallant knight, with other visitors, was then at the castle, who, presuming upon his address, which was somewhat winning, made repeated advances, which by her were met with all possible encouragement; they frequently had private interviews, and their illicit connexion was suspected by every one but him whom it most concerned. This once begun, vice succeeded vice; and Margaret always consoled for her lord's neglect in the arms of another, which gratified at once her unchaste desires, and her great revenge.

She now, in company with her lord, visited Bosmora, on the celebration of Matilda's birth-day, where the youthful Donald excited her warmest admiration; and when she found he did not, or would not understand the advances made to him, she ascribed it to his fear of giving offence; and resolving to procure an interview with him, she mixed a strong soporific in the drink of her detested husband. Thus making herself secure, she conducted the object of her passions even to her very chamber, where, for the first time in her life, she experienced a refusal, which aroused all the malevolence of her nature; for, supposing Donald's coolness towards her to proceed from his affection for Matilda, she vowed vengeance on her innocent head; and, uttering dreadful threats, the interview intended for love terminated in hate.

Upon their return to Duncaethal, the alteration of her lord's behaviour struck her forcibly. He became attentive, and seemingly affectionate, which gained imperceptibly upon her heart, not naturally hard; for had her headstrong disposition been duly checked in its earliest appearance, she might, by the virtues of her mind, have added lustre to the dazzling beauties of her person. This altered conduct of Duncaethal's was only an artifice to win her to his purpose; and it too well succeeded; for, in an unlucky moment, being thrown off her guard by his pretended affection, she signed an article, by which she bequeathed to him, at her decease, the whole of her jointure. This was what he wanted, and her fate was now decided. He had cast his eyes on the fair Matilda, and waited but the signing of this deed, by his devoted victim, ere he removed her, in a way that should not impede his intended offers to the heiress of Bosmora. Two days after, a certain drug was procured by Dargo, which, being infused into her wine, caused her to rave in the fever of delirium. Her confessor, from the neighbouring convent, for a rich reward presented him by Duncaethal, who too well knew the force of a bribe, administered a draught, which caused the appearance of death, and giving out she had fallen a victim to pestilential disease, prevented the approach of servants, and avoided her being laid in state, which would have discovered the fraud, and defeated the diabolical schemes of the villainous Duncaethal. No one, except Gertrude, was permitted to enter the apartment, who, being old and almost blind, was not feared by this triumvirate of wretches. A coffin, with a sufficient quantity of weight in it, was conveyed to the tomb of Monteith, with all the mockery of woe and solemnity of religion.

After the departure of his master, Dargo visited the apartments in the east wing of the castle, whither they had conveyed the wretched woman during her counterfeit death, from which she had not yet recovered. Placing a lamp on the table, he retired, and shortly after she awoke, and looking round her in great amazement, she suspected the deceit which had been made use of; then, raving with all the frenzy of a maniac, she struck her head violently against the wall of her prison, wishing indeed to end her being, rather than drag on a miserable existence, deprived of the blessing of liberty. Her loud screams alarmed the villain Dargo, who now proceeded to gag her mouth, lest she should be heard by any of the servants; this was almost an unnecessary precaution, for her place of confinement was situated at the very extremity of the inhabited part of the castle.

Duncaethal soon returned, exulting in the success of his

diabolical scheme, and repairing to her prison, where Dargo, after allowing her to take refreshments, had left her in a state incapable of speaking, or even using her hands, she started from her seat at the sight of her detestful tyrant, and endeavouring to speak, which being unable to effect, the wretch laughed at her defeated efforts, and, in a voice of derision, said—"Is this Monteith's heiress, that vain beauty, who was wont to reign paramount in the gay throng of visitors which infested my castle and devoured my substance? Pity 'tis she cannot express herself with the same fluency of eloquence she was used. I prithee, good Dargo, unbind her mouth, for I think she will make no ill use of this indulgence; if she should, we can easily silence her again."

The ruffian now ungagged her mouth, when, disdaining the idea of a tear staining her cheek, or a sigh to ruffle her bosom, she, with a haughty dignity of manner, and commanding tone of voice, said—"Insulting, barbarous wretch! dearly wilt thou repent this treatment! for deeply will my noble father revenge my cause, when he learns the base conduct practiced against his child!"

"Thou weak woman," returned he, "canst thou for a moment suppose I have not taken means to prevent his ever knowing it? Thou shallow defeated fair one, thy foolish sire is mourning over the tomb, which he is led to think contains thy remains."

"Then," exclaimed Margaret, clasping her hands in frantic grief, "I am for ever lost!"

"Thou art," returned he, "while I enjoy that fortune, which gratified vanity, not love, caused you to bequeath me in case of your death. Short-sighted woman, know that when you signed your hand to that instrument, you signed the deed for your own death."

"Wretch!" returned she, "waited you but for that to complete your horrid purpose?"

"I did," answered he; "nor is that all—another possesses that love once your's! The fair Matilda, Bosmora's heiress, is to reign sole mistress of this castle and of my heart." He now left the room, first telling her violence would be of no use, unless to be again punished by a bandage across her mouth, which, on the slightest noise or intimation, should be replaced by Dargo, who would be in the adjoining apartment.

She profited by the hint and remained silent, except muttering bitter threats of vengeance against the innocence of Matilda, should she by any chance ever be liberated. "Oh!" said she, "what would I give for my freedom, to be able to repay my wrongs in the blood of my rival—my double rival, both with him I loved, and with him whom I hate! Oh for revenge!—revenge!—revenge!"

A lucky thought now struck her—and when Dargo again visited her, she, throwing all the softness she could so well assume into her voice and manner, besought his pity. He was deaf to her entreaties, till she thus proceeded—"Dargo, in a secret repository of my own apartment, I have concealed a thousand angels, and a diamond ring of immense value; help me to escape, and half of the money, together with the ring, shall be your's."

The wretch listened to this proposal with some attention, and saying—"But when my lord shall know of your flight, my life will pay the forfeit, lady; I cannot consent to release you, unless you take a solemn oath never to discover yourself to him by word or action, directly or indirectly so long as you shall live."

"I consent," said the delighted Margaret, "and do here most solemnly swear that I will never make known my existence, but quit Scotland for ever, and end my days in some religious house in a foreign land."

"I then will aid your escape: I shall easily persuade my lord you are dead, as he this night desired me not to return to his presence till I had taken your life—Yes, he commanded me to murder you! But how shall I procure the reward if it be in a secret repository, lady?—how can I find it unless you direct me?"

"Oh, fear not!" said the discerning Margaret, who was aware of the crafty wretch she had to deal with; "you shall, when all in the castle are wrapt in sleep, conduct me to the room, for no one but myself can discover the secret spot where it is concealed."

He was obliged to consent to this measure, and telling her he would soon return, withdrew to acquaint Duncaethal that she was no more. He had ordered him to dispatch her, for he was ever in dread of discovery, as guilt ever is suspicious; and he long ere this had ended poor Agnes, but her quiet resignation to her unhappy lot lulled his suspicions. Add to this, Dargo could not, when company arrived to celebrate his nuptials with Matilda, which he was resolved should take place, as he felt assured he should possess her; and thus determined, he concluded to end the unhappy life of Margaret.

When Dargo entered the room, he eagerly inquired—"Well, is it done? is she dead?"

"She is, my lord, and buried," answered the other.

"Buried!" said the baron, "where?"

"Why, my lord, I did not think it proper to murder her in that apartment she was in, as I could not there conceal the body; so I betrayed her into the subterranean, by the pretence of assisting her to escape—there, my lord, I plunged my poniard to heart; she now lies beneath the flooring of the bottom dungeon: shall I conduct you, my lord, to the spot, for I have so concealed it from the eye, that no one can discover it but myself?"

"No, no, my kind fellow!" said the wretch; "she is at peace, and I care not to behold her grave!" A demoniac smile passed his features as he put a well-filled purse into the hands of this miscreant, who, in hopes of possessing the five hundred angels of Margaret, had thus deceived his villainous master.

When all was still, he again repaired to her prison, where, first making her swear not to alarm the inhabitants of the castle, conducted her through the corridor to her own apartment, and standing at the door, waited for her return with the prize which was to be his, that in value exceeded all that had ever been presented him by his master.

She shortly appeared, and, showing him the glittering ring, said—"Dargo, art thou deceiving me, or wilt thou conduct me from the castle?"

"I will, lady," replied he.

"Well then," said the politic Margaret, "give me thy dagger, and when thou hast brought me without the walls, thou shalt receive thy reward."

Content with this arrangement, he led her from the castle, when, finding herself enlarged, she gave him the promised prize, retaining, by his consent, the dagger. With a bounding heart she proceeded onwards, while Dargo stole to his bed, well satisfied with this night's enterprize.

CHAP. X.

Like to the Pontick sea,
Whose icy current and compulsive course
Ne'er feels retiring ebb, but keeps due on,
To the Propontick, and the Hellespont;
Even so my bloody thoughts, with violent pace,
Shall ne'er look back, ne'er ebb to humble love,
'Till that a capable and wide revenge
Swallow them up—Now, by yon marble heav'n,
In the due rev'rence of a sacred vow,
I here engage my words—

SHAKESPEARE.*

MARGARET, elate with her liberty, walked with tolerable brisk pace. She had about her person jewels to a large amount, and fifteen hundred angels, in addition to the sum which Dargo supposed her to have; for she did not think it proper to make him acquainted with all she possessed, lest he should extort from her a greater reward than what she proposed. This treasure had been presented to her by her father, unknown to Duncaethal, who, during her confinement had searched the little cabinet for her jewellery; yet some of the richest remained in the secret drawer, which escaped his notice, not supposing it contained such a concealment.

A pelting storm overtook her in the forest, through which, without knowing whither to bend her steps, she was quickly hurrying, and, under the wide-spreading branches of an aged oak, the once proud heiress of Monteith sought shelter from its fury. Here it was that, kneeling, she again vowed destruction on the authors of her degradation. "Yes," said she, "I am dead to the world! I will cast off my woman's attire, and with it all the puerile fears and timid delicacy of my sex! I have sworn never to discover myself to Duncaethal or any one—I never will; but, in the disguise of another, I will sting him to the heart! I will be his bane!—his curse! Matilda, Donald, beware! Dreadful is my fate, dreadful shall be my vengeance!—direful, deadly, and horrid!"

Her fiend-like passions distorted her countenance as sternly she again pursued her way. Daylight appeared as she gained the outskirts of the forest, and perceiving a neat white cottage, she thought of taking some rest ere she fixed upon any plan relative to her future proceedings. On reaching the door, she gave a gentle tap, and it was instantly opened by an old woman, who asked what she wanted, at the same time expressing surprise at her rather strange appearance. Margaret silenced all further inquiries by the timely application of a piece of gold, and asking if she might rest herself, as she felt greatly fatigued.

"Your ladyship shall have my humble couch, in welcome," said the old woman; "there is no one at home but myself."

Margaret being conducted to the apartment, threw herself upon the bed, where she forgot her cares in a sound refreshing sleep. When she awoke, the first thing that met her sight was a mean suit of male attire, hanging against the wall, at the foot of the bed; calling the old woman, she asked to whom it belonged?

"To my son," answered she, "who had not long been gone to work, in the wood, when your ladyship came."

"Will you sell it?" asked Margaret.

"Sell it, lady! gramercy, what use will it be to you?"

Margaret told the old woman that she had fled from the pursuit of one who sought her life, and she wished to disguise herself; then putting in her hand a couple of pieces of gold, six times more than they were worth, she asked no further questions. She left her to array herself in them, which she quickly did, and cutting off her fine long hair, she put on a highland cap, as worn by the peasants, and concealing her wealth in her clothes, she set forth from the cottage, with many blessings from the old woman, who said she made a bonnyer lad than her son Michael.

After walking a great distance, she perceived a quantity of berries which grew around, and plucking some, pressed out the brownish liquid that they yielded—with this she disguised the snowy delicacy of her skin. She was on the point of pursuing her journey, when the voices of men attracted her ear, and stepping behind a tree, overheard one of them say—"I tell you, comrade, the trade is a very good one; who do you think would work, when he can be so well paid for doing nothing, as a body may say? Think you I would stick at any thing for money? No, not I, i'faith! though our chief, Morven, being unluckily wounded, and lies here hard by, we live in a state of idleness, as a body may say."

A thought entered the prolific brain of Margaret, and advancing, said—"Which of you will conduct me to Morven, the noble chief of your band?"

"Ah!" returned they, "who art thou that dares thus undauntedly address us? Know you who we are?"

"I do," said she; "are you not a brave set of men, who live by taking from others what they can very well spare?"

"We are," answered they; "and now, youth, who art thou?"

"One who fain would be of your noble calling," said she; "but come, conduct me to your chief."

"Come on then," said they.

They led her to a kind of hovel, where, on a bed, lay the wounded Morven, attended by an elderly-looking woman, who was administering to him medicine, unconscious of his real way of life, or even caring, so long as she was well paid for her trouble. He was wounded in an attack, with the other two, who, being overpowered by superior numbers, fled, and left their chief for dead; but, on returning to the spot after the victors had departed, they found he still breathed, and, conveying him to this cottage, said he was their master, who had been wounded by a robber in the wood, it being at too great a distance to think of conveying him to the abbey. Whether the cottagers believed this or not is uncertain, but they did not think fit to express any doubts, as they were well rewarded.

When Margaret entered the room, she expressed a desire of speaking in private. Morven, desiring all to withdraw, then requested the purport of this interview; to this Margaret answered—"I am a nobleman, that has been basely wronged by the united houses of Duncaethal and Bosmora; I loved the beauteous daughter of the latter, but my offers were scorned for a mean youth—a peasant boy; let me be admitted into your band, by which means I can get her into my power, and I'll reward you amply."

"My lord, you shall have our assistance; but why wish to join our band, for we will follow your directions?"

"Because," returned she, "in disguise I can act unknown; as the heir of——but no matter who I am—here's a hundred angels to divide amongst the noble fellows who shall assist me," putting into his hand a purse for himself.

"Marry, my lord, your argument is very powerful, and you shall have all the aid our band can afford; and, as I am incapable of attending at the abbey, the rendezvous of our band, you shall act as chief, and by my orders they will obey you as myself."

"Revenge will then be mine!" said she.

"It will, my lord," returned the other; "but I beg pardon, what should you like to be called, as it is necessary you should be distinguished by some appellation?"

After passing a moment, she recollected the Venetian letter, and she said—"My name shall be Darthalgo!"

"Very well, my lord," answered the chief, "it shall be that. Would you please to retire for a moment, while I commune with my men?"

She complied, and summoning to his presence the two robbers, he thus begun—"My boys, here's a lucky day's work! here are an hundred angels to be divided among the band." He then gave these instructions on how they were to act towards the stranger, who he said was a powerful baron, who had promised to reward them well, if they assisted him in the purpose for which he had assumed this disguise.

They readily agreed to all their chief proposed; then, setting forth for the abbey, promised to return the next day to see how he fared. Upon their arrival at the rendezvous, she was introduced to the rest of the band, and then conducted to a room full of arms of every description. After selecting a dress, which she thought the most terrific, she arrayed herself in it, together with bushy hair and a large beard, which she discovered among the various disguises made use of by the band on particular occasions; she added a black patch on the right side of her forehead. Thus metamorphosed, who could recognize the once-lovely heiress of Monteith? She soon became acquainted with the manners of the banditti, but never accompanied them on any of their excursions for plunder; neither would she allow them to be a spy upon her actions.

In this manner, week after week passed on, without any opportunity occurring by which she might ensnare Matilda, until the fatal night in which the castle was attacked, when, scouting round in company with one of the robbers, she beheld the motions of Duncaethal, and giving directions to her companion, rushed in at the private door, which had been thrown open by the terrified domestics, and being well acquainted with the interior, made for the apartment of Matilda, where finding her in a state of insensibility, caught her in her arms, and, snatching up a half-extinguished torch, hurried down among the subterraneans, whence she hoped, as soon as animation should revisit her, during the confusion to convey her safely away. Matilda's scruples, however, prevented her; and with bitter execrations, on account of her views being thwarted, she left the castle, and, seeking her companion, mounted her horse and rode away.

She now turned her thoughts towards Duncaethal, whither she felt assured Matilda would be conveyed, and reconnoitering the spot, a loud noise caused them to start; and having left their horses in the forest, they sought to conceal themselves in what appeared to be a natural cavity of the earth, but was, in fact, the passage leading to the door of the subterranean, which, by the quantity of rubbish that appeared, seemed as if it had not been made use of many years. Thus, by mere chance, she discovered the passage by which she so often afterwards made her secret and nocturnal visits to our poor heroine, and learned the confinement of Donald, by overhearing a conversation between Dargo and his lord, relative to their future proceedings towards that unhappy youth.

In her different visits, she covered herself with a long white robe, stained on the breast with blood, in case she was ever seen by any of the inhabitants, they would suppose her to be a ghost; this she always cast off and left behind the picture (the device of which she had discovered when she inhabited the apartment) whenever she visited Matilda. On the evening she had quitted Matilda, at hearing the voice of Duncaethal, she plucked the beard from her face and quickly putting on the robe, appeared to her guilty lord as the spirit of his murdered wife! The event answered equal to her wish, and she had the pleasure of seeing Duncaethal writhing in the agonies of conscience stained with blood, as he sunk prostrate to the earth; then repairing to the trap, which she had discovered one night in her researches, she rejoined her companions, whom she told that she had not succeeded with Matilda according to expectation, and that they must return another night; then presented them with a well-filled purse, which not only prevented them from murmuring, but won their hearts. Thus did Margaret, by timely bribery, gain the esteem of the ruffians, who thought her a worthy generous nobleman, and would, if required, have sacrificed their lives in her defence.

At last, by various stratagems, she ensnared the person of Matilda, whose blood, though she had at first resolved, she now hesitated to shed; for though the inmate of a banditts' cave, yet did she start at murder, and what she oft intended to perform, her hand would shrink from. Often did she say to herself—"Margaret, thy wavering spirit shames thee! Can thy miseries be washed away but by blood? Impossible!—therefore she must die!" And one night, being rather more than usually determined, she went to the cell of Donald, and bidding him follow, resolved before his face to end the life of her victim. Her dagger was raised for that purpose, when the old woman rushed in with intelligence of the abbey being attacked; in this dilemma she knew not how to proceed; she dared not to meet the presence of Duncaethal, who she rightly conjectured had come for the purpose of recovering his prisoners, when she recollected the secret entrance behind the altar, where she concealed herself, and was shortly joined by two of the band, who, finding the day against them, sought here for refuge.

After the abbey was evacuated by all but the old hag, whom Bosmora suffered to remain, they ventured to steal from their hiding-place. These two ruffians, who often had assassinated in the dark, had not the courage to stand the issue of the battle, but had fled after the first onset, under the idea that they were attacked by royal troops. The politic Margaret knew better than to undeceive them, for she feared, when they should know it was through her the band was routed, they would refuse again to assist her, and perhaps by her life revenge themselves for the injury.

"Fool that I was," thought she, "so often I've had it in my power, not to revenge myself for all the sufferings caused me by her life, and that of the upstart Donald; but she shall not yet escape my vengeance!"

She now, in concert with the two robbers, in disguise, wandered round Duncaethal, till that day when they seized poor Matilda and her maid Venella; the latter Margaret would willingly have dispensed with, but was obliged to retain her, lest she should be the means of discovering the perpetrator of this action. She concluded that they would not suspect her when once they found the abbey vacant, which, by her instructions to the old woman, they would, no doubt, suppose it to be.

Judge then her disappointment and rage, when, on repairing to the ruin, she found Matilda had again escaped her! With many useless exclamations of regret, they retraced their way to the cave which Morven had fixed upon for their future residence. Unluckily, during their absence, he had been informed by a wood-cutter, with whom he fell in conversation, who were the real besiegers of the abbey. "Ah! ah" continued the man, ignorant of who he was addressing, "the rogues will all swing for it, I warrant them! Do you know that one of them conveyed away the heiress of Bosmora? By saint Andrew, he had a liquorish tooth! Don't you think so?"

"Pray how do you know all this?" said the other.

"Know, quotha! why because some of the guards passed by my cottage, who had the rogues in custody, and were conducting them to the punishment they deserve."

Morven walked away, and soon as his two comrades returned, accompanied by Darthalgo, he regarded not the latter by any pleasant looks. Margaret's suspicions were aroused, and, pretending fatigue, retired to an outer cave; but instead of resting on the couch, she listened through a chink of the door, and overheard their conversation, the subject of which was revenge for the loss of their companions, by her death.

She, unperceived, left the cave, and taking a horse that was near, mounted it, and swiftly pursued her way to Duncaethal, covering herself with a long plaid cloak to conceal her strange habit. Upon her approach to the castle, she alighted at the door of a cottage, and asked for a little water, which being granted, she inquired if lord Duncaethal was married yet to the heiress of Bosmora?

"Not yet," said the cottager, "but he will when the trial is over."

"Trial!—what trial?"

"Why didn't you know, stranger, that the tyrant lord who wedded the heiress of Monteith was a usurper?"

"A usurper!" said the astonished Margaret.

"Yes, stranger, a usurper; and a youth, called Donald, is proved to be the lawful heir of Duncaethal."

"Indeed!"

"Yes, stranger, it is true; and at this very moment they are trying the usurping lord for unlawful possession," added the cottager.

Margaret, thanking her informer for his politeness, quitted the door, and, after a moment's pause, she said—"And is vengeance at last snatched from me? He once escaped a blow aimed by my hand, but he shall not escape another! I must perish in the attempt; but my long-cherished revenge, at least on him, shall sweeten my fall." She now rushed amongst the throng into the hall, and fell by her own hand, after dealing retribution on the guilty Philip. She fell in the pride of her days, a dreadful example of the bitter effects of an ungoverned temper and unrestrained passion. Peace to her sad remains! "We war not with the dead!"

Alexander, in a few weeks, received the hand of his beloved

Matilda. The gloomy halls of Duncaethal were again filled with aged bards; the gates were again open to hospitality; the wretched never went unrelieved from the portal; while meek-eyed benevolence, and genuine charity, presided in the person of Matilda.

Lady Agnes and the baron lived to witness the continuing glory of their families, in the persons of a grandson and daughter. The former inherited all his father's virtues; the latter, all her mother's beauty, chastity, and goodness. Old Allen and Jannet finished their days beneath his roof, while Venella and Robert, who were shortly united, dwelt in happiness and prosperity; the latter often indulging in his natural propensity of feasting and drinking in the halls of his lord.

Thus did Alexander, happy himself, by the happiness which he caused to others, sink gently into the vale of years. While surrounded by his lovely offspring, he sat in his hall, and listened to the song of minstrelsy, as touching the golden strings of the harp, they recalled to his mind—

> "The time which has rolled away;
> The deeds of the days of other years."*

FINIS.

NOTES

PAGE

2   *this first offspring of my brain:* The jury is out as to whether or not this
    is Smith's first or third novel as two other novels—*The Misanthrope
    Father, or, The Guarded Secret* (1807) and *The Castle of Arragon, or, The
    Banditti of the Forest* (1809-10)—ascribed to a "Miss Smith" might
    not be the production of *Mrs.* Smith. She may be suggesting in this
    instance, however, that this was the first that she wrote, a factor
    that might help towards resolving the issues. See pages vii-viii in
    James D. Jenkins's Introduction to *Barozzi; or The Venetian Sorceress*
    (Chicago: Valancourt Books, 2006) who delineates the nature of this
    dispute.

3   *epigraph:* These lines are spoken while no one is onstage by King
    Henry in *Henry VI, Part 2,* Act III, Scene 2, in regard to who mur-
    dered the King's uncle Humphrey, Duke of Gloucester.

4   *first epigraph:* These lines, like those that preface Volume II, Chapter
    9, derive from Act I, Scene 1 of Thomas Otway's *Venice Preserved*
    (1682). They are recited by Jaffeir who eloped with Belvidera,
    daughter of Senator Priuli. Three years later, the now penniless
    Jaffeir comes to beg mercy of his father-in-law for the sake of his
    wife and child. In the course of making this request, Jaffeir reminds
    Priuli that he actually saved Belvidera during a shipwreck. Priuli
    rebuffs and curses Jaffeir who, he says, stole his daughter from him.
    He suggests that they now live in penury.

4   *second epigraph:* These lines derive from Act II, Scene 1 in John
    Home's famous tragedy, *Douglas* (1756), and furnish Norval's self-
    description after he saves the life of Lord Randolph.

5   *Sat, like Patience on a monument, smiling at grief:* This line derives
    from Shakespeare's *Twelfth Night* and concerns Viola who never
    expressed her love for Duke Orsino. The full statement reads as
    follows: "She never told her love, but let concealment, like a worm
    i' the bud, feed on her damask cheek: she pined in thought, and
    with a green and yellow melancholy, she sat like patience on a mon-
    ument, smiling at grief."

11 *epigraph: Othello,* Act III, Scene 3. This marks a turning point in
    Shakespeare's play as Othello, feeling that the dastardly Iago has
    provided him with incontrovertible evidence of an affair between
    Desdemona and Cassio, vows revenge.

21 *epigraph*: This is one instance where Smith gets her sources wrong. This is Colley Cibber's rewrite of *Richard III*. The scene takes place in Act V on the eve of Richard's battle with Richmond. Richard experiences a disturbing night of dreams whereby he is visited in turn by the ghosts of each person he has murdered.

28 *first epigraph*: These lines derive from *Romeo and Juliet*, Act I, Scene 4 and involve Romeo discussing his love for Juliet with Mercutio.

28 *second epigraph*: These lines are from Ossian's (James Macpherson's) *Lathmon*, which relates the invasion of Ireland and subsequent imprisonment of Lathmon, a British prince.

38 *epigraph*: These lines, like those that preface Volume I, Chapter 5, appear in *Lathmon*.

49 *epigraph*: These lines also derive from Ossian's (James Macpherson's) *Berrathon*, named after an island in Scandinavia where Fingal is generously entertained by Larthmor who is later imprisoned by his own son Uthal. Uthal also proves to be an inconstant, treacherous lover (like Smith's Duncaethal) and he is later defeated in single combat by Ossian.

67 *epigraph*: This is a confused epigraph combining lines from Shakespeare's *Richard II* and *Macbeth*. Both characters are haunted by nightmares relating to their crimes.

75 *epigraph*: These lines derive from John Home's *Douglas* (1756) and recount the tragic fate of Lady Randolph. This work was first produced in Edinburgh among a storm of applause and protest and arguably inspired James Macpherson's Ossian cycle.

89 *epigraph*: This is another incorrectly ascribed epigraph. It actually derives from Act II, Scene 1 of Nicholas Rowe's *Jane Shore: A Tragedy in Five Acts* (1714), an adaptation of Thomas Heywood's *Edward IV (Part II)*. Jane Shore was a married woman who became the mistress of Edward IV. After his death, she was the mistress of Thomas Grey, 1st marquess of Dorset and, subsequently, Lord Hastings. Probably for political reasons, she was accused of sorcery by Richard III in 1483, placed in the Tower of London, and then forced to do public penance as a harlot. While she then attracted the king's solicitor, Thomas Lynon, their proposed marriage never transpired and she died in poverty.

96 This word is virtually obsolete and means, according to the *Oxford English Dictionary*, "dewy, moist, dank; resembling or falling like dew."

96 *epigraph*: These lines derive from Act II, Scene 1 in John Home's *Douglas*, and are spoken by Glenalvon, Lord Randolph's heir.

Glenalvon becomes envious of the young Norval, who turns out to be Lady Randolph's son, and by way of treacherous machinations, slays him.

103 *epigraph*: This citation, which derives from *Richard III*, Act IV, Scene 4, provides yet another instance of Smith's reliance on an imperfect memory for her epigraphs. There are misspellings accompanied by crucial missing lines. A more complete extract of these lines, spoken by Richard's own mother, the Duchess of York, reads as follows:

"Tetchy and wayward was thy infancy;
Thy school-days frightful, desp'rate, wild, and furious;
Thy prime of manhood daring, bold, and venturous;
Thy age confirm'd, proud, subtle, sly, and bloody . . . "

114 *epigraph*: These lines derive from a British national ballad called *Richard Plantagenet; a Legendary Tale* (1774) signed by a "T. Hull". Richard Plantagenet was the 3rd Duke of York and father of Edward IV and Richard III. Richard Plantagenet was a key figure in the Wars of the Roses but he suffered death in battle and never became king.

120 *epigraph*: These lines also derive from the British national ballad *Richard Plantagenet* (1774).

130 *epigraph*: These lines are spoken by the magician Prospero in *The Tempest*, Act IV, Scene 1.

135 *perdue*: This means "in concealment or ambush."

136 *abacot*: The word "abacot," which derives from Henry Spelman's *Glossarium* (1664), refers to "a cap of state, wrought up into the shape of two crowns, worn formerly by English kings."

139 *epigraph*: These are George, Duke of Clarence's words in *Richard III* from Act I, Scene 4 as he recounts a night of horrible dreams to his keeper Brakenbury, the Lieutenant of the Tower of London, during which he was tormented by some of his victims.

140 *versal*: This is a colloquial abbreviation of the word "universal".

145 *epigraph*: This serves as another example of Smith combining quotes from two different works by the same author. In this case, she cites Ossian's *Oithona* in the first few lines and then *The Song of Selma* in the last three lines. *Oithona* recounts the very dramatic tale of Oithona, the courageous daughter of Nuäth and beloved of Gaul, a soldier of Fingal's. Oithona is raped and carried off by Dunrommath. Although advised to remove herself from the battle involving Gaul's retaliation against Dunrommath, Oithona disguises herself as a soldier and is mortally wounded. *The Song*

of Selma articulates lamentations about Fingal and his now dead soldiers, among them Morar whose dead father is also envisioned here.

151 *epigraph*: These lines prefacing the chapter recounting a fuller history of Margaret of Monteith derive from Act I, Scene 1 of Thomas Otway's *Venice Preserved* (1682). They are recited by Jaffeir who eloped with Belvidera, daughter of Senator Priuli. Three years later, the now penniless Jaffeir comes to beg mercy of his father-in-law for the sake of his wife and child. Priuli rebuffs and curses him, suggesting they live in penury.

160 *epigraph*: *Othello*, Act III, Scene 3. These are Othello's words to Iago as he rages about his wife's imagined infidelities and envisions his revenge, a suitable passage prefacing a fuller account of Margaret's attempts to take her revenge on her treacherous husband Duncaethal.

168 *The time which has rolled away*: These closing lines are actually misquoted. They derive from Ossian's *Carthon: A Poem*. The original lines read: "A Tale of the times of old—the deeds of the days of other years."